Shadowboxer

Praise for Jessica L. Webb

Troop 18

"*Troop 18* is the third in the Dr. Kate Morrison series and is another winner…The story is a fascinating mystery that had me stumped and I loved how it was told in a very understated way with so much going on under the surface."—*Kitty Kat's Book Review Blog*

"Jessica Webb, you are so good! I love a book that makes you feel, even if it hurts."—*The Romantic Reader*

Lambda Literary Award Winner *Pathogen*

"Where did Jessica Webb come from? This is the second Dr. Kate Morrison book, the first is *Trigger*, and it was amazing. A reader should really read them in order, because they are both fantastic. I would sign up today to read the next ten books Webb writes." —*Amanda's Reviews*

Trigger

"The book reads very well and is full of heart pounding, adrenaline racing moments. I have zero clue if human bombs can be actually made, but Webb 100% sold me on the possibility through her story. I was held captive throughout the book, desperately needing to know how this was all resolved…This book has action out the wazoo, but it doesn't stop there. Mystery, intrigue, and a fantastic couple are in full force as well."—*The Romantic Reader*

"[A] really clever, intricate, and extremely well developed story line that has conspiracies, betrayals, and enough excitement to whet any reader's appetite. I cannot commend this book highly enough." —*Inked Rainbow Reads*

Lambda Literary Award Finalist *Repercussions*

"[A]lthough this is such an action-packed book, Webb still balanced it with some romance in such a way that the chemistry leaps off the pages in this intense, steamy kind of way. Webb is someone you can count on for accuracy and realism in her books, which I love because it makes it so much easier to fall into the story and forget the world around you. Her dialogue is well written and sounds conversationalist. She has a fast pace, good writing style, developed characters, plenty of action, and an exciting plot."—*Artistic Bent*

"I loved this book! The author has balanced suspense and romance perfectly. The plot is edge-of-your-seat exciting. The writing immerses the reader. The action is plentiful with lots of twists and turns and there are some very interesting, creative ideas within the book."—*Melina Bickard, Librarian (Waterloo Library, London)*

"*Repercussions* by Jessica L. Webb is nothing short of phenomenal. This book is everything you want and more. It is one delicious story, with amazing characters and an exciting plot…I could go on for days about how freaking fantastic this one is. All of Webb's books are home runs, but somehow, someway, she took it to the next level with *Repercussions*. This book is going to hook you on by the first chapter. A roller coaster ride of awesomeness is awaiting you with this book."—*The Romantic Reader*

"Jessica L. Webb can write a psychological thriller like no other in lesfic. This is her fourth book, and every time she manages to deliver an amazing story…She's one of a few authors that I trust she's going to take me on an imaginative and entertaining journey. Ms. Webb delivers again a pair of multilayered and authentic main characters with amazing chemistry and a plot with enough twist and turns to keep the reader turning pages."—*Lez Review*

By the Author

Dr. Kate Morrison Thriller series

Trigger

Pathogen

Troop 18

Repercussions

Shadowboxer

Shadowboxer

by

Jessica L. Webb

2018

SHADOWBOXER

ISBN 13: 978-1-63555-267-6

This Trade Paperback Original Is Published By
Bold Strokes Books, Inc.
P.O. Box 249
Valley Falls, NY 12185

First Edition: September 2018

Credits
Editor: Jerry L. Wheeler
Production Design: Stacia Seaman
Cover Design by Melody Pond

Acknowledgments

A big thank you to my beta readers—Jen; Meredith; Katie; my parents, Ron and Val; and my sister, Rebecca. Thanks to my entire extended wacky family for being proud of me. Thanks to my readers, who lift me up with their reviews and comments and emails. Thanks to everyone at Bold Strokes Books for everything you do to get our books out into the world.

Special thanks to Katie for helping with the title and the cover.

Finally, thank you to my editor, Jerry. This partnership means a lot to me. Thank you for being you.

For my wife, Jen. For making the shadows less scary.

And for all of us who have ever felt like we're not enough.
We are. We got this.

CHAPTER ONE

Jordan—Six

Six years old and it's a warm time. Jory kicks the legs of her chair and hums a song they learned in school about God and all his creatures. Mama hums a different song, and Jory stops to listen, her legs still thumping, thumping, thumping. She's cooking supper, Mama is, onions on the stove, something with apples and sausages. Mama is smiling, and Jory almost remembers a time Mama didn't. A cold time when Mama never got up and Daddy cursed such big words and limped and yelled and Steven hugged her and Jakey growled and brought them cold food. Jory shivered. Maybe a bad dream, that cold time, maybe not the for real world with the leaves changing colour outside, that big *chlorophyll* word Mrs. Keenley used today in class and laughed when everyone tried to say it. Mrs. Keenley has a good laugh. It makes Jory warm and makes her forget she might remember cold times. Jory loves her teacher in a secret, proud way in her heart.

She loves her mama, too, and Jory looks up at her from under her dark eyelashes, so long and dark like her daddy's. Her blue eyes were his, too. A gift, he tells her, the long sight and a long life. Steven has long sight, but not Jakey. Jory worries about Jakey, her biggest brother, nineteen and already working the docks. What about his long sight and long life? Mama laughed when Jory cried about it long ago. She's too big to cry now, but then she cried and Mama said not to worry, all her babies were warriors like the Cressidys before them. She'd turned Jory's arm over and showed her the veins in her wrists and arms and hands.

"See?" she said. "Warrior blood."

"Let me see yours," Jory cried, fascinated.

Mama turned her arm over, and Jory did not see the faint tremor as she put her skinny arm next to her mama's. She traced the dark blood veins through her wrist.

"Warrior blood," Jory whispered. "But less, Mama? I've got less because I'm one-half Cressidy and one-half McAddie?"

"No," Mama whispered. "That is the magic of warrior blood. All you need is a drop."

Jory stared now at her hands and kicked the legs of her chair as Mama hummed in the kitchen. Just a drop, and she had a half. She was just about to ask about warrior blood because Mama didn't mind questions in warm times, when the back door opened too hard and hit the wall. Mama stiffened and Jory shivered. Daddy muttered a dark sound outside of warm time and clanked, clanked, clanked as he limped into the kitchen carrying a box.

He looked like her warm time Daddy who had walked her to school that morning but wrong somehow, different, weighed down with that box. Jory could read, smartest in her class Mrs. Keenley had whispered to her, but the words on the box were not what frightened Jory. She remembered its shape. That sound of clinking bottles and the smell of them as they were stacked on the rotting front porch until Jakey, always so angry, carried them away.

Jory stopped kicking her chair and bowed her head, dark curls hiding her face. She gripped her wrist and shut her eyes as Mama and Daddy's words got louder and angrier and the smell of burning onions made her eyes tear and she sat so still and so still until Steven came home. He tugged her sleeve and pulled her out of the kitchen and hugged her against his skinny twelve-year-old body, one half-full just like her, and they stayed like that, pretending cold time had not just walked through their door.

❖

Jordan hung up the phone in her cubicle, rubbed her dry eyes, and pushed her hand through her short-cropped curly dark hair. It had taken over an hour to find a foster home that would take a young teenager who needed an emergency placement. She'd finally found one, but after a late night of studying, an early class at Dalhousie University, eighteen phone calls, and endless bureaucratic paperwork, Jordan felt like she'd already fought a few rounds. And her day was nowhere near to shutting down. But you didn't go into social services to have a regular schedule. Jordan took it as a good sign that even in moments like this, she didn't question her drive to become a social worker. She'd get there. And she'd still have days like this.

Her timing always ever so exact, her colleague Cay walked into their tiny, shared cubicle.

"Show time, chicken."

Jordan grunted at the older woman and Cay laughed, her wrinkles dimpling and dancing across her broad, dark face.

"Snap out of it, darling, and quick. We need the clean, tough, articulate Jordan Pauline McAddie to show up at the gym in an hour. Impress the hell out of these suits, and we might have a private avenue of funding instead of having to beg for scraps from Children and Youth Services. A whole twelve months of funding for your gym, your program, your kids."

"Ours, ours, and ours," Jordan said as she stood up and grabbed her black leather jacket.

JP's Gym had been hers for the past four years, but she never really thought of it that way. She often wondered if the last of her earnings from her short boxing career should have gone somewhere else. Maybe she could have gotten a real apartment, not the slapped-together but homey space above the gym where she lived. But then the kids would come tumbling and swearing and swaggering into the gym for their evening practice, and Jordan would remember why she'd purchased this building and stressed over the monthly bills.

Jordan checked the pockets of her jacket for her keys and wallet before tugging it on, feeling the newness of the leather as it settled on her shoulders. An indulgence, this jacket, given the steady level of debt accruing from her master's studies and the fact that her car needed repair. She knew exactly how much food this jacket could have provided for the street kids she supported. She felt a little sick as she tugged it across her chest, smoothing it down over the plain black shirt she'd carefully chosen this morning along with dark grey pants that were not quite jeans but close enough. This was as close to an effort as the suits, as Cay called them, were going to get.

Cay eyed the jacket critically, and Jordan tried not to fidget under the scrutiny.

"It's perfect, you know," Cay said finally. "Stop hating yourself."

A mind reader, Cay.

"Fuck off," Jordan muttered, and Cay laughed.

"I said articulate, not muttering and sullen. The kids have got that covered without your help."

Jordan laughed out loud as they walked through the sea of cubicles and offices that housed a myriad of social services. The community centre where Jordan ran some of the other teen programs was right next door. Jordan had worked here for seven years as a crisis and intake worker until Cay suggested she look into part-time studies at the local university. Her life was a balancing act with work and the gym and her studies. Jordan was busy. And for the most part, she was happy.

Jordan waved at Tim and Kayla at the reception desk and felt her phone vibrate in her back pocket and she pulled it out. A text from Madi, one of Jordan's kids. Former kids, Jordan reminded herself as she pulled up the text. Madi was twenty now.

Where r u?

Jordan shook her head as she thumbed out an answer.

On our way. Patience, grasshopper.

Jordan didn't hear back. Interesting. She would have expected an expletive and emoticon-filled response. Madi's silence was telling.

"What is it?" Cay said. The day was already cold, and Jordan tugged her jacket across her chest again, preparing for the chilly ten-minute walk to the gym at the edge of downtown. Wind pulled at her hair, but she'd had it cut recently so it couldn't do much damage to the short curls or the neatly shaved swath around her ears and neck.

"Madi," Jordan answered Cay. "She's nervous."

Cay said nothing. She had her head down in her characteristic dash to whatever needed doing next. Jordan was momentarily suspicious Cay hadn't taken the opportunity to rail at street kids having no home, no food, no hope. But they had a cell phone.

"Why's Madi nervous?" Jordan pushed.

Cay stopped abruptly just before they reached the gym doors. Jordan could hear the bass from the warm-up music thumping from out here.

"This wasn't my idea," Cay said.

Jordan noted her friend's unease and felt herself absorb the edges of it.

"This meeting? I know that. Children and Youth Services were contacted about a donation. I'm assuming Campbell has something to do with it, since it's politics," Jordan said, referencing their big boss.

Cay said nothing, just kept glancing from Jordan to the gym doors and back again.

"Cay, spit it out."

"There was a meeting already. Campbell and this company."

Jordan still didn't understand. "So?"

Cay sighed. "And Madi."

Jordan felt the burn of anger start as a tremor in her hands.

"What do you mean?" Jordan controlled her voice. She'd had a great deal of practice.

"I don't know the details. I overheard Campbell talking about a new avenue for funding involving Madi as a sort of poster child—" Cay put up a hand when Jordan growled. "Hang on. It involves top executives as part of an outreach or mentorship program. When I asked Campbell how Madi was pulled in, he told me to keep it to myself. Said he wasn't going to let your overprotectiveness of an independent adult who was no longer a Crown ward get in the way."

The anger spread, gaining tension and momentum as it traveled up Jordan's arms and across her biceps until it settled in a seething mass across her neck and shoulders. It was true, Madi was no longer part of the system, but it didn't mean she didn't need someone looking out for her.

"Do you know if Madi's agreed to anything?"

Cay shook her head. "She hasn't been around this week for me to ask."

Brilliant and tough and alternately raised by the system and the streets, Madigan Battiste was a poet whose small frame belied a voice and a message that could punch you in the gut so hard it would leave you breathless. Jordan smiled to herself. And Madi could punch, too. She checked her watch.

"Let's go find out what this is."

Cay put a hand out and tugged gently at Jordan's sleeve. Some of the fire had returned to her eyes. "Don't go looking for an opponent if there's not one there."

Jordan grimaced. She hated that she still needed the same advice as her kids. "Yeah, yeah."

Cay rolled her eyes and opened the door, hissing, "Articulate, McAddie."

Jordan laughed and entered the gym.

The space was wide and open with one ring along the back wall and workout and sparring stations spread throughout. It was ugly but clean. None of the equipment was new, but when Jordan pulled in a breath, the smell of cleanser balanced the smell of sweat. Nineties-era rap reverberated off the walls and the ceiling, the voices of kids high and excited as they warmed up, yelling along with Maestro Fresh-Wes to drop the needle. Jordan guessed it was Rupert's turn to choose the warm-up music. Show up to train four days in a week, and your name went into a draw to choose the music. Only once had the music ever caused a fight. Surprisingly, it hadn't been the Gregorian chanting that ended in violence.

"Jordan! Jesus, finally."

Madi jumped up from a seat outside the change rooms. She was dressed in her characteristic head-to-toe black. Skinny jeans and a plain black tank top. Her pixie-like face was framed by long dark hair and flashing grey eyes.

"Hey, Madi."

"Every other fucking day you show up early, but not today." Madi shoved her hands into her back pockets, her eyes bright and fierce.

Jordan assessed the young woman, checking her pupils and reading her body language out of habit. Madi was stressed but not high. Anger masked her nerves, but she seemed in control. Jordan relaxed. It had been a long time since she'd seen Madi high.

"I'm here," Jordan said. Staying calm helped the kids stay calm. Usually. "What's up?"

"This meeting. It's weird. I mean, it's fine. These guys are bringing in a boatload of money for the gym and the program. So it has to be worth it, right?"

Jordan felt two steps behind already. She hated that feeling.

Cay jumped in. "Let's hear what they have to say before we answer that question. You get to draw the line, Madi. It's your life."

Madi rolled her eyes, but she relaxed her shoulders a little. Power and choice were commodities on the streets. Jordan and Cay tried to give them for free wherever they could.

"Sierra's with the suits," Madi said. "I should get back. As her manager, I should be there."

Madi was a graduate of the youth boxing gym program. She still worked out at the gym, but she was also unofficially mentoring with Jordan to be a general manager. At twenty, Madi had the charisma and brains and heart to be whatever she wanted to be. But the world held few opportunities for a young woman with only a high school degree and a complex host of mental health needs. And now that she was an adult, at least in the eyes of the system, Madi could no longer access services through Jordan and Cay. It had been a rough year of transition. Jordan's counterpart in adult services, Helena Cavio, had taken Madi under her wing. Jordan and Madi were still working out their shift to friendship.

Jordan looked over by the ring where a small group gathered. A man and a woman in casual business wear stood talking with Sierra.

"You've met them already?" Jordan indicated the group by the ring. It wouldn't do Madi any good to let her discomfort show.

Madi shrugged. "Yeah. They seem copacetic."

Cay laughed and Jordan grinned. Madi finally smiled.

"Lead on, Ms. Battiste," Cay said. "You can be in charge of the introductions."

Kids called out to the trio as they made their way back to the boxing ring. The warm-up was almost complete, and soon the kids would start their circuits, taking turns as coach and boxer at each station. It was a way to address the power struggles, but it was only partially successful.

An older man with neatly styled white hair and a plain suit turned and smiled as they approached. Jordan suspected this was Tom Lawrence, president of the Centera Corporation, the company looking to buy some good PR by offering to fund the youth boxing program for a year. At least, that was Jordan's cynical take on it. Jordan shifted her attention to Sierra, who looked relieved at their arrival. She was sixteen and strong and already had a left hook that made Jordan wary. Right now she looked like a scared kid.

Madi started the introductions, her voice rising above the din of the gym and showing none of her previous nerves. But the words and the sounds were suddenly drowned out for Jordan, a mere buzz in the background as she took in the other person standing silently in the group.

She was tall, close to Jordan's height, and dressed simply in dark grey pants and a white button-up shirt with the sleeves rolled up. She had dark blonde hair that barely reached her shoulders. Then the woman turned fully around and Jordan took in the blue-grey eyes she had looked into a hundred times before. Jordan tried to swallow as her heart bottomed out, then pounded painfully against her ribcage. Ali Clarke, the first girl Jordan had ever loved, was standing in her gym.

Ali's smile was full of confidence and knowing, the expression of a woman who knew exactly where she was in the world. The pictures in Jordan's mind of Ali just as confident and sure at seventeen were rapidly replaced by this living, breathing, beautiful woman.

"It's traditional in our culture to shake hands, Jordan."

Madi's sarcasm cut through Jordan's thoughts, and she realized Ali was holding out her hand. Jordan mumbled an apology and shook Ali's hand, the contact far too brief to bring Jordan any joy or clarity.

"I've taken Ms. McAddie off guard, I think." Ali's voice was smoother than Jordan remembered, as if she'd modulated out the elation of childhood.

"A little, yes." That seemed inadequate, but Jordan was suddenly very conscious of the group surrounding them. "It's good to see you again."

"You know each other already?" Cay said.

The beat of silence was so brief, but Jordan felt the weight of years.

"We were in our final year of high school together," Ali said. Her tone was easy and conversational. Her eyes held a different message, but Jordan was unsure she could decipher it.

"Another Saint Sebastian graduate? Excellent!" Tom, the CEO, looked genuinely pleased. "Alison has told me a great deal about that school."

"Just my final year of high school," Jordan explained. The all girls private school trained elite athletes, and Jordan had attended only part of one year. Her world had just fallen apart and one of the trainers from the boxing gym, a cop and his wife, had taken her in, convincing Saint Sebastian to give her a scholarship and a chance. She'd shown up late in September, battered and angry, focused on her goal of doing whatever she needed to get the hell out of Halifax and away from her family.

"Madi, why don't you take Mr. Lawrence and Ms. Clarke on a tour of the gym, and then we can all meet up in the office," Cay said.

Jordan was thankful Cay had stepped in to lead this meeting. She was thrown by Ali's sudden presence, a whip backwards to a time of intense happiness and bruised anger.

After a quick and curious look to Jordan, Ali followed Madi and her boss. Jordan and Cay fell in behind as Madi explained the set-up of the boxing program, focusing on the mentoring and co-op systems Jordan had implemented to try and provide structure and opportunity for the kids who came through her gym.

"Anything I should know?" Cay said.

I just shook hands with my biggest regret.

"No."

"A no which means yes," Cay sighed. "My favourite kind."

Madi continued to lead the group around the gym, drawing the details into a story as only Madi could. Jordan caught a glimpse of Ali's face in profile as she listened to Madi's speech, steeling her stomach against an unexpected sensation of sudden nausea.

Jordan had always thought Ali Clarke was golden. She was athletic and fearless, stubborn and intelligent. She set goals and climbed toward them with precision and pride. At seventeen, Ali's privileged upbringing had afforded her a status that never once diminished a rigid moral compass of right and wrong. Ali never seemed to falter. To eighteen-year-old Jordan, a tough exterior hiding the softness of her internal bruises, Ali shone like a summer sun in a Maritime winter.

Jordan had walked away from that sun fourteen years ago and wondered if she'd ever been warm since.

"You're scowling."

Jordan blinked into the present. "I'm not."

Cay arched an eyebrow. "She's beautiful. I can't help wondering why that makes you grumpy?"

Jordan had to laugh. "It's a long story."

"The best kind. Let's have coffee this week, and you can start at the beginning. Right now, however, I think Madi's gym tour is done and you're up next."

Jordan checked on the group ahead. Madi was answering questions but kept giving Jordan quick glances. She obviously needed a rescue.

"Got this," Jordan muttered to herself.

"It's only the future of these kids riding on your shoulders," Cay stage whispered. "Don't screw it up."

Jordan grinned at Cay, then squared her shoulders and shook out the tension in her arms. All eyes turned to her as she approached, and Jordan took the three short steps to remind herself why she was here. Soon she would be a social worker, fighting for her kids and the resources that could give them a chance. This was about their future. Past was past.

"I was thinking now that you've had a chance to see the gym, we could head upstairs to the office to talk about what you're proposing. We might actually get to hear ourselves think up there."

"It smells better, too," Madi added.

The group laughed and Jordan smiled at Madi, whose eyes were bright with her recent success. Jordan anchored to that look. Madi and the others needed Jordan to be strong and certain, not tangled up and tripping over history and regret.

Jordan led the group up the metal staircase to the second-floor office and general meeting room. Her own apartment was on the other side of the whitewashed cinderblock wall. The room was pretty banged up and dingy but serviceable. Jordan gestured for everyone to take a seat, but Tom was distracted by the pictures, medals, and awards along the back wall. There was an eight-by-ten black-and-white photo of Jordan during a match. Her face was half-hidden behind her glove and one tattooed, muscled shoulder. The look in Jordan's eyes was calculating and focused.

"Ms. Battiste was telling us you made a career out of boxing for a period of time," Tom said.

Jordan stole a quick glance at Ali, who was already seated across the table. She looked politely interested. The strangeness of casually discussing what had driven them apart was nearly overwhelming.

"Yes, I toured the professional circuit for a few years when I was younger."

"You fought as the Dock Rat, is that right?"

"I did. It was a nod to my working-class upbringing." The answer she always gave. No need to explain she'd felt no better than a dock rat for so long. Working class meant living below the poverty line during cold times, and part of her always feared she would never be any better.

"And would you consider it a successful career?" Tom said.

Jordan had no idea how to measure success. She'd won bouts, even a few championships. She'd learned what to do with her fear, even if she'd never completely conquered it. She'd fought and learned and made her way out of Halifax. And she'd gained enough insight to know when it was time to come home.

"Yes, I think so. Boxing gave my life structure, it gave me a goal, and in the end, it gave me the financial means and the confidence to finish university and buy this gym. So yes, it was a success."

"Thank you for answering that. I recognize it was a personal question, but I'm insatiably curious about how people define success."

Jordan didn't know how to respond. She wasn't sure what to make of this man. Where she'd been expecting bluster and self-aggrandizement, she found thoughtfulness and a good listener.

"What weight class did you compete in?"

"Welterweight."

Tom raised his eyebrows. "Really."

Jordan laughed. "I had more muscle mass back then. And my coach wanted me to fight just outside my weight class."

"He wanted to push you."

"Bento wanted me to focus. He thought matching me with opponents heavier than me would force me to keep my head in the game." Jordan hesitated. The answer was incomplete. She saw Madi looking at her expectantly from the corner. "He wanted me so scared of getting pounded that I'd have to fight my way out of the ring every single time."

Jordan was acutely aware of Ali sitting across from her. They'd spent hours talking about courage and fear and skill and focus. Ali had always believed Jordan could fight. Maybe even right up until the moment Jordan had run away.

"Did it work?" Madi said. She knew a lot of this story, most of the kids did. "Pitting you against ogres. Did it work?"

"That's a good question," Jordan said with a quick grin. "I learned a lot about controlling fear from Bento and from boxing. But I really needed to learn what came after I succeeded at survival. Those lessons took a lot longer."

Madi rolled her eyes and Jordan laughed. Jordan knew Madi hated being preached to. She also knew Madi would give a sharp retort or insult whenever a moment cut just a little too close. Jordan respected those boundaries.

"Would you say you incorporate a lot of your coach's methods into the boxing program?"

Jordan wondered where the CEO was going with this line of inquiry. She needed this meeting to go well to secure the funding for the next year, but she wasn't prepared to defend her practices to a third party who likely knew very little about social services.

"He's not evaluating you, if that's what you're worried about," Ali said from across the table. "Tom is fascinated by organizational leadership and the psychology of workplace hierarchy. I keep telling him he should have been a psychologist, not a CEO."

"Your opinion has been noted, Ms. Clarke," Tom said wryly. "I believe you even sent me a memo to that effect on legal stationery when you finished your law degree a few years back."

"And yet you still haven't given me control of the company. Interesting."

Tom laughed as Ali grinned. Even though Ali's smile wasn't aimed at her, it did absolutely nothing to control the spinning of Jordan's stomach.

"You get to talk to your boss like that?" Madi said.

"'Get to' might be stretching it a little. I've worked with Tom since I graduated from college. I've learned where the line is and not to cross it."

"That sounded like a lesson. Hang on." Madi pulled out her phone and fiddled with it. Then she looked up at Ali with a false eagerness that made Jordan squirm. "Okay, I've got my notes app open. Lay some more wisdom on me, O mentor."

Madi's declaration was met with silence. Cay looked concerned and Tom contemplative. Then Ali laughed, Madi grinned, and the tension broke.

"I think we're going to get along just fine," Ali said.

"If I may interrupt this meeting of the minds for a moment," Tom said. "I think it's important to note this mentorship initiative is not about Alison mentoring you, Ms. Battiste. The exact opposite. You have been chosen to mentor Ms. Clarke."

"I don't get it," Madi said. "You mean in boxing?"

"In whatever wisdom and knowledge and life experience you have to share. That's not up to me to decide. It's not even Alison's choice. You are the mentor, she's here to learn from you."

Jordan could read Madi's agitation in the slight shift of her posture, the way she flicked her fingers on the table, the tilt of her head.

"Maybe you could fill me in on some of the details, Tom." Jordan would normally not interfere, but she thought Madi could use a moment to listen before she was expected to react. "What obligations are you placing on Madi and the gym with this mentorship program? It would be helpful to understand the expectations."

Tom looked surprised. "No obligations at all. The funding is in place for a year regardless of what happens from here on out."

"Then why are you here?" Madi said. "You have to *want* something out of this, even if you're telling me I don't *need* to do anything."

Madi's question was met with silence. Tom seemed at a loss, and Jordan didn't exactly blame him. She doubted his business skills extended to dealing with mouthy young adults.

"Centera fucked up," Ali jumped in. Tom winced. "Big time. We're a holding company, so we don't produce anything. We just buy up the stocks of other companies and take on their risks. But our investors walked a grey legal line to try and make our last quarter look more profitable than it really was so our shareholders wouldn't freak out. While they were busy trying to defend the legality of their action, we failed to recognize we had quite resoundingly crossed a moral line. We put our customers' data at risk and narrowly avoided selling them out to a third party. It was a legal nightmare, and we barely emerged unscathed."

Tom picked up the story. "And then we walked right into an ethical dilemma. Do we tell our stakeholders and customers? The crisis was averted, but we sell them trust and security. A disclosure would be disastrous."

"But failing to disclose and being discovered would have meant the end of Centera Corporation," Ali said. "Years of legal battles, our names raked through the mud, blacklisted from our place amongst the top international holding companies."

"Let me guess," Madi said. "You did the right moral thing and told everyone you fucked up. And they were unhappy. Now you're trying to win back their love and trust by throwing money bombs at street kids."

Tom's shoulders seemed to droop and Jordan nearly felt sorry for him. But Madi was dead on as usual, and Jordan wanted to hear how the CEO of a massive multinational would react to being called out.

"Yes," Ali answered.

Madi narrowed her eyes like she didn't trust the direct answer.

"Another guess, here. You were voluntold to be part of this little community outreach project."

"Yes."

"Did you fuck up? Is that why?"

Ali shrugged. "It doesn't matter."

"It matters to me."

Ali half smiled and gestured at Madi. "Get your notes app open. I think you'll want to write this shit down." Ali leaned forward. "It doesn't matter which individuals screwed up. I work for Centera. I *am* Centera. One of us falls, we all fall."

Jordan expected another string of curses from Madi. She'd spent her entire life surviving and looking out for herself. Boxing had taught her to channel some of her anger. Coaching, mentoring, and managing had taught her it was okay to take a risk and care about others, to twine your futures together, even for a short time. Madi was incredibly protective of the teens in the gym, but she hadn't yet learned those lessons and wasn't comfortable with caring.

"For me, this isn't about buying back trust," Tom said. "I want to change corporate culture, Ms. Battiste. I *need* to change corporate culture. We have become too concerned with pushing the legal boundaries of what we can do to make more money and have lost sight of who we are ultimately serving. So I am embedding a dozen of my top executives in communities across North America. I want them to listen and learn and return to the office with a perspective of people and society we are sorely lacking. There will be no cameras or media announcements. Each executive is expected to maintain a journal and will give a short presentation at our AGM in Chicago next year. You are welcome to attend. Your insight and judgement would be welcome."

Jordan slid the facts around in her head like tiles in a game, not only Tom's words but his obvious passion to do better. Jordan trusted it. She wasn't sure what Madi thought.

"I bet your shareholders are unhappy," Jordan said.

"They think I'm absolutely off my rocker," Tom announced happily.

Madi was still looking at Ali with suspicion. Ali seemed relaxed, perfectly comfortable with the scrutiny.

"So you're just going to follow me around and become inspired by my story and my struggle to survive, is that it? Maybe by the end we're braiding each other's hair and you're offering to pay for me to go to university because you're so moved by everything I've taught you. Sound about right?"

Ali's expression didn't change, and she didn't look to anyone else for support. Jordan respected her for that. "You're here at the gym four or five times a week, is that right?"

"Yes," Madi said.

"I thought I'd start by coming by for a few practices. I'm interested in seeing how the coach and boxer roles coincide with your friendships. I thought we'd start there. Is that okay?"

Madi cocked her head to the side. "Yeah. Sure."

"As for the other, I'm a lost cause when it comes to anything to do with hair. But if that's what you want to teach me, I'm up for the challenge."

Madi nodded but said nothing. Jordan was pretty sure Ali confused her. It took a long time for Madi to trust anyone, and she gave them a hell of a ride along the way. This could get interesting.

"You're here for a year?" Jordan's thoughts were still on how this whole program would affect Madi, weighing the pros and the cons. She hadn't considered how Ali might perceive her question.

"I'm committing to this mentorship for a year, yes," Ali said. Jordan tried not to squirm at the correction. Ali's voice softened just a little when she continued. "I'll be working part-time at our Halifax office for the first six months, but I'll still need to travel fairly frequently back to my main office in Chicago."

Jordan nodded a short acknowledgement like she hadn't just heard Ali Clarke was walking back into her life.

"Well, then," Tom said. He leaned back in his chair, obviously pleased with where this conversation had gone. "I'd like to thank you all for your time. I'm heading to the West Coast tomorrow morning, but I'll be checking in regularly with Alison to see how her homecoming is going and how things are working out with Ms. Battiste."

They pushed aside their mismatched chairs and shook hands, all the social niceties that Jordan had come to learn and respect.

"I'll answer your question," Madi said, remaining seated.

"Madi?" Jordan said.

Madi had her eyes fixed on Tom. "You asked Jordan if she used any of her coach's methods in the boxing program with the kids. With us."

"Yes, that's right. I did ask that," Tom said.

"The answer is no. Jordan already knows we can survive tougher opponents. She's teaching us to focus, not fight. She's teaching us to expect more from ourselves and the people around us. And she would never use fear as a teaching tool. None of us would be here if she did."

Jordan thought she might cry. Right here in front of Madi, the bright fierceness in her eyes a perfect match for her voice. She was going to cry in front of Cay, in front of the CEO of a multi-million-dollar company. In front of Ali Clarke.

Then Madi stood and grinned, breaking the tension. She nodded toward Ali.

"You might want to start your journal with that mic drop moment." Madi walked toward the door with a wave. "See you at practice tomorrow."

The adults were left staring at each other, the kid having walked out of the room with all of their words.

CHAPTER TWO

Constable Rachel Shreve was sitting on the step outside the gym when Jordan showed up the next day. Rachel was in a T-shirt and jeans, short hair tucked behind her ears, gym bag by her feet. Her eyes were closed and her head tilted back in the sunlight, a half smile on her face. Jordan had always thought the cop was attractive. Rachel was also a good friend, a huge asset as a volunteer at the gym, and married to one of the nicest men Jordan had ever met.

"Tell me you're dreaming about Adam," Jordan said.

Rachel opened her eyes and laughed. "If I was, I wouldn't tell you."

Rachel was a community officer who'd started her career on the very same streets where Jordan and most of her kids had been raised. Now that Rachel had two youngsters at home, she was making her way to the investigative branch of the Halifax Police Department. The move would be a good one for the young cop, but Jordan would miss her on the streets, knowing she always looked out for her kids.

Peppy music drifted out from the gym, punctuated by gleefully shouted instructions. Jordan rented out the gym to a mom-and-me boxercise class a few times a week, one of the ways she kept the bills paid and the doors open. She had a partner, Sean, who ran all the adult programming at the gym, arranging scheduling and membership. He'd even recently brought Jordan a proposal for small classes and private clients. But as much as he wanted to make JP's Gym lucrative, he respected Jordan's primary objective was to run the programming for vulnerable youth.

"You're here early," Jordan said, taking a seat beside Rachel.

"Yes and no. I've got some official business to get out of the way before practice tonight." Rachel hurried to clarify. "Everyone is fine, but I just wanted to check in with you about something I've been hearing on the street."

Jordan turned her face into the October afternoon sun and let her heart rate return to normal. After a restless night followed by another busy day, the sun felt good against her cheeks. She'd lain in bed for a long time last night, thinking about Ali. She could feel her presence somehow. Something tangible was in the air, as if Ali's arrival in the city had changed the molecules. Eventually she'd gone to sleep, frustrated by her inability to put Ali's presence into perspective. Jordan had focused on work all day today, trying not to become distracted by the clock.

Rachel pulled her phone out of her pocket and scrolled through a series of images. Then she passed her phone to Jordan to take a look.

"Do you recognize this symbol? Is it at all familiar to you?"

Jordan was looking at a picture of a tattoo. Stylized sun rays on one side and what looked like sword points or knife points on the other. It was simply designed and looked professionally done, unlike some of the horrible ink she'd seen come through her gym. But Jordan didn't recognize the symbol.

"No, sorry. It doesn't look familiar," Jordan said as she handed back the phone.

"I guess it's too much to ask if you recognize the tattoo artist?" Rachel said.

Jordan shook her head. "It doesn't look like a street tat, that's pretty much all I can tell you."

"It was a long shot, thanks." Rachel sighed and put away her phone. "This symbol was spray-painted in a dozen places around the downtown core last night. Mostly tourist spots but also the food bank and a methadone clinic."

"Seems pretty random."

"I think so, too. Or maybe it's not. The tattoo is from a resident who lived at one of the homeless shelters. He was found non-responsive a few weeks ago, and we investigated cause of death. Turns out it was medically related, not suspicious. But that symbol really stuck in my mind."

"Think it's a gang tattoo?"

Rachel blew out a breath. "God, I hope not. We're finally getting things under control the last few years with the Halifax-Toronto trafficking pipeline. I'd hate to think something else is moving up to take its place."

Jordan felt the same way. They were constantly on the lookout for gang activity, especially around the girls.

"I'll keep an eye out."

"Thanks, friend," Rachel said and closed her eyes again. "Hey, I've never asked you about your ink. Did you get any of it done in Halifax?" Rachel said.

"Just the one between my shoulders," Jordan said. It was a detailed tree with reaching branches and anchoring roots. Her brother Steven's initials were set into the whorled knots and branches.

"And the rest?"

Jordan pushed her T-shirt up over her shoulder and looked at the half-sleeve on her left arm. She touched it lightly, smiling. It was a tableau of water with cranes in the distance and a sky that was half storm and half sunshine.

"I got these done in New York. A woman I met on the boxing scene." Then Jordan blushed and Rachel laughed.

"A boxing fan, huh?"

Jordan smiled. It was hard to feel too embarrassed around Rachel. "Nadia grew up around boxing her whole life. She was an artist and a philosopher and a psychic."

"A psychic boxing fan. Did she predict your wins?"

"No, nothing like that. She came up to me after a bout, told me we should have tea and talk. My coach said I should go, said no one ever turned down Nadia Sokolov. So we talked and drank some strange herbal infusion. I told her about my childhood, about how boxing scared me. When she asked me about my deepest desire, I told her I wanted to run away from my life."

Rachel remained quiet. Jordan had already trusted her with some of the darker moments of her past, including her brother Steven's death when she was fifteen.

"Was that really your deepest desire?"

"Yes. In a way." Jordan didn't add that what she'd really wanted back then was to be with Ali, somewhere far away from Halifax and from boxing. Jordan tilted her head back and blinked into the afternoon sunlight. Ali was here. She swallowed and continued her story. "Nadia turned my story into the design for this tattoo. She believed we carry our past, present, and future around with us, and our stories deserve to be told in some form or another."

"That's a beautiful story," Rachel said softly. "Thanks for sharing it."

They sat in silence in the sunshine as the boxercise class wrapped up, the sound of the dance music replaced by laughter and conversation.

"I imagine that would be a hard story to tell your kids," Rachel said. "But I wish they could hear it, you know?"

Jordan did know. "I wouldn't have heard it at their age. I wasn't ready. And I'm not an artist or a storyteller. I just want to keep them alive so they can hear it when someone like Nadia walks into their life and asks to hear their story." Jordan wasn't sure she was making any sense. Past and present still seemed so mixed up, a whirl of emotion instead of reason. Jordan hated this off-kilter feeling. She dropped her head and sighed.

"Sorry," Rachel said quickly. "That was a little intense for a Thursday afternoon."

Jordan laughed. "No, you're good. Really. Just a lot going on these days."

She was grateful Rachel let it pass. Moments later, the gym doors opened and moms with strollers and babies and bags pushed out into the afternoon sun, their faces bright with exertion and endorphins. Jordan envied them their chemical high. She checked the time on her phone. She could still get in a workout before the kids arrived.

"Want to spar today?" she asked Rachel.

Rachel grinned, and her eyes flashed with the challenge. "Yeah, definitely. Just don't flatten me."

Twenty minutes later, they had changed into workout gear and warmed up. Jordan checked in with Sean, who was heading home to feed his kids. He'd be on-site later for the adult gym time, once her teen program was done. Sean was an easy-going guy and had always reminded her of Steven. Not in their looks—Sean was a ginger from a long line of Irishmen—but his temperament. Like Steven, Sean was laid-back, solid, and empathetic without being overbearing.

Once Jordan finished talking with Sean, she pulled on her cracked and worn sparring gloves. They felt comfortable and she had never once felt the frisson of fear and self-loathing her boxing gloves had once elicited.

Rachel already had her mouthguard in and her gloves on. She'd been training with Jordan and her kids for five years, and she'd even tried fighting a few real bouts before she got pregnant with Hannah. Rachel was small but completely driven to excel. She fought with a joy Jordan knew she could never match. She grinned as Rachel threw shadow punches.

"I'm on defense," Jordan said, mouthguard only half in. "Chase me." Jordan pushed in her mouthguard the rest of the way and raised her gloves.

Rachel moved in fast, but Jordan easily sidestepped her opening gambit. They were only sparring, aiming for light blows that would score points if anyone had cared to keep track. Rachel tried to back Jordan against the ropes to slow her footwork so she could land something. Jordan danced out of reach, weaving once under Rachel's outstretched arm in a showy move that would have earned her a blistering lecture from Bento if she'd ever tried it in a bout. But this wasn't a real match, and Jordan felt the edges of lightness as she continued to take Rachel's punches on her gloves, her body warming. She anticipated another of Rachel's punches, allowing Rachel's sparring gloves to touch her high on the shoulder before she landed a three-punch combination on Rachel's torso. Then Jordan pivoted away to the other side of the ring, leaving Rachel frustrated and laughing.

Jordan heard the kids enter the gym, but she wanted Rachel to be the one to end the sparring session. Sometimes defeat was easier when you were the one allowed to admit it. Jordan took a few more punches on her gloves, narrowly avoided Rachel's surprise right jab, and managed to score another point before retreating to the other side of the ring. Rachel followed, but seemed to think better of it. She stepped back and touched her right glove to her left shoulder, signaling the end to their sparring session. They met in the middle of the ring and embraced lightly before walking to the ropes, pushing off their gloves, and spitting out their mouthguards.

"You're barely sweating," Rachel complained good-naturedly as she used her T-shirt to wipe her face. "One day I'm going to take you down, McAddie."

Jordan laughed. "That's the spirit." She cuffed her friend lightly on the shoulder. "Thanks for the spar. I needed that."

Rachel grinned.

"Hey, Jordan. We doing ring work tonight?"

Jordan looked through the ropes to see Rupert and Sierra looking up at her hopefully. Sierra was already in loose shorts and a T-shirt, and Rupert held a plastic bag in his fist. The likelihood he'd washed his gym clothes from yesterday was slim.

"Sure," Jordan said, making a quick decision. Better to work out with the kids than sit around watching Ali all night. "But get warmed up first, at least half the circuit."

Rupert and Sierra high-fived. Sometimes they were simply puppies, tumbling and cheerful and energetic, but those puppies had teeth and claws and a history of hurt. Jordan never forgot that.

Jordan jumped down off the mat and found her water bottle. Kids were still trickling in, and Jordan could hear the slam of car doors as foster parents or older siblings dropped them off. A few graduates came in, waving at Jordan. The space between childhood and adulthood didn't exist for them in the same unyielding way it did for government services. What Jordan wanted to provide for all the kids she supported, regardless of when they turned nineteen, was constancy and care. She considered it a success when the graduates returned.

"Hey."

Jordan tried not to flinch when she heard Ali's voice, unexpectedly close and undeniably familiar. When she turned around, the laughter in Ali's eyes said she'd failed miserably.

"Hey," Jordan said. She couldn't think of a single other word to say.

"You always did scare easily," Ali said.

"And you always found it weirdly entertaining." She wondered, maybe a little late, if she should be encouraging this connection. That's why she'd been awake so much of the night.

"You've got more ink than I remember," Ali said, nodding at Jordan's bicep.

Jordan looked down briefly. "I had no ink when you knew me."

"True. But it was just a matter of time."

Before Jordan could interpret Ali's words, Madi approached.

"How well do you two know each other, exactly?" Madi said, pulling her long hair into a braid. She obviously intended to work out tonight.

"Just our last year of high school," Jordan said. Her being gay wasn't a secret and never had been. Specifics were not necessarily open for discussion, however.

Madi continued to eye Jordan and then Ali while she tied off her braid and tossed it over her shoulder. "It's cute the way you think that answers my question. I'm trying to establish the nature and depth of your history, not the exact year you met."

Jordan loved this kid. She really did. But she absolutely did not want to answer this question. Ali clearly had other ideas.

"We dated. I guess we weren't that much younger than you."

Madi gave Jordan a triumphant look before turning her attention more fully to Ali.

"So we're talking young love, then. What was Jordan like? I'm imagining she was angry and wounded, maybe discovering her sexuality, all seething—"

"Enough, Madi," Jordan said, smiling even as she put down the boundary. "My story and my life."

Madi grimaced at Jordan, though she clearly wasn't surprised by the rebuke. "Fine. But if you really don't want everyone to know Ali is your ex, you're going to have to stop looking all dopey and bashful when she's around." Madi jerked her chin over at the circuits where most of the kids were now warming up. "These guys will know in five minutes you've tapped it."

"Madi." Jordan's voice had an edge this time.

Madi threw her arms up in surrender. "I'm out." She walked away, smiling.

Jordan watched her go. She did not want to look at Ali.

"She's a firecracker, as my dad would say."

"Yeah, she is. And incredibly bright with very high emotional intelligence." Jordan took a breath and turned to Ali. "Which she uses for good and evil."

"Maybe she should be a lawyer," Ali said.

"You should tell her that."

"I will."

Someone cranked the music, and Johnny Cash came blaring through the speakers.

"Nice warm-up music," Ali said.

Jordan said nothing. She suddenly wanted to be away from Ali; away from the uncertainty of what to say and how to act; away from the constant awareness that she needed to apologize to Ali for walking away when they were younger.

Running, Jordan thought to herself.

"I should go," Jordan said awkwardly. "You know, get the kids organized."

"Sure." Jordan thought she caught a moment of doubt in Ali's expression. That couldn't be. Ali Clarke was never uncertain. "I'll catch up with Madi."

Jordan nodded and turned to go, uncomfortably relieved to have Ali out of her line of sight. It was going to be a long night. And an even longer six months.

"Hey, JP!"

Jordan's heart bottomed out and rebounded, and she closed her eyes at Ali using her old nickname. But they weren't seventeen anymore.

"Can I buy you a beer later?"

Jordan shook her head slowly. "*I'm* buying," Jordan said. Ali grinned and Jordan tried desperately to school her expression before she approached her kids.

Rupert and Sierra were waiting impatiently for Jordan in the ring. They were throwing imaginary punches at each other from opposite ends of the ring, laughing and trading insults. Rupert was smiling, and right now he looked like a boy with a crush. Sierra seemed to like the attention. Jordan made a mental note to check in with Cay, who was her social worker. At sixteen, Sierra had already had a baby removed from her care. She had committed to getting her life back on track and getting her baby out of the foster home. Jordan and Cay planned to help get her there.

"I'm going to take you down," Rupert called across to Sierra, throwing a wobbly right hook that left his head wide open.

"Not with that, you're not," Jordan said as she climbed into the ring. It was easier to focus with the music and the noise of the kids in the background. "Sierra, tell him why you'd have him on the mat with that throw."

Forty-five minutes later, Jordan was sweating from keeping up with the teenagers. They were still dancing and throwing punches but had focused their energy and aim with her guidance. Sierra had an athlete's ability to read her opponent and knew when to stay out of the way or move in. When she timed her right hook accurately, it was killer. Rupert, on the other hand, was a solid block who could take a blow and follow up without faltering. He'd once told Jordan that boxing fit his life philosophy: don't let anyone knock you down. It wouldn't work in a real match, but Jordan had to hand it to the teen. He'd committed valiantly to a life course.

The music dropped noticeably, signaling the fifteen-minute cool-down. Groans and cheers bounced around the gym. Jordan gauged the clusters of teens scattered around the equipment. Tonight had been a good night. Jordan caught sight of Ali. At some point, she'd pulled off her button-up shirt and was now just in her tee. She'd been holding a bag and kick gloves for Madi as they'd paired up for a circuit run. Jordan couldn't read Madi's body language, but the two of them were still together, and that was a good sign.

"Rupert and Sierra, can you grab the food from the fridge?" Jordan tossed them the key to her apartment. She knew the kids talked about who Jordan trusted with her apartment key, even just for the five minutes it took to grab their post-workout snack and return.

Rupert and Sierra high-fived and ran off. *Puppies*, Jordan thought again. And then, because she'd wanted to all night, Jordan walked over to Madi and Ali.

"Jordan, tell your ex to bring workout gear next time," Madi said as she sat on the floor and stretched.

"Madi, you can call her Ali or Ms. Clarke," Jordan said before turning to Ali. "Ali, bring your workout gear next time."

Ali threw her hands up. "Madi has berated me sufficiently. I'm bringing workout gear tomorrow."

Madi leapt up from the mat with an agility Jordan envied. "Tomorrow I'm coaching. You can find a circuit partner, probably. Or follow me around." Madi shrugged. "Doesn't matter to me." Jordan caught the mildly embarrassed look on Madi's face. Interesting. When she turned back, Madi had controlled her expression. "Food's here. It will be gone in about two and a half minutes, so get in there if you want some."

Ali waved away the offer and Madi shrugged and left, leaving them alone.

"Firecracker," Ali confirmed. "She's great."

Jordan's heart swelled at the approval in Ali's tone. Then her head warned caution.

"Madi's a great human being. And incredibly complex."

Ali looked at Jordan carefully. "I won't hurt her, JP."

"Never said you would." She wanted to tell Ali to call her Jordan. It seemed childish, but more than anything, she wanted Ali to see her as an adult. A functioning, successful adult. Jordan breathed deep into her core as shadows of doubt and uncertainty darkened her thoughts.

She turned when Ali gave a low whistle. Jordan followed her gaze to see the kids gathered around the foldout table, grabbing carrot sticks and apples and handfuls of almonds. The ranch dip would be gone by now. Jordan tried not to calculate how much of her paycheck she spent every month on ranch dip.

"That's one of the things Centera's donation is helping pay for," Jordan said. "It's the only time some of them see a vegetable."

"That's awesome," Ali said, still watching the cluster of teens fighting over the food. "What else?" She suddenly seemed all business, but Jordan recognized the light in her eyes. She was pursuing something.

"Nothing flashy," Jordan said with a shrug. "Gym time, mostly. I can't legally make money off the program, but I offer the gym to the Ministry of Children and Youth Services at cost. I'm hoping to get a washer and dryer in here at some point so the kids can take turns washing their clothes while they work out."

Ali wrinkled her nose. Jordan tried not to feel defensive and failed.

"They're street kids, Ali. A lot of them, anyway. It's not their fault."

Jordan had never been that kid, not really. She'd had brothers who looked out for her when her parents couldn't. But she knew the humiliation of powerlessness and poverty. She felt the weight of Ali's judgement, for herself and her kids.

"Sorry. That was an unnecessary reaction," Ali said. "I'm just not used to being around teenagers. They're…fragrant."

Jordan allowed a smile, but she was torn. She knew she should give Ali some leeway, allow her to be the decent human she'd always been. But Ali knew very little about this world. Caution settled like a resolution in Jordan's thoughts. It was comforting. It was distance.

"Jordan, do you have a minute?"

Rachel approached and her posture was tense, her expression focused. She'd disappeared halfway through the workout. Jordan assumed she'd got a call-out.

"What's up?"

Rachel looked up and was about to speak when she saw Ali.

"Hi. Sorry, I'm interrupting."

"Not a problem," Jordan said. "Rachel, this is Ali Clarke. She's partnering with Madi for the mentorship program. Ali, this is Constable Rachel Shreve."

The two women shook hands. Rachel smiled warmly, but Ali seemed a little stiff.

"Do you mind if I steal Jordan away for a minute, Ali?"

Jordan began to worry.

"No, not at all. I'll leave you two alone."

Jordan watched Ali walk over to the chaos around the snack table. Jordan admired her courage. She focused back on Rachel.

"What is it?"

"Probably nothing. That symbol I showed you earlier? Turns out the mayor's office and all sixteen regional councilors received a fax earlier today with the sun symbol and the words 'lighting the dark to help you see.' "

"Sounds vaguely ominous. But who sends faxes anymore?"

"Someone who has access to the main branch of the library, since that's where we traced the sending number."

"So, it's still just a weird event. Sounds less like a gang, if you ask me. They don't tend to worry about faxes, regional politics, and being helpful."

Rachel smiled, but she seemed to do it just for Jordan's benefit. "I guess you're right."

"Anything you want me to do?"

Rachel put her hand on Jordan's arm, squeezing gently. "No, friend. Just keep an eye out and listen for anything the kids are bringing in about this. I..." Another hesitation. Very unlike the confident constable.

"Say it, Rach."

"Something's up. Something…organized. I don't know what yet. But the gang task force is saying they've got nothing new. No new activity, no increase in trafficking or prostitution. Other than the influx of opioids, which is true in every municipality across the country, the gang scene is low and slow, as they put it."

"Organized but not a gang. Is that it?"

Rachel grimaced. "I know it doesn't make any sense. It's just petty crimes. But it's the targeted nature of those petty crimes that's making me nervous. That symbol is making me nervous." She shrugged. "Maybe I'm off."

"Trust your instincts on this, Rach."

Rachel looked away for a moment, doubt causing her posture to slump. Then she turned back to Jordan and smiled slightly. "Yeah, okay. But maybe I'll wait until I have more information before I bring it up with my supervisor."

"Fair enough, Constable," Jordan said, trying to keep Rachel in a positive headspace. Self-doubt didn't look good on her. "Be good to yourself."

"You, too. I'm going to go home and put my babies to bed. See you tomorrow if I can make it."

"I'll see you then."

Rachel left and Jordan took a moment to try and clear her head before heading over to the table where a handful of kids still lounged. Ali was talking with Madi and Sierra. Sierra was showing Ali something on her phone. Probably pictures of her little girl, Brooklynn, if that smile on her face was any indication.

Madi looked up first when Jordan approached.

"Everything okay?"

Jordan touched her lightly on the shoulder. Madi was tense.

"Yeah, Madi. Everything's okay."

Madi gave Jordan a long look, as if testing the veracity of Jordan's statement. Then she turned away.

"I'm out. Places to be, people to do. Sierra, you coming?"

Jordan caught Ali's expression of surprise but Ali just blinked and said nothing. Madi was going for shock value. It meant she'd had a good night with Ali. Now she was going to attempt some self-sabotage. But it wasn't going to work if Jordan could help it. She wondered at herself. She'd gone from wanting to protect Madi from whatever this mentorship was to wanting to pin Ali down and hold her to her promises.

As Madi rounded up the last of the kids and clanged the gym door closed behind them, Jordan rubbed her hands over her face. Long day, so little sleep. And a beer with Ali. She looked up to see Ali watching her.

"You still up for a beer? I'll understand if you're not. You look beat."

Maybe she should take this offer of distance. Establish a boundary, draw a line between past and present. But she really, really didn't want to.

"Give me ten minutes to shower?"

Ali looked down at her own T-shirt and pulled it away from her body. Jordan tried and failed to not watch Ali running her hands over her stomach.

"How about you meet me at the Anchor Inn Pub in half an hour? It's next to my hotel."

"Yeah, okay. Perfect," Jordan said. Of course Ali was staying at the swankiest hotel in Halifax.

Ali dropped her hand and said nothing. Jordan wished she'd leave. And briefly, so briefly, wished she'd never arrived.

"You can pick somewhere else. I just thought—"

"No," Jordan interrupted, feeling like an ass. "It's good. See you there in half an hour."

Another drawn-out pause. Jordan felt the weight of their uncertainty.

"Just a beer, Jordan," Ali said quietly.

Jordan could not hold her gaze. She picked up the remnants of the veggie platter and wiped the table down quickly with a napkin. Arms full, clearly ready to go, Jordan met Ali's eyes.

"Just a beer sounds great."

❖

The Anchor Inn Pub pretended to be a local bar with history. Every detail had been designed to make the tourists in the neighbouring hotel feel like they were part of the seaside city's local flavour, including the shiny black anchor on a pedestal outside the heavy wooden front door.

Jordan, in dark jeans and a black shirt under her leather jacket, snorted quietly as she parked her car up the street. Cay would give her a hard time if she saw Jordan here. But the chance of running into anyone she knew was slim.

"Jordan, hello."

Jordan turned at the sound of her name to see a familiar figure approaching from the street.

"Helena, hi," Jordan said.

Helena Cavio was a petite woman with thin, straight brown hair that fell just below her jaw, her bangs blunt across her forehead in a style either fashionable or uncaring. Given her intense focus and commitment to protecting and supporting the vulnerable in their community, Jordan guessed the latter. Her clothes were always clean but worn. Helena was often slightly awkward, a fierce champion for her clients but a bit of an oddity with her colleagues.

"Out shopping?" Jordan said, indicating the large reusable shopping bag Helena had over her shoulder.

Helena's eyes lit up.

"I've just picked up a few maps for a project we're doing in our support group. We're discussing what it means to have a home, to be home."

Jordan smiled at Helena. They'd always gotten along well in meetings and the working groups to which they both belonged.

"That sounds incredible. Maybe it's something I could adapt with the teens? I'd love to hear more about it, but I'm just heading in to meet someone." Jordan sheepishly indicated the Anchor Inn behind them, though she doubted Helena was the type to judge.

The look of excitement dimmed a little on Helena's face.

"Yes, of course. We can connect whenever you'd like."

A figure emerged from the dark street.

"Let me get that for you, boss."

Helena smiled at the man who took the bags and propped them over his shoulder. Jordan thought he looked familiar, but it took a moment to place him.

"Creaser?"

The man looked up and smiled. Everything about James Creaser had always been good-natured.

"Jordan. Man, I haven't seen you in ages." Creaser turned to Helena. "Jordan and me grew up together, same neighbourhood. She's good people."

"Thanks, man. So are you," Jordan said. Seeing Creaser made her think of late nights hanging out at the park, a sense of boredom and danger and belonging. "It's good to see you."

Helena looked back and forth between the two, her smile serene. "Yes, good people. Well, we should go set up for a meeting. Have a good night."

Creaser waved cheerfully and followed Helena into the night.

As she headed into the bar, Jordan considered Creaser and their shared history in one of the rougher neighbourhoods of Halifax. Knowing what she did now, Jordan suspected Creaser had Fetal Alcohol Spectrum Disorder. He had struggled in school, but he was always wanting to please the people around him, which often made him the fall guy. And he couldn't predict future consequences for his actions. Jordan was happy to see he was his same happy-go-lucky self, connected to community services like Helena's.

The bar was sticky warm and smelled of shrimp and garlic and hops. The combination made Jordan's stomach rumble, despite her resistance to the pub itself. Ali was already seated along the wall under black-and-white photos of Halifax Harbour. She was dressed simply, her hair still damp and tucked behind her ears. It made her look younger, like the teenager Jordan had once known. Jordan wasn't sure if that made this easier or harder.

"Don't be mad, I ordered shrimp," Ali said, by way of greeting.

Jordan laughed and took off her jacket, pulling herself into the booth opposite Ali.

"It does smell good. Why would I be mad?"

"Because I promised just a beer," Ali said.

She really was beautiful, Jordan thought. The bar was evening dark, each table lit with one overhead light and a glass globe lantern. The candlelight made Ali's skin glow, the shine of her smile matching the expression in her eyes. Seeing that look again and knowing it had once belonged to her was joy and agony.

The waiter approached with menus, the specials, and a dizzying list of local craft brews on tap. Jordan ordered a lager from Lunenburg, just down the coast. Ali ordered amber ale from a brewery only a few blocks from where they sat. When the waiter left, Jordan found just enough courage to jump in.

"I assumed the 'just a beer' comment had more to do with our conversation and less to do with what we ordered."

Ali looked briefly surprised, then gave a short laugh. "I thought maybe I'd leave it open to interpretation."

"Meaning you'd let me take the lead?" Jordan had the sense she wasn't being fair, that she was pushing. But she didn't stop.

"Showing up unexpectedly, not just in your city but in your gym, and then directing what we were going to talk about seemed overly presumptuous. Even for me."

"So, you knew it was my gym before you arrived."

"Yes."

"Did you tell your boss to send you here?"

Ali seemed to catch the anger in Jordan's tone. Ali flexed her jaw but kept the same even modulation in her voice.

"I didn't seek you out, Jordan. I knew Tom wanted me back in my hometown. He liked the symmetry of it. And he knows I…" Ali hesitated, then carried on. "It doesn't matter. When the description of the program at JP's Gym came across my desk, I knew it was you. I did some research to confirm."

Jordan didn't say anything. The obvious next question hung between them, so she waited.

Ali was about to speak when the waiter returned with their drinks. They thanked him but left their beer untouched.

"Not contacting you first to give you a heads-up was childish," Ali said. "And I apologize."

Ali turned her pint glass in slow circles on the table but kept her eyes on Jordan.

The apology made Jordan feel a hundred times worse, not better. Jordan rubbed the back of her head roughly, then sat up a little straighter.

"I'm a complete shit. I owe you an apology for running away. For not really explaining why I had to leave. For leaving you a letter and then not contacting you. For…" Jordan trailed off and then shrugged. "For a million things. I'm sorry."

Ali nodded slowly, her expression never changing. Then she picked up her pint glass in a salute.

"To forgiveness," Ali said.

Jordan raised her glass, and they clinked.

"Forgiveness."

They both drank to absolution, as tentative and shallow as it was in its current state. Jordan was grateful for the sharp, cold taste of the beer on her tongue, and she pulled in a long gulp. Ali lowered her glass and tilted her head to the side, as if in silent reflection. Then she tilted her beer slightly toward Jordan before she spoke.

"You broke my heart."

Jordan almost choked, and Ali grinned. Maybe she was forgiven, but Ali was not going to make this easy. In some ways, it made Jordan feel better.

"I know. I'm sorry. I really am."

Better or worse to admit she'd broken her own heart the day she walked away? To admit that the current state of her heart was still suspect? No. Jordan knew she wasn't ready for that.

"We were kids, Jordan. I'm not kidding about the forgiveness."

"It was still a shitty thing to do. Especially to someone who meant so much to me."

Ali said nothing, and Jordan risked another sip of her beer. She felt more vulnerable than she had in a long, long time. She wrestled with it in silence, waiting for Ali to say something.

"You really love those kids."

It wasn't the conversation Jordan was expecting. But it was easier.

"I do. Some I've known for a long time now. Working with them isn't always easy. Loving them is."

Ali looked surprised, and Jordan lifted her chin. This was what she wanted Ali to see. Jordan was more whole, more grounded, just *more* than the angry teenager Ali had known.

When Ali didn't add anything, Jordan jumped in.

"What about you? You told Madi you've worked with Centera since you left college?"

Ali took a drink of beer before answering.

"Eleven years. Worked there through both my MBA and my law degree."

"Impressive," Jordan said. She'd always known Ali would climb. "You must love it if you've been there that long."

Ali gave a tight smile. "It's been home for a long time." She seemed to relax a little. "Tom's a good guy, he really is. I've learned a lot from him."

Jordan knew there was more. She didn't know Ali well enough any more to push.

The platter of garlic shrimp arrived with skewers of vegetables and a pile of rice. The waiter dropped off two plates, and Jordan and Ali served themselves.

"Tastes as good as it smells," Ali groaned, popping an entire shrimp into her mouth. "Thank God."

Jordan took a bite of the grilled zucchini, wondering at Ali's strange expression. "What?"

"You're willingly eating vegetables? That's a thing you do now?"

In reply, Jordan stabbed at a red pepper and ate it.

"I'm an adult. Adults fucking love vegetables."

Ali leaned back in the booth and laughed, and Jordan's heart swelled at the unrestrained sound.

"There you are," Jordan said softly. She recognized the girl she'd known, recognized their last summer together in that laugh.

Ali looked startled. "Sorry?"

"I..." This was overstepping, creating bonds when she meant to be traveling the line of present, not past. "You looked like your high school self just then. That's all."

"I don't the rest of the time?" Ali grinned and patted her stomach. "I haven't had a six-pack since I was a senior in college."

Jordan laughed with her. "I wasn't referring to muscle tone." Ali raised one of her eyebrows suggestively, then laughed when Jordan blushed. "Fuck off," she mumbled good-naturedly. "You know that's not what I meant."

"You look exactly the same as when you blushed in high school, JP."

Jordan kept shaking her head, but she was smiling. She and Ali were talking about the past as a warm time, not the brittle coldness of how it ended. Jordan felt the need to apologize again. She wondered if that feeling would ever stop.

"Ali, I—"

Ali stopped her with a raised hand. "Can we leave it right now? The archaeological dig." She smiled oddly, and Jordan wondered if she was trying to soften her words. "I'm really enjoying getting to know

Jordan McAddie as she is now." She paused and looked out across the restaurant, then back again. "I didn't know if I would ever get the chance."

Relief and regret and the painful beginnings of hope twisted in Jordan's stomach. She took a steadying breath, willing the hope to die down. "Yeah, okay. Let's do that." She didn't know if this was the start of something new or the delayed but final chapter, but her heart was very clear which she wanted it to be.

CHAPTER THREE

Jordan—Nine

Nine years old and the sun is warm on Jordan's face as she rides in the passenger seat next to her dad. He's picked her up from school for a dentist appointment, and Jordan is secretly thrilled and proud her dad has shown up and signed her out and taken her to Dr. Singh on time. He's on a swing shift. No point in taking her back to school, so they stop for ice cream. Jordan doesn't tell her dad the cold hurts her teeth where they just filled three cavities. She bites the frozen chocolate pieces and winces and smiles at her dad and wonders why pain always comes with happiness.

They walk down to the docks, and her dad waves to the guy at the security booth who shakes his head and makes a show of pretending not to see Jordan. Her dad points out the cranes, the efficient layout of the shipping yard, and all the precautions that keep the workers safe. The sun glints off the water and the windows of the booth of the crane operators, sitting up so high they must feel like they're floating. Jordan wants to be up there moving freight, listening to the gulls and the hum of the machine, and the horn on the freighters as they power into port.

The sun is warm, her fingers sticky with ice cream, and her dad is here, talking just to her. She lets slip her dream. He laughs and Jordan's chest hurts. She wonders if it's the bones around the heart that snap and not the heart itself because that's what it feels like. Worse when her dad's friends come by and he shares the joke and they laugh. The docks are not for scrawny smart girls, they tell her. Jordan's dad must see the hurt because he stops laughing and waves away his buddies. He puts his arms around her shoulder and steers her out of the gates, and she tries so hard not to cry. You're a dock rat, he says. Like he's explaining the world to her. You're wily and smart, getting into everything. Use your brain and get away from the docks.

Jordan swallows and nods and gulps back her tears. So angry at herself for ruining this warm time. For letting dreams rise to the surface like the puff of cloud in the sky. Dreams carry weight. Dreams carry risk. The dock rat won't forget that again.

❖

No good phone calls came at 4:11 in the morning. That was Jordan's first thought as she surfaced from a deep sleep to her phone buzzing and flashing on the table by her bed. Anxiety spiked in her body. Was her dad sick again? One of the kids? Madi?

"Yeah, hello."

"Jordan, it's Constable Frederickson. Really sorry to wake you this early."

Jordan knew him. He'd been on the force forever.

"It's okay," she said, clearing her throat and sitting up in bed. Her apartment was dark, the whitewashed cinderblock walls reflecting some of the glow from the streetlights outside. "What is it?"

"We've got a bit of a situation down here in the Heights. We've rounded up a bunch of guys for public mischief, but one of them's a kid and won't give us his name. We've got no one reported missing, no contact from any group homes. Could be a street kid. Just wondering if you could give us a hand. I know you see a lot of these guys in your gym."

Jordan rubbed her face. "Group homes won't be a doing a check until six thirty. What does he look like?"

"Tall white kid, maybe sixteen or so. Dark hair and brown eyes maybe? Hard to tell in this light. Wearing jeans and a hoodie."

"Constable Frederickson, you just described the entire teenage population of the Halifax Regional Municipality." Jordan got out of bed and turned on a light.

Constable Frederickson laughed. "Don't I know it." He cleared his throat. "Look, I really don't want to process this kid if I don't have to. My call is going to sit in queue for half a day before anyone's got the time at community services. I just thought…"

"I got it, Constable. Give me ten minutes."

"Sure, thanks, Jordan. We're at West and Langford. I'll tell the guys at the barricade to let you in."

Jordan picked up her jeans from where she'd thrown them the night before. Barricade? She shook her head. "See you soon."

It was cold and damp when Jordan left her apartment a few minutes later, having pulled on a hooded sweater and rubbed the sleep from her eyes. The metal stairs clanged loudly in the grim dark of post-night and pre-dawn.

As she drove through the empty Halifax streets out to the nicer neighbourhoods of the Heights, Jordan considered what she was driving into. This wasn't her job, not entirely. There were community services youth workers who were on call to the police. But Halifax, even as the capital of Nova Scotia with a population at just over four hundred thousand, was still a small town in many ways. The Maritime code stuck, looking out for your own, knowing your neighbours, asking for a favour because you knew it would be returned. Some of the old-timers like Frederickson shrugged off protocol when they could get the job done. It was a community, and Jordan was happy to be a part of it.

Jordan saw the flashing lights when she pulled onto Langford. One orange barricade and a cop in a high visibility vest blocked the road. Jordan rolled down the window, gave her name, and the cop waved her through. The neighbourhood was a pricey one, all multi-story homes with wide driveways and landscaped yards. It wasn't far from where Ali had grown up, Jordan thought, as she pulled her car over and parked behind one of the cruisers.

At first, the scene in front of her made absolutely no sense. A pyramid made up of at least forty or fifty recycling and waste bins sat in the middle of the street. Jordan could make out the relatively new wheeled green carts tilted at odd angles and stacked against the square blue recycling bins. The tower reached nearly fifteen feet in the air. Cops stood in clusters around the base, which took up most of the width of the street. Flashes from cameras went off and homeowners were standing on the sidewalk, most taking photos with their cell phones.

"Jordan, thanks for coming down."

Constable Frederickson walked over with his hand extended. Jordan shook it, then jerked her chin at the pyramid.

"What's with the art installation?"

"Art, right," Frederickson snorted. "Just public mischief. Something to do on Thursday night when you're drunk."

Jordan couldn't believe the size of the recycling bin tower. It would have taken a pretty concerted effort to amass that many recycling bins and construct a pyramid before getting caught.

"That would be hard to execute drunk, don't you think?"

"I don't know, we all did stupid shit when we were drunk as kids, eh?" Frederickson looked to Jordan for confirmation. Jordan just smiled and kept looking at the tower. "At least we were smart enough to stay away from the high-end homes. Folks are pissed about this, and it'll be our fault somehow. We'll have the mayor on this by seven a.m., betcha a pint of Propeller." When Jordan still didn't reply, he waved her on. "Come on, I'll take you to our lad."

Jordan softened a little at Frederickson's term of endearment. About ten people were seated along one of the curbs, spaced a few feet apart with a handful of cops near enough to discourage any talking. Frederickson pointed to the guy on the end with his hood up and his head in his hands.

"There he is. Won't tell us his name. Said he had nothing to do with it, and he doesn't want to talk."

Jordan walked over and sat down on the curb next to the hooded figure. Frederickson followed, looming above them in a way that annoyed Jordan.

"Hey, buddy," Frederickson said. "Hood off." The guy pushed his hood back and glared up at Frederickson. "You know him, Jordan?"

At the mention of her name, the kid looked at her with surprise and then relief. Then his face set back into an angry, resistant mask.

"Yeah, I do. Give us a minute, Frederickson?"

The constable hesitated then backed off a few steps.

"Hey, Seamus."

Jordan didn't remember his last name. He'd come into the gym only a handful of times, obviously looking for entertainment and socialization instead of work and instruction. He was disruptive but not aggressive, a pain in the ass more than a criminal.

"Hey, Jordan," Seamus said miserably. "They said they were

calling someone. Didn't know it was you." He looked up hopefully. "Can you get me out of here? I didn't do anything, I swear it."

That didn't mean a thing to Jordan. Not at all. Lying was a skill, like fighting or evasion or knowing when to run.

"It's not me you have to convince." She indicated the cluster of cops just a few feet away. "They don't want to pull you in, but you're not giving them much choice."

Seamus hung his head but didn't speak.

"Where are you staying these days?"

"With some friends," Seamus muttered.

"These friends?"

Silence.

"Well, these friends are all over eighteen and about to be processed. No idea if they'll get charged or spend at least part of today in jail. So, I imagine you have two choices. Let me find you an emergency placement"—she held up her hand as Seamus snorted and swore—"or let Frederickson call the juvenile detention, and they can start processing you for that."

"No way. They said another infraction or whatever, and they'd be taking me to Westwood. I'm not going there."

Westwood was the full-care facility for youth who needed more intensive intervention than community resources and group homes could manage. Jordan knew it was unlikely Seamus would end up there. That facility was for those too violent and explosive for a group home setting. As far as Jordan knew, Seamus didn't have that kind of record.

"I don't know what else to tell you," Jordan said. "Your options are on the table." She didn't want to perpetuate the idea Westwood was a horrible place to be avoided at all costs.

"Can't I just stay with you? I could sleep at the gym. And I'll figure out something in the morning."

He wasn't the first kid to ask, but it wasn't a solution. Jordan had drawn that line years ago.

"Emergency placement or let them process you," Jordan said.

"Fuck," Seamus muttered and dropped his head in his hands. "Fine. But not Grange House. Hanson's there, and he's a dick."

"I'll see what I can do. What's your last name, Seamus?"

"Harrigan," Seamus said before pulling his hood up and dropping his head into his hands.

Jordan clapped Seamus on the back and stood. She pulled out her phone as she walked toward Frederickson, logging into the database to see if she could find him a space. Preferably not Grange House.

"Seamus Harrigan, sixteen, I think," Jordan told Frederickson. "My guess is group home runaway, but I'll know more when I get into the database."

"Let me guess. He's just along for the ride and didn't have anything to do with this," Frederickson said, indicating the recycling bin tower behind him.

Jordan kept scrolling and reminded herself not to react overprotectively.

"Seamus has been crashing with some of these guys. He could have been in the middle of this, or he could have just been along for the ride. I don't know." She found the list for emergency placement and sighed in relief when it wasn't Grange House. "I'll take him over to Hart House. He'll be registered there if you need to follow up. His social worker is Alice Robinson. Or you can give me a call." She flashed Frederickson a grin. "Preferably not at four a.m."

Frederickson laughed as he wrote down the info.

"You're a champ for coming out here, Jordan."

"I'm a champ who needs coffee," Jordan said, checking the time. Nearly five. She'd give the staff at Hart House another hour before she called. She had no real reason to wake them up any earlier than necessary, and Seamus wasn't in a hurry.

Jordan looked up at the massive recycling bin tower, now roped off with police tape. She knew nothing about structural engineering and supports, but this pyramid had been put together with some impressive precision. As she walked around the base, her shoe kicked something metal and sent it spinning. Jordan stopped it with the toe of her sneaker and rolled it over. A spray paint can.

Frederickson took a glove and picked up the can at Jordan's feet. "We found a few of these. So it's definitely art." He snorted and called for one of the junior officers to take the can and put it with the others.

"Taggers?"

"Dunno. Looks like the lads were doing a preschool art project to me." He indicated Jordan should follow him and they moved around to the far side of the tower. "See?"

The streetlights didn't quite reach, and it was darker on this side of the tower but Jordan could still see the broken-up arcs and whirls of the spray painted bins.

"That's going to piss off the residents more than the four a.m. wake up," Frederickson said. "They'll have dirty recycling bins."

Jordan didn't answer. The spray paint didn't look like the regular graffiti of local taggers. She looked at the broad swath of bins that had lines and streaks of paint. It didn't look much like anything. Except…

"Think we can get some of that light over here?" Jordan said.

Frederickson looked at her sharply, then called for the light stands to be moved around to the far side. Jordan walked backwards as the cops set up a couple of light standards around the base. She was another fifteen feet away when she saw it.

"Frederickson. A minute?"

The older cop hustled over. "You see something?"

Jordan pointed at the roughly outlined half rays, half swords sun. "I was asked about this symbol. It was graffitied on a bunch of places downtown earlier this week? And some connection to politicians. Constable Rachel Shreve showed it to me yesterday."

"Yeah, I saw a report about that graffiti. Good find. I'll see when Shreve's on shift."

Jordan stared at the painted bins as Frederickson typed awkwardly into his phone. What had seemed like a joke or just mischief a few minutes ago somehow seemed sinister under the harsh police lights in the pre-dawn cold. Jordan shivered. Maybe Rachel had been right. Jordan got the sense of something starting, something shifting, something moving in the dark and beginning to take shape.

Frederickson began talking into his phone, then moved it away from his mouth to address Jordan. "Thanks a million, eh? Why don't you check in with Constable Smith to sign off on the kid and get out of here. Go find a coffee and a sandwich."

Jordan found the young cop with the paperwork, signed to take Seamus into care, then collected the youth, who looked like he'd fallen asleep sitting up. He shuffled along silently beside her as they walked to her car and got in.

"Breakfast?" Jordan said as she started her car and turned the heat to high.

Seamus shrugged. "Whatever. Nothing's open."

A rejection and an acceptance. Identifying wants and needs meant showing a vulnerability.

"There's a diner across the bridge in Dartmouth that serves all day breakfast. Or the all-night McDonald's on King. You choose. Both have coffee, and that's all I care about."

"Fine. Diner."

They drove in silence. Jordan wanted to pester him with questions about who he'd been staying with and what he knew about the sun symbol. He was already mad at Jordan for hauling him back to a group home, so the chances of him opening up about his life were pretty slim. She figured she'd test the waters once he was full of bacon and eggs.

The bridge across Halifax Harbour was nearly empty, with just a few commuters, produce vans, and delivery trucks making the early morning trip. The dock shift started at seven, Jordan knew that. Her dad had been out the door at six fifteen every morning. When he'd been working, anyway. Before he showed up drunk to work and taken a fall. Her dad's supervisor had lied on the paperwork to get him disability. Jordan had been ten. Her father had never worked again.

Jake did, though. Jordan wondered if her brother was on morning shift today as she shifted gears and pulled onto the bridge. He'd been doing swing shifts forever, two weeks on mornings, two weeks on late. Over twenty-five years at the docks, working the cranes, loading and unloading the multicoloured shipping containers from the ships. Jordan had wanted to do that when she was a kid. The orange cranes had their own kind of power and magic. She'd always been amazed how something so big could be commanded by something so small. She'd loved the precision of the stacked shipping containers, always wanting to sort them by colour even though her dad laughed and Jake scorned her six-year-old imagination.

Steven had never laughed at her. He'd brought her pencil crayons and helped her label them: crane orange, shipping container blue, security fence grey, anchor white. Steven had always tried to create a space for Jordan's imagination. He'd been the only one who consistently worried about her having a childhood. That safety had died when Steven had. Space for dreams had also died. After that, she'd filled the hole with goals, with a show of strength, with boxing her way out of Halifax. With running away.

The last double thump of the tires on the bridge's metal grid and the even hum of pavement pulled Jordan from her thoughts. Steven had been gone seventeen years. And it was probably time to call Jake and check in.

"You've got a shitty job."

Jordan glanced at Seamus and laughed. "Not really."

"You got a phone call in the middle of the night from the cops. You're stuck with me until you can drop me off at a group home. And you don't even know me." He sounded resentful. He sounded confused.

"I know you well enough. And I'd rather the cops call than tie you up in the system. And I definitely don't mind an excuse to have pancakes and bacon."

Seamus didn't say much, just pulled his toque off and ran it through his fingers before pushing it back onto his head until it sat just right.

"Jail or bacon. Those were my choices tonight." Jordan wasn't sure if it was a question or a reflection. "Whatever. I'm glad you have a shitty job, then, so I can have bacon. But aren't you, like, rewarding my bad behaviour or something?"

Jordan pulled into the small parking lot beside the unassuming red brick diner.

"I have no idea what happened out there tonight or how you got involved with that group of guys. I do know you're underage, underfed, and the last thing you want is for me to take you to the group home. I'm hoping if I fill you up with bacon, you'll be too fat to run away again."

Seamus's eyes lit up, and he seemed to be working hard to fight off a laugh.

"That's your plan? Bacon fat? What kind of shit-ass social worker are you?"

Jordan flashed him a grin and opened her car door. "The kind who's not a social worker yet. Come on, kid. Let's go eat."

❖

Meet me 4 lunch.

Jordan looked down at the text from Madi on her phone. It was nearly two in the afternoon, and Jordan had spent most of the day at her desk. After dropping Seamus off at Hart House, she'd gone home to shower. Then, feeling restless, she'd come into the office early.

I brought my lunch today. Jordan texted back, trying to focus on her computer screen. Paperwork was endless, but at times it was easier than dealing with crisis after crisis and feeling like you never had a solution to any of it.

If U choose shitty PBJ over me, our friendship = over.

Jordan laughed. That's exactly what she had in her lunch today. That and a handful of vegetables. It was pretty depressing.

What if I'm busy? Now Jordan was just teasing Madi.

There was text silence for a bit and Jordan began to worry she'd run Madi off. Then a pic came through. A meme with a tiny kitten with big eyes that said, "why u no love me?"

You win. Where do you want to meet?

Tell Tim U R expecting me.

So Madi was already here at the front desk, but she hadn't pushed or manipulated her way back to Jordan's cubicle. She'd respected a boundary. It was a good sign.

Jordan grabbed her jacket and phone and closed her laptop. Getting away from her office suddenly felt like a very, very good idea.

"Hey, Mad."

Madi, leaning against the front desk, looked at Jordan shrewdly.

"You look like a vampire emerging from its lair. You sure you can go out into the sun?"

"Are you saying I look tired?"

"I'm saying you look like shit."

Jordan shook her head and spoke to Tim, who was grinning behind the counter. "Back in twenty or so. I've got my phone."

Tim waved them away, and Jordan and Madi walked out into the street. Traffic surged and ebbed and filled the street with sound and gas fumes as pedestrians flowed in and around the busy downtown core. Jordan followed Madi in silence, the sound of a lumbering truck filling the air too much to talk until they'd turned the corner.

"Up the hill, really?" It wasn't actually possible to go anywhere in Halifax without climbing a hill. They were the tiny San Francisco of the Maritimes.

Madi walked backward to give Jordan the full effect of her eye roll.

"Dude. It's food truck Friday. It's worth the climb to the Citadel."

Friday already, Jesus. How had that happened? Jordan rubbed her eyes and thought vaguely of the burn in her quads as the hill got steeper. She should run tomorrow. Maybe even a distance run if she got enough sleep tonight.

"Food trucks are always worth the climb, yes," Jordan said. "I've taught you well, grasshopper."

"That's why I keep you around. These pearls of wisdom."

They walked together in silence, and Jordan began to wonder if Madi had a reason for this outing. She considered asking but figured Madi would get around to it eventually. Or if Madi just needed to know someone wanted to spend time with her, that was okay, too.

"I'm thinking deep fried," Madi said. "Pickles, maybe. Or a corn dog. Or both."

Jordan grimaced. The grease from her delicious but massive early morning diner breakfast was still sitting with her.

"Well, I'm heading to the Greenery," Jordan said, indicating the brightly painted green food truck, one of eight trucks parked alongside the roped-off Citadel at the top of the hill.

"Deep fried everything at your disposal, and you choose kale." Madi sounded truly disgusted.

"Hey, I had a greasy breakfast. Life is all about balance, Madigan Battiste."

Madi stuck her tongue out.

The lines were short, and Jordan and Madi ordered their food and waited along with the families with young kids and a handful of government employees with their ID tags around their necks. Once they'd picked up their orders, they wandered away from the noise of the generators and people to a couple of benches.

"So was your greasy breakfast with Ali? You refusing to cook for her the next morning, or something?"

Jordan stabbed at a forkful of Caesar salad and chewed before answering.

"You're digging. And not particularly subtly."

Madi licked some yellow mustard off her finger but said nothing.

"I had breakfast with a client. Kid needed a good meal, I needed coffee. It just so happened that two eggs, a pancake, and four strips of bacon were also consumed."

Madi gave a half smile, and they ate in silence. It was overcast today and a wind that hinted at cold swept across the large, open space of the Citadel at their backs.

"What's it like being a good person? Like, all the time."

"I'm not."

"But you are," Madi said. She seemed to be getting agitated. "All the fucking time. You feed a kid breakfast, you spend half your time chopping vegetables and pouring ranch dressing, you watch Sierra like a hawk in case she's starting to slip, and you want to be ready to catch her or steady or whatever."

Madi took a breath, like she was just warming up. Jordan considered interrupting but thought better of it. "You spend time with an ex, which is obviously making you six kinds of fucking uncomfortable, but you do it anyway because it's an opportunity for the gym and the kids. And me. And you answer my text in the middle of your stupidly long work day and hang out with me because you know I'm needy with a history of coming completely unglued and unbalanced at any goddamn time."

Madi glared at Jordan over her half-eaten corn dog, then suddenly dropped her glance. Jordan wondered where to start, how to drill down to the heart of what was bothering Madi.

"Know what I was thinking as we were walking here?" Jordan said.

Madi continued to pick at her food, not looking up.

"I was grateful to have a friend who could force me away from my computer and my spinning thoughts about how ineffective I feel most of the time. Someone who knows me well enough to know I'm likely going to sit at my desk eating a PB&J sandwich. Which is a damn depressing way to spend a Friday."

"But it's weird, right? I mean, you bought some street kid breakfast this morning because he was hungry, and you're buying me lunch now. What's the difference?"

"The difference is you're no longer a client. The difference is you have my personal cell number, which I gave you with the blessing of my supervisor and your aunt. The difference is I chose to leave the office because getting outside and having lunch with you sounded like a really great idea. Because we're friends."

"But we're not really friends," Madi said quietly after a moment.

"You don't entirely trust me. You know every damn thing about me. My entire life history including every foster family, every drug addiction, every diagnosis. And I only know pieces of you, professional pieces."

Jordan didn't know what to say. Madi was right, of course.

"It's not about trust," Jordan said. "Maybe I'm just taking some time shifting from the relationship we had to being friends. Some of it is habit and some of it is self-preservation. I'm sorry if that's hurtful."

Madi threw her balled-up napkins on the table and stared out across the city. Jordan wasn't sure if she'd said the right thing or the wrong thing.

"You trust me?" Madi said. "You didn't used to."

"I used to worry you wouldn't see the danger in front of you. That's different. I trust you can handle yourself. I trust that we're friends." Madi closed her eyes briefly, like something Jordan had just said hurt. "Do you trust me?"

Madi opened her mouth to respond but snapped it shut. Jordan could almost hear her caustic, sarcastic, automatic response to what she obviously considered a stupid question. But she paused before answering. "Yes."

"Good." Jordan smiled.

"So if you trust me, are you going to tell me about spending the night with Ali?"

Jordan laughed and Madi grinned, whatever had been bothering her moments ago thrown to the wind.

"You really want to know about my night?"

"Dude, yes."

Jordan pushed her empty cardboard carton aside and looked seriously at Madi. "It was me, a beer, and my *Quantitative Approaches to 21st Century Social Work* textbook."

Madi looked horrified. "Hot ex-girlfriend in town who is still clearly hung up on you, and you're reading a fucking textbook? Jesus, McAddie. You're a menace to yourself."

Jordan shook her head. She warred with herself for only a moment, thinking of their conversation about trust before asking her question.

"You think she's still hung up on me?"

"I'd say you are eighty percent of the reason she's even here. That's my quantitative analysis."

Jordan didn't believe it. Ali had an impressive career, a condo in Chicago, and a long list of degrees. This small-town hometown seemed to hold only memories.

"I think maybe she's looking for closure," Jordan said, thinking out loud. That completely lined up with why Ali was back in Halifax and, briefly at least, back in Jordan's life. Jordan's heart hurt, though. She didn't want it to hurt.

Jordan glanced at Madi, who was sitting quietly, clearly waiting for Jordan to continue. "I basically ran away from our relationship. Ali had her pick of three elite colleges in the U.S. Full athletic scholarships, really good opportunities. My boxing career was just getting started. She had plans for staying together and making it work. All I could think was that I was weighing her down. So, I left her a note and I left town. This week is the first time I've seen her since."

"You're a fucking idiot," Madi said, but without any heat.

Jordan gave a short laugh. "Oh, yeah."

"More specifically, you let your negative predictions about the future make decisions about your present."

It was interesting, hearing her own words used back on her. Not particularly comfortable, either.

"You're a pain in the ass," Jordan grumbled. "And you're right."

"And you're still being an idiot if you think she's just here for closure."

Jordan looked away from the intensity of Madi's conviction. This was too close and too hard. She breathed in the smell of grease, sea air, and the damp wood of the bench.

"I really don't know, Mad," Jordan said quietly.

Jordan expected more cursing and getting called out from Madi, but she sat quietly until Jordan's phone chimed. She grimaced and pulled it out.

"It's Tim. I should get back."

They started walking back down the hill.

"Thanks for getting me out of the office," Jordan said.

"Thanks for buying."

"I'll see you tonight?"

Madi looked away. "No, I took a shift at the mall tonight. Next week, for sure."

"Okay."

Madi looked back at Jordan suspiciously. "No lecture?"

Jordan shrugged. "Nope. Just let me know what you want me to tell Ali."

"Tell her whatever you want. My whole life story, if that will make you happy."

"Yes, that seems like a reasonable thing to do in the circumstance."

They were almost back at the office when Madi suddenly stopped and leaned back against the building. She fiddled with her phone, and then she pushed her hair out of her eyes and looked defiantly up at Jordan.

"Fine. You tell me why I'm not going to be there tonight."

"You had a good time with Ali the other night," Jordan said immediately. "I think that makes you nervous, so you want to warn her off and let her know you aren't reliable. Which you are."

Madi gave her an incredulous look. "Except I'm not. Since I'm skipping out tonight."

"To take an extra work shift. You're not going out to party. Which is where you would have been a few years ago." Madi still didn't say anything. "Sierra thinks you're reliable. Most of the kids at the gym do."

Madi picked at the corner of her sparkly phone case. She was moments away from swearing or leaving.

"Ugh, I hate this honesty shit," Madi finally said. "Fine. Tell Ali I needed a break from all her awesomeness. It's basically true. Oh, and I'll be back on Monday."

"I'll do that." Jordan sensed Madi needed to be done. "See you, friend."

Madi's expression softened for just a fraction of a moment. "Yeah, see you."

Jordan pulled open the door of her office, still thinking about the exchange with Madi. Their relationship had changed over the years. Jordan had known her since she was thirteen years old, tiny and explosive and sharp. She was still all those things but tempered by time and meds and therapy along with the arrival of an aunt who gave her some solid ground. And by Jordan and Cay's war of constancy. Jordan had always been there for Madi. She would always be there for Madi.

"Hey, Jordan," Tim called out. "I put three calls through to your voicemail. None said urgent, so I didn't forward to your cell. And Cay's looking for you."

Jordan approached the desk as Tim reeled off the various callers since she'd left for lunch. He was sorting through the mail, and he picked up a thick yellow envelope. Jordan glimpsed a line of ink on the back of the package as he flipped it over. Her brain lit up with a warning.

"Tim, put the package down, please."

Tim put the package on the counter and took a step back. "What is it?"

Jordan picked up two pens and flipped the envelope over on the counter. A bladed sun was sketched in dark ink on the back. A frisson of fear coursed through her chest, but when Jordan spoke, her voice was calm.

"We need to call the police."

CHAPTER FOUR

"Okay, here's what we know."

Rachel balanced on the edge of Jordan's desk. She'd arrived in full cop mode about half an hour after Jordan had called. Cay sat in her chair with one leg tucked under her, chewing on the edge of her coffee lid in agitation.

"Is it a threat? We wouldn't still be here if it was a threat." Cay's voice was jumpy, with none of her usual calm.

"No, Cay. It's not a threat. As far as I can tell, there is no danger here."

Jordan knew Rachel wouldn't lie, but she could sense her uncertainty.

"Let her talk, Cay," Jordan said gently, nodding at Rachel to continue.

"It's a plain piece of paper with the words 'We're hungry' printed in the middle."

No one said anything. Jordan could hear the voices of the other uniforms still at the front desk.

"That's it?" Jordan said. "The package seemed thicker than one piece of paper."

"The paper was in the middle of a bunch of folded grocery store flyers. We've taken it all in, but I've got to tell you the only reason this is getting any kind of attention is because the same symbol was sent to the regional councilors earlier this week."

"And the recycling bins," Jordan said. She wished she'd picked up a coffee at lunch. "From last night. Yesterday night? Sorry, it's blurring."

"What are you talking about?" Rachel said, her voice sharp.

"In the Heights. The recycling bin tower. It had the same symbol." Rachel clearly had no idea what Jordan was talking about. "I told them to call you."

"You were there?"

"One of our kids was involved, and they didn't want to take him in. Frederickson called me instead of waiting for the court system to wake up."

Rachel pulled out her phone and started scrolling. "I need to make some calls."

"Sorry, Rach. I assumed you knew."

Rachel put her phone to her ear and waved Jordan's apology away as she walked out of the office.

Jordan and Cay stared at each other in silence. Cay had stopped chewing on her coffee cup, but she still looked unsettled.

"You good?"

"Yeah," Cay said. "Just freaked me out a little." She laughed and sat up. "I watch too much TV. That's the problem."

"You and your crime shows," Jordan said. She never understood how Cay could do the job she did every day and still go home and watch that kind of misery on TV.

Cay sniffed and tossed her orange hair behind her shoulder. "You know how I feel about a man in uniform."

Jordan laughed and turned back to her computer to try and focus on her paperwork until they heard anything more from Rachel. Her phone rang a moment later.

"Jordan McAddie speaking."

"Very official, JP."

Jordan felt her cheeks warm. She wondered how long until she got used to hearing Ali's voice again.

"Hey. What can I do for you?"

"Sorry to track you down at work, but I don't have your cell number."

"Oh. It's fine. And I should remedy that." Jordan gave her cell number and tried to ignore Cay's curious glance off to her left.

"Thanks. I just wanted to let you know I can't make it to the gym tonight. I've got a conference call with our Southeast Asian partners, so the timing isn't going to work."

"Sure, that's not a problem."

"It is, actually. I told Madi I was going to be there. I made a commitment."

"It's okay, Ali. Madi took a shift at work tonight, so she's not going to be there either."

"Oh."

Jordan couldn't tell if Ali was relieved or disappointed. "Madi said to tell you she needed a break from your awesomeness, and she'll see you on Monday."

Ali laughed and Jordan smiled at the sound. "Then I'll stop feeling guilty."

"Yes, definitely."

An awkward pause had Jordan trailing her thumb over the ridges and scars of her desk.

"What are you doing this weekend?"

Jordan let out a breath. What to do with the fact that she'd been hoping Ali would ask?

"I've got a final paper due next week, so mostly coursework. You?"

"Coursework?"

Another reminder that she and Ali did not really know each other at all.

"Um, yeah. I'm taking my Master's of Social Work at Dal."

"I didn't know that. Jordan, that's great."

Jordan squirmed. The accomplishment seemed so small compared to Ali's. She searched for condescension in Ali's tone, the sickly sweetness of being patronized.

"Are you liking the courses? Are they applicable or more theoretical?"

Those were good questions. Jordan relaxed a little. "A bit of both. And I'm liking both, actually."

"I want to know more," Ali said, her tone so definitive it made Jordan smile again. "How about a road trip tomorrow to Mahone Bay? I haven't seen the fall scarecrows in almost twenty years. And you can tell me about your courses. And, you know…your life." Ali's voice trailed off at the end. Wistful, somehow.

Jordan didn't hesitate. "Is nine too early to pick you up?"

"Make it eight, and I'll bring breakfast."

"Deal."

Jordan hung up the phone and stood staring at the beige handset for a long time. She was trying to define the feeling in her chest. No, her whole body. Warmth and excitement replaced worry and guilt. But caution was present, too, a lifelong adherence to not putting your trust in hope. But caution could have a place with happiness.

"She's making you less grumpy, I see," Cay said. "She should stick around, that Ali Clarke."

Jordan blinked and focused back on her desk, the sounds of the office buzzing around them, and Cay's curious expression.

"We're going to Mahone Bay tomorrow," Jordan said.

"That sounds lovely," Cay said casually, then turned back to her computer. "Don't forget to let her see how wonderful you are."

Jordan shook her head at her friend and opened her email. She scanned the staff notices and Ministry updates, and then she opened an email from a local social services group she belonged to, where people posted links to resources and asked questions about waitlists and support groups. The subject of one of the posts was "weird delivery," and it had been posted that morning by a mental health worker who worked in a seniors care program. Jordan clicked on the post, then opened the picture embedded in the email, instantly recognizing the package, the flyers, and the typed note with the words "We're hungry."

Jordan swiveled her monitor to the left. "Cay, take a look at this."

Cay's eyes went wide when she looked at Jordan's screen. "Who sent that?"

"Program lead at Barrington Senior Care."

"Take it to Rachel."

Jordan opened the email app on her phone as she walked to the front desk. Rachel was sitting on a bench by the front window, her cell phone pressed between her shoulder and ear, taking notes on a small notepad on her lap.

"I don't have anything more yet, I'm afraid," Rachel said when she hung up.

"I do." Jordan opened the email. "Another agency received a similar package today."

Rachel's eyes went wide as she took the phone from Jordan and scrolled through the short message.

"Tell me about this group."

"It's pretty informal, maybe thirty or forty members all having some tie to social services in the region."

"Did you post about the package?"

Jordan tried not to be hurt that her friend thought she would do such a thing. "No."

"Sorry," Rachel said. "I just needed to check."

"No problem," Jordan said. Rachel was stressed, and Jordan felt responsible.

Rachel scrolled through the message before she handed the phone back to Jordan. "Can you post a message to the group? Ask them if anyone else has received a package. Put my contact number on there."

Jordan opened up a new message and typed rapidly. She showed Rachel the message, then hit Send when she nodded her approval.

"What is this, Rach?"

Rachel sighed. "I wish I knew. But it's starting to look more like a protest than a gang."

The graffiti, the recycling bins, the packages. All messages? Protesting what?

"So what's next, then?"

"Business as usual, Ms. McAddie. Same advice as a few days ago. Keep your eyes open, and let me know if anything comes up."

Jordan looked down at the picture on her phone. She wanted to see through the message to the intent of the sender. Not possible, so she closed the email app and shoved the phone back in her pocket.

"Come by for dinner this weekend?" Rachel said as they walked toward the front door.

"I've got plans, actually. But thanks for thinking of me," Jordan said.

Rachel gave her an appraising look. "Ali?"

Jordan scuffed her feet like an embarrassed child. She laughed at herself and stopped, looking up to meet Rachel's gaze. "Yeah."

Rachel smiled. "Have fun, my friend. I mean it."

"Roger that, Constable."

Rachel sketched a salute on her way out the door. Jordan stood for just a moment in the warmth of the foyer, taking in the fall sun. Something was happening. A slight shift in the ground under her feet, a rumbling of an approaching storm. Combined with the pull in the air of having Ali back in town, Jordan felt nerves and anticipation like the moments before a fight. Dread and excitement. She shivered and blinked into the sun. Then she turned back to her desk and the familiarity of work.

❖

Jordan's phone was ringing when she got out of the shower. The Friday night workout at the gym was often sparse because the kids wanted to launch into the weekend early. Jordan usually took Fridays to run her own circuit, and her muscles were pleasantly sore.

She walked across her small apartment in a clean T-shirt and boxers and picked up her phone.

"Hey, Mom."

"Hi, sweetheart. It's Mom calling." Jordan smiled into the phone. Her mother was incapable of any other phone greeting. "I hope it's not too late. I tried to wait until after your gym session with the kids."

Rosa McAddie had been sober for seventeen years, and Jordan was still getting used to her mom being aware of her schedule and her life.

"You timed your call perfectly," Jordan said, walking into her kitchen and opening her fridge. "How are you?"

"I'm good. I was supposed to volunteer down at the seniors centre this afternoon, but they have a viral outbreak or something, so they're under quarantine."

"That's too bad," Jordan said, half listening as she searched her fridge for food. She closed the door and snagged an apple from the bowl on the counter. "Did you get out shopping or something instead?"

"Oh, no. I didn't have a list ready or anything. I told the respite worker not to come, but she insisted we use your father's hours this week. You know what Joan is like."

Jordan didn't, not really. But she murmured her agreement, feeling guilty and grateful someone in her mother's life insisted she get out of the house. The respite worker would stay with Jordan's dad while her mom shopped, or volunteered, or occasionally took a class at the community centre. Her dad mostly sat in his chair, but he was sometimes unpredictable when left alone, trying to make himself something to eat or wandering off. And he got agitated when Jordan's mom wasn't around. Jordan and Jake had both tried sitting with him, but that never worked. He didn't like being alone with either of them, so he'd begin mumbling about Steven and the docks and unfairness.

"So, I was thinking," Jordan's mom said, bringing Jordan back. "Maybe you and I could go to the farmers' market in the morning?"

The Halifax Seaport Market was a massive space on the harbour, taking up almost a full block. It was a mix of fresh produce, seafood, and hundreds of artisans. And it would be packed on a Saturday morning. Jordan's mom rarely went to the market. It was an indulgence when they lived on such a limited budget. But if she was asking to go, she was wanting to treat herself.

"I'd really like to. Let me just see if I can rearrange my plans for the morning."

"Oh, no. No, no, don't do that. I can just head to Atlantic Foods and maybe pick up some crullers for your father. No need to rearrange anything."

"Mom, stop fretting for a moment."

Her mother laughed. "Jordan McAddie, you say that like it's possible."

Jordan laughed too, warmth filling her chest. She allowed it to enter and stay there, a skill she'd had to learn and practice.

"I'd like to go to the market with you, so let me just see if I can push back my plans a bit. Unless..." Jordan swallowed against the sudden image of shopping at the market with her mom and Ali. It was a perfect moment in her head, with the noise of the crowd and the view of the water through the windows. She and Ali standing back and drinking coffee while her mom sorted through bunches of kale and rainbow chard. An ache so fierce in her chest at this image, this rightness, this *family*, made Jordan take a step back.

"Jordan? I don't want to be a bother."

Jordan took a breath. She thought about Madi calling her an idiot. Letting negative predictions about the future run her life.

"Would you be okay if I asked someone to come with us? I made plans for the morning, but I'm wondering if she'd like to come."

"Yes, of course," Jordan's mom said, sounding surprised.

Another breath. Why did this conversation require so much bravery? "Do you remember Ali Clarke? From high school?"

"Your girlfriend. Yes, I remember." Her mom's voice was softer now. Pain and regret from the cold times of Jordan's childhood.

"She's back in town for a little while. I'll see if she'd like to come with us."

"That would be lovely. Perfect, really." Jordan's mom cleared her throat, a definitive sound that moved them both away from hurt. "You just let me know. I'll be awake for another hour or so."

Jordan hung up the phone and bit into her apple. She was putting off calling Ali. She was putting off denying a hope and a want. It was far worse than rejection.

Jordan finished her apple and rinsed her hands. She shook out her arms and took a steadying breath. Then she called Ali Clarke to invite her on an outing with her mom.

❖

Jordan pulled up outside the hotel just before seven the next morning. Ali was waiting outside in jeans and a sweater, and her smile was warmth and joy as she climbed in the car.

"Good morning," Ali said, holding up a paper bag. "I brought chocolate croissants."

"Good morning. And thanks for breakfast."

Jordan pulled onto the street, concentrating more than she really needed to in the light morning traffic. She was working so hard at playing it cool. Ali had no such concerns, apparently.

"Is it weird I'm so excited about this?"

Jordan laughed. "Which part? The croissants, the early morning, the ride in my old car? Or is it the chance to spend an hour or so pressed up against the Haligonian hippies and hipsters? With my mom, of course."

Ali laughed, and Jordan shot her a grin. Making Ali laugh had always made her feel powerful, evidence she had influence over this magnificent creature. She'd felt that same shiver of power when Ali's breath would catch when Jordan kissed her.

Jordan hit the brakes a little harder than she needed to and pulled herself back from the memory of kissing Ali.

"Sorry," Jordan murmured.

"No problem. And to answer your question, I'm excited about doing something so normal. And so Halifax."

Jordan angled her car up the hill, deciding to go through downtown, which wouldn't see much traffic until later in the morning. She scanned the streets and side streets out of habit, looking for her kids, a face she recognized, a way to help. This, she realized, was her normal. And likely it didn't match any definition of Ali's.

"What would you normally be doing on a Saturday?" Jordan said.

"Working," Ali said, looking out the window. "It's the quietest day at the office. If not working, then working out. I still golf. Sometimes I'll see friends. My parents, when they're in town." Ali shrugged. "I'm not home enough to have a weekend routine, I guess. My life is very corporate America." She said the last part dryly. Jordan sensed her deflection.

"Does it make you happy?"

Ali folded the top of the bakery bag over and creased it carefully before looking at Jordan and answering. "No. Not anymore."

The words were a heaviness, and Jordan absorbed the edges of sadness she guessed Ali did not want to acknowledge. At least not right now.

"Thanks for answering such an invasive question."

Ali laughed lightly. "And before I've had coffee, even."

Jordan turned left up at the light. "We should remedy that. We'll need fortification to get through the morning."

"It makes a difference that we've got history, I think." Ali said after a moment of silence. She glanced sideways at Jordan. "Answering questions about myself. I'm not trying to impress you with how together I am, my address, my degrees. How my booze collection far outweighs the food in my fridge." Jordan raised her eyebrows, and Ali laughed. "You're either a gourmet chef in your spare time or you brag about eating takeout for all your meals. There is no in between."

"Really?"

"Really."

"So what does it mean that I'm taking you to McDonald's for coffee?"

Ali pretended to think about. "That you're normal."

"Fuck that," Jordan muttered.

She noticed a clump of people sitting in a vestibule outside the Lucky Seven convenience store, the only open store at this hour. They were likely hoping for some change. She scanned their faces, looking past their uniforms of hoodies and jeans and dirty jackets. She recognized at least one of the kids. She pulled up next to the curb and put on her four-way flashers.

"Give me a minute," Jordan said to Ali before she opened her car door. She called over the hood of her car. "Hey. I'm heading to McDonald's. You guys want anything?"

There was silence for a minute before the expressions of the teenagers went from defiance and suspicion to nearly childlike joy. A chorus of "Jordan!" and "Fuck, yeah" rang out before they called out their orders, one kid getting cuffed in the side of the head for ordering a cheeseburger while the breakfast menu was still up.

Jordan repeated the order to make sure she got everything, then she ducked back into her car.

"Shouldn't add too much time to our trip," Jordan said as she pulled back onto the street. She could feel Ali watching her.

"This is your normal Saturday morning?" Ali said.

It wasn't, exactly. But scanning the streets for her kids, feeding someone who looked hungry? That was her life. "Yes."

Ali didn't say anything, but Jordan felt a momentary anxiety at the evidence of the stark differences of their lives.

Jordan pulled into the McDonald's drive-thru and soon was handing Ali bags of food and trays of coffee.

"I got it," Ali said, balancing the two trays of coffee on her lap and pressing the giant paper bags of breakfast sandwiches and hash browns against her side. She looked so serious in that moment, committed to holding on to breakfast for a bunch of street kids. Jordan quickly picked up her phone from the console and snapped a picture.

"What the hell was that?" Ali laughed.

"Your boss said you needed to keep a journal. I thought you could use some photo evidence."

"Drive, McAddie. You massive pain in the ass."

Feeling lighter then, happy and connected, Jordan drove back the way they had come. The kids crowded around the car as soon as they pulled up. Jordan handed the bags of food through the window as they jostled and pushed, drawn by the sight and scent of food. They looked tired, Jordan thought. She wondered if any of them had slept the night before. But she laughed when one kid shoved an entire hash brown in his mouth, then danced around because it was so hot. His friends laughed and the group moved off down the street, waving their thanks to Jordan.

They drove in silence, Jordan half worrying about the kids she'd just left, half worrying about what Ali thought of her. After a moment, Ali pulled Jordan's coffee out of the tray, pushed back the opening in the lid, and handed it to Jordan.

"Thanks," Jordan said. "Your shotgun skills are excellent."

"Ivy League schools teach you everything," Ali said.

Soon, they'd left the downtown core and pulled into the blocks of low apartment buildings and tightly packed, run-down townhouses of Jordan's childhood. These streets were nearly dead. The only evidence of life they saw was a stray cat and someone sitting on their front steps in their pyjamas, smoking a cigarette.

"Your parents still live in the same place?"

"Yes."

Ali had been here only twice, as far as Jordan could remember. Both brief visits for Jordan to pick something up that she'd needed. As a teenager, Jordan had only felt shame. She had perspective now, a broader understanding of her family dynamic, addictions, and cycles of poverty. She read about it, she lived it, she helped her kids live through it. But driving Ali to the heart of her childhood still made her stomach tremble.

"There's my mom," Jordan said as she pulled into a parking spot outside the townhomes. Rosa McAddie was already making her way down the front steps of number eighteen Cobden Street. She was wearing a sweater and a jacket, her purse slung protectively across her chest. Jordan jumped out of the car, and she heard Ali get out as well. Rosa's eyes lit up at the sight of Jordan. Jordan smiled and gave her a kiss on the cheek.

"Hi, sweetheart."

"Hi, Mom." It had taken Jordan years to see every day of connection and love as a gift instead of a stark reminder of what she had not been able to count on growing up.

"Hi, Mrs. McAddie, I'm Ali Clarke."

"Hello, there. Yes, I remember you, Ali Clarke." Rosa peered up at the two of them. "Yes, I distinctly remember you two towering over me. And you've both grown. And I think I've shrunk."

Jordan felt a momentary giddiness. Maybe this was going to work. Maybe her past and present could fit in this moment and be okay.

"It's good to see you again. And we brought coffee and chocolate croissants."

"You do know how to do this right, don't you?" Rosa said approvingly. "Then let's go, I want to be there before the crowds."

They walked back to the car, and Rosa waved Ali into the front seat, which Ali protested. Rosa ended the argument by climbing in the back and putting her seat belt on. Jordan shrugged and got in, starting up the car's engine in the quiet morning.

"Ah, yes. Thank you," Rosa said as Ali handed back her coffee. "This is a treat."

"It's one of my favourites," Ali said, sorting through the contents of the bakery bag. Jordan worried she was being condescending, but she saw no deception when Ali looked up. Good.

"Tell Ali why you love McDonald's coffee when you go to the market, Mom," Jordan said, heading toward the harbour.

"Because it tastes good and it's cheap." Rosa sniffed, but Jordan could see the light in her mom's eyes when she looked in her rearview mirror.

"And?"

"And because I love walking around the crowds with my $1.79 double-double and seeing the look of horror on people's faces as they sip their five-dollar organic lattes. It makes my day."

Ali burst out laughing, and Jordan checked her mother's pleased expression.

"You're a shit disturber, Mom."

"Thank you, sweetheart."

Ali passed around the chocolate croissants, and Jordan ate the flaky, sugary pastry with one hand, navigating through the city with the other while her mom and Ali kept up a constant patter of conversation. The sun had already broken the horizon, pushing orange light onto the greyness of the morning as Jordan parked in the giant lot, waving away her mom's concern with the price of parking. A steady trickle of people were already heading into the market as Jordan, her mom, and Ali made their way in with their coffees.

Jordan would have found the market overwhelming if she wasn't already familiar with the space. Rows of produce vendors lined the long space, their tables loaded with baskets and crates of pale yellow and bright orange carrots, sixteen kinds of tomatoes, and a stack of leafy greens Jordan couldn't even identify. Barrels of earthy potatoes and bright red apples were spaced every few feet, their round bellies protruding into the walk space. Rosa's eyes were bright as she walked between stalls, picking up vegetables and chatting with the vendors.

Jordan and Ali hung back, sipping their coffees and looking at the artist stalls along the outside wall. A woman sat on a paint-splattered kitchen chair with a sketchbook and a pencil in her hand, looking perfectly at ease among the clamour of trade. She smiled benignly when Ali and Jordan stopped to check out her work before they moved on to the man in a ragged fisherman's sweater planing wood, his handmade fiddles hanging off homemade wire hooks on the stall around him. Ali stopped to chat as Jordan took a step back to look for her mom. She was buying sweet potatoes not too far away, and Jordan walked over to take the first heavy bag from her.

"Thanks, sweetheart. I won't be long. Just maybe a few more things for this week."

"There's no rush, Mom. Dad is covered, and we're not in a hurry."

They moved aside as a woman pushing a massive double stroller with two crying babies wound her way through the crowd. Rosa looked over to where Ali was smelling a block of chunky, handmade soap.

"Ali is having a good time, then?"

"Yes, I think she is."

Rosa looked up at Jordan and a sadness passed through her eyes. It was fleeting, and Jordan wondered if she should acknowledge it.

"How long has it been since you've seen her?"

"Fourteen years."

Rosa gave her daughter an appraising look, and she seemed to hesitate before she spoke.

"Have you missed her?"

"Ah, Mom," Jordan said, a little embarrassed. She rubbed the back of her neck with her free hand. "I don't know how to answer that."

Rosa smiled. "You just did, sweetheart." Rosa took a sip of her coffee, then consulted a crumpled list in her hand. "What do you think about inviting Ali over for dinner? Your father will have been out for a walk, so he'll likely take an early meal and go to bed."

Jordan wasn't sure who she disliked more in that moment. Her father for making his wife a prisoner to his self-ravaged brain and body or herself for making her mother compartmentalize her life between husband and her surviving children.

"Mom…"

Rosa raised her hand. It was steady. Jordan still evaluated her mother's steadiness, a childhood full of worry. "I don't need an apology. Your father is happy to see you, but I know spending a lot of time with him is problematic. For both of you. I'm saying I'd like to have you and Ali over for dinner tonight, but your dad will only be there for a short time. If that works, wonderful. If not, that's okay, too."

The crowd was getting busier, and Jordan and her mom shifted away from a handful of women with woven baskets tucked in the crook of their arm.

"I'll check with Ali."

"Well, that's good. I'll head down to the meat and cheese section next if you two want to catch up with me there."

"Okay, Mom. And thanks."

Rosa smiled and tugged on the strap of her purse before following the walkway toward the meat, cheese, and seafood section. Jordan took a moment to watch her go before turning back to find Ali.

"Look at these," Ali said when Jordan found her eyeing a selection of handmade pottery. "See the tiny lobsters in the pattern? I wonder if I could get them home without breaking them."

Jordan's stomach went cold at the word "home." Home for Ali was a high-rise condo in Chicago. Home was a group of friends who talked about wine over expensive meals at nice restaurants. Home was not Halifax.

"Jordan?"

Jordan blinked, and the sound of the market filled her head in a rush. She was being an idiot. Again.

"Sorry. Yes, they're adorable lobster mugs."

"Adorable. Hmm. I don't usually go for adorable in a coffee mug. But these are so…Halifax."

"Won't go with your current décor?" Jordan hoped she sounded light and funny. She must have missed because Ali shot her a quick look before placing the mug carefully back amongst its brethren.

"I had an assistant a few years back who loved to decorate. She and I were friends, I guess. So, I gave her a budget, she asked some questions, and then my condo was decorated. It's nice." Ali sounded utterly noncommittal about the whole thing. Disconnected.

"But would it be nicer with a set of adorable lobster mugs? That's the real question."

Ali laughed. "You know what? I think it would."

Jordan sipped her coffee as Ali chatted easily with the artist, who carefully wrapped four lobster mugs in paper and nestled them at the bottom of a brown paper bag. Ali completed the transaction and took a business card. Jordan indicated which way they should head to catch up with her mom.

"Feel better?"

"Actually, yes. I'll get to take a piece of home with me home." Ali gave a short laugh and shook her head. "You know what I mean."

Jordan did, or at least she thought she did. The word had already come up so many times today. Jordan wanted out from under the weight of it, but her next question was laden with the reality and complexities of home.

"My mom would like to invite us over for dinner tonight."

Ali looked at Jordan briefly as they dodged a tiny, toddling human waving a crust of soggy bread over its head, chortling madly.

"What are you thinking?" Ali said.

It was a fair question.

"I have a lot of thoughts about it, but mostly I'm thinking if that's how you'd like to spend this evening, that would be nice."

Ali said nothing and Jordan reminded herself not to hold her breath. The meat section wasn't quite as busy, the long glass cases filled with rounds of smoked ham and kielbasa. Jordan spotted her mom reaching up to a Styrofoam plate with cubes of cheese. Jordan knew she wouldn't buy any of them, but she loved to sample the flavours. Jordan had always thought her mother should have been a chef. She loved being in the kitchen, loved to taste and experiment. She loved to serve her family. All of Jordan's warm time memories of home involved her mom in the kitchen.

"You're smiling," Ali said.

"It's been known to happen."

"Good. Because here's what I want."

"Lay it on me."

"I want to co-opt your day. Completely."

Jordan laughed. "I like this plan already."

Ali's eyes were bright with laughter. "Right now I'm going to go tell your mom I would love it if she cooked for us, but I'm paying for ingredients." Ali waved away Jordan's obvious protest. "Then after we take your mom home with her groceries, you're going to drive us to Mahone Bay and we're going to wander in the sunshine and you're going to tell me about your life. Maybe we talk about past regrets. Maybe I kick you for breaking my heart when we were teenagers. Maybe I don't. Half the fun will be not knowing. Then we have dinner with your parents."

Jordan laughed, the sensation in her chest a joyous mix of warmth and comfort and excitement. She knew this person. She liked her. And they had the whole day ahead of them.

"Yes. To all of it."

As Ali's gaze rested on Jordan's face, the corner of her eyes crinkling with her smile, Jordan wasn't sure exactly what she was agreeing to. But in that moment, she didn't care.

Chapter Five

We should follow up with that, see what it means for our budget next year."

Cay followed her whispered words with a hard nudge, and Jordan crash-landed from her daydream back into the convention hall meeting room.

"What?"

Cay sighed. "Have you heard anything the Ministry rep has said in the last hour?"

"Um. No."

They were at an all-day joint Ministry meeting. Normally, Jordan liked these days, because she got a chance to connect with other programs and municipalities, to find out about joint initiatives, and to glean meaning from the often vaguely worded but passionate updates from the various provincial Ministries.

Not today. Her mind was occupied by Ali Clarke today.

Saturday had been a perfect day, like nothing Jordan had ever experienced. They'd driven through the country on the narrow Fishermen's Memorial Highway, the multitude of evergreens making up for the near sparseness of the trees that had dropped their leaves early this fall. Jordan had told Ali the Farmers' Almanac called for a harsh winter and Ali had laughed. They'd talked about their shared history growing up in the Canadian Maritimes. Ali said early in her career she'd been told she was too friendly, and she needed to change that if she was going to get anywhere in business. She confessed that seeing tartan and hearing bagpipes sometimes still made her teary. She admitted she rarely ordered lobster on any menu because nothing could compare to lobster season in the spring back home.

That word continued to haunt Jordan throughout their sun-filled day. They'd walked the streets of Mahone Bay, checking out the scarecrows dressed as pioneers, fishermen, and even clowns displayed throughout town. With Ali's insistent questioning, Jordan talked about the days, weeks, and years after she'd left Halifax. She detailed all the travel, the training, the bouts. She talked about depression, though she hadn't known enough to label it at the time. They laughed about her crush on the coach's wife and how she had used Jordan's obvious infatuation to keep her in line and on task. Crystal Fernando was the reason Jordan had finished her first two years of university by the time she and the boxing world had split ways. Ali asked how she'd felt when boxing was done. Relieved and lost, Jordan had said. And ready to come home.

They'd ended their day at her parents' home. Rosa had been cooking all afternoon, and the house smelled of sweet potato and spices. Jordan and Ali had spent a short time talking to Alfred McAddie, who sat in his chair in clean plaid pyjamas and a hoodie, his hands shaking as he reached for his can of light beer. But his eyes had been sharp, at least for a little while, as he'd asked about the scarecrows and if the town had fixed the on-ramp to the highway. The ramp had been fixed at least seven years ago, but Jordan dutifully answered the question. Their conversation was calm and polite, but her dad seemed happy and Ali seemed relaxed. Jordan tried to see this moment, with all its discomfort and buried history, as the gift that it was.

"You might want to pay attention for this, buttercup. They're talking about you."

Jordan's heart jolted in her chest. Her boss, Campbell, was up at the podium now, talking about the new initiative with JP's Gym and a private corporate enterprise. Jordan could feel the eyes of colleagues and strangers as she stared at the front, like she was listening carefully to Campbell's boasts about forging community relationships and furthering their goals of ending the cycles of poverty by targeting youth programming. Jordan could feel the heat in her cheeks. She wished Campbell had given her a heads-up about this.

"It looks like lunch is rolling in," Campbell said, "and I know I'm about to lose you all to sandwiches and cookies, but please feel free to direct any questions about this new enterprise to me, Cay Rawlson, or Jordan McAddie. We'll reconvene in an hour."

The din of a hundred voices released from their morning of silence was stark and almost overwhelming. The crowd surged in polite but focused urgency to the back of the room, where long tables draped with white cloths had been set up with platters of sandwiches, bowls of iceberg lettuce salad, and plates of cookies. Jordan stayed in her seat, smiling at people she knew and trying to get her head in the game. She answered a few questions from people who said they wanted to know more about the gym program or just wanted to give her a hard time for having a starring role in the day's agenda. She was just waving off a laughing colleague when she felt the seat next to her being pulled out. Helena Cavio sat down and folded her hands in her lap.

"Jordan."

"Hi, Helena. How are you?"

"I'm fine, thank you," Helena said gravely. Of course, Helena said most things gravely. "Though if I hear the phrase 'aligning with the Ministry funding model' one more time, I'm going to scream." Jordan laughed but stopped quickly when she noticed Helena had not joined her. "I wanted to ask you about this corporate partnership and how it came to be."

Jordan tried to decipher Helena's expression. It was difficult to hear in this noise but she wondered if she'd just heard judgement.

"Apparently Campbell was approached by a corporation with ties to Halifax—"

"Which one?"

"Centera Corporation. They're running a pilot project with their senior staff, embedding them in various community groups and having the community mentor them. They picked the youth boxing program."

Jordan recognized she was now selling the mentorship program she herself had initially doubted. It was entirely possible it was Ali's involvement that had won her over.

"You have no concerns about allowing a corporate enterprise to dictate the directives of a publicly funded program?"

Definite judgement. And a hint of bitterness. Jordan took apart the words as she calmed the immediate defensive response that sprang to her lips.

"I've had plenty of concerns," Jordan said calmly. "I'm content with the intent of the mentorship, the level of commitment by those involved, and the direction of the funding."

Helena shook her head and picked up a pen from the table, rolling it between her fingers like a cigarette. Jordan's stomach began to rumble as more and more people passed them with plates piled high with food, but she was too polite to end this conversation. And she liked Helena. They had often been on the same side of some intensely passionate arguments at meetings exactly like this one.

"Multinational corporations can't possibly understand what it is that we do," Helena said, her eyes slightly unfocused as she stared into the distance. "We are *not* a blip on their radar. We are not clients or partners, and yet they think they can show up and *take* from a community they've given nothing to. Ever. And we're supposed to shake hands and thank them." Helena dropped her pen and shifted to stare at Jordan. The intensity of her gaze made the mildest alarm bells ring in Jordan's head. "You be careful, Jordan. Don't forget the mission and the goals and the kids."

Jordan did not appreciate this lecture, but she still aimed for calm. "You know my priorities, Helena. Always."

Helena relaxed just a fraction, and she nodded once. Sharply. "Yes. I've always been able to count on you."

Jordan smiled. "Besides, I know the senior staff they've got embedded at the gym. Ali Clarke. I knew her when we were teenagers. She and Madi seem to be making a good connection—"

Jordan stopped as Helena stood abruptly.

"Madigan Battiste? You've connected her to Madigan?"

Jordan didn't think it was particularly important to point out none of it had been her idea.

"I'm watching out for her, Helena," Jordan said quietly as she also stood. "I always will."

Helena looked blankly at Jordan for a moment, then scanned the room, as if reminding herself where they were.

"Yes. My apologies." Helena gave Jordan the smallest of smiles. "I'm sure it will all work out, as they say."

As Helena walked away and Jordan went to join the long, snaking line waiting for lunch, she reflected on Helena's warning. So much of their work boiled down to "us" and "them." Her own life straddled both worlds, the giving and receiving of help. She shared that connection with some, but not all, in the social services community. She wondered if Helena's background was the same, if that was why her fight for the vulnerable populations they served seemed more passionate and personal.

Jordan ate the chewy sandwiches and boring salad while trying to listen to the conversation around the table in the noisy conference room. A commotion, a slight but noticeable increase in noise and hurried movements ran through the mostly seated crowd. Waiters in white shirts and black vests had been clearing some dishes, but a few more now entered carrying large platters covered in silver domes. They moved quickly, set them down on half a dozen tables around the room, and then left. Jordan felt a niggling in her stomach, the sense of something off, but she was distracted by a server coming to clear her plate. Jordan looked up and smiled her thanks.

The mood in the room shifted abruptly when someone at a nearby table lifted one of the silver domes. A pile of hypodermic needles poured out onto the white tablecloth, and a woman shrieked as people hastily pushed back from the table. Jordan felt the tension, panic, and uncertainty as more lids were raised and more hypodermic needles covered the tables.

"What the hell's going on?" Cay said, turning in her seat to get a better look. "Needles? That's horrible."

People were crowding the tables as others were trying to back away, some snapping pictures with their phones and quite a few making their way to the exits. They blocked Jordan's view as she tried to visually track down the waiters who had delivered the platters to the table. But the room was too chaotic, and the only wait staff Jordan saw were two huddled at the back, watching in horror.

Moments later, Campbell hurried up to the podium.

"Okay, folks. We obviously have an issue here. Please touch nothing on the tables and calmly make your way to the exits. The Halifax Police Department are on their way. Calmly, folks, please."

Jordan stayed in her seat as throngs of people tried to exit all at once, the noise level rising until it was nearly uncomfortable. She couldn't look away from the pile of needles on the adjacent table. Most were capped, some weren't. All were unwrapped. Jordan wondered if a note was amidst the needles. No, she knew there was a note. Another hand-delivered protest.

"Come on, Jordan," Cay said. "Let's get out of here and let the police handle this."

Jordan didn't move. Something was sitting off-centre in her chest, an extra beat of her heart or an unneeded breath in her lungs. A message, an alert from her body to pay attention. Everything faded as she replayed the scene of the platters being delivered to the tables. The uniforms that were not quite uniforms. The hurried movements.

"Jordan?"

Jordan looked up into Cay's concerned eyes.

"They were teenagers," Jordan finally said. "The people who delivered these needles were teenagers."

Cay stared at her blankly. The room was nearly empty save for a handful of concerned hotel staff conferring with the Ministry leads.

"Are you sure?"

"Yes. I'm sure of it. And, Cay…" Jordan struggled to pull her thoughts into alignment. To say what needed to be said despite the sickness in her stomach. "It's a weekday. What teens aren't in school?"

"Ours," Cay said. Her shoulders sagged. "They could be ours."

Jordan stood and put a reassuring hand on Cay's shoulder.

"Let's go talk to the police."

❖

"You're sure you didn't recognize any of them?"

Jordan gripped the tiny china cup in her hand, idly wondering if she could break it. The cop she was talking to was paid to be suspicious. It was his job.

"Yes. Like I said, I didn't recognize any individuals, but I've worked with enough teenagers to know when I'm around them."

The cop kept looking at Jordan with his pen poised over his notebook, as if this would encourage Jordan to somehow know more than she did.

"And like *I* said, you're not actually protecting anyone by not giving names. We'll treat them properly, but we've got to follow this up."

Jordan looked down into her cup as anger surged up through her stomach. She tilted the one drop of cold coffee around the bottom of the cup before looking up again.

"Message received, Constable Marco."

The cop was confirming Jordan's details when Rachel walked over.

"Marco, have you got Ms. McAddie's statement?"

"We just finished up, Constable."

"Good. There are sixteen more witnesses we need to interview." Jordan caught the look of annoyance that passed quickly over the young officer's face. Apparently Rachel caught it, too. "I'm coming to help, you nimwit," Rachel said, part admonishment and part fondness. Constable Marco managed to look sheepish. "Let me just follow up with Jordan, and I'll be right behind you. And remind me to teach you how to roll your eyes at a superior officer without getting caught."

Jordan shook her head at Rachel as Constable Marco walked away.

"What?"

"You're a piece of work."

"Yeah," Rachel snorted. "I'm a piece of work that isn't likely to put her kids to bed anytime this week."

"This thing keeps getting bigger, doesn't it?"

"Bigger…maybe," Rachel said, her voice contemplative as she looked over the crowd of social workers and officers. "Louder, I think. Like they're starting to find their voice. Shouting." Rachel finally zeroed in on Jordan. "What are we going to do when they start screaming?"

Jordan swallowed and tried to find the words to reassure her, but Rachel beat her to it.

"Forget it. I'm tired and rambling."

"No, you're tired and worried. And it's me you're talking to, not nimwit Constable Marco, so you're good."

Rachel cracked a smile. "Thanks for that." She surveyed the room again, and Jordan noticed this time her gaze was sharper, more focused. "I'm hoping we get some more details from these interviews. We've got hotel security footage from the entrances and the lobby but not the hallways or conference rooms." Rachel took a breath. "And a task force. I just got word the city wants a task force created. I'd like you to sit on it."

"Me?" Jordan couldn't think what she could possibly add to a police task force.

"We need community representation. We're pulling in some of the beat cops, but if they're protesting community treatment and services, we need some of that perspective."

"Is that what it is? A complaint against community outreach?"

Rachel took out her phone and scrolled until she found a picture she showed Jordan. It was a plain piece of paper with the sun symbol and large printed letters that said, "OUR HEALTH AND SAFETY."

"Jesus," Jordan muttered.

"So, the task force," Rachel said, putting away her phone. "You'll be on it? We could use your perspective."

"I guess," Jordan said. Uncertainty threaded its way through her body. She felt pulled somehow, as if being tugged across an invisible line. Us and them. Jordan pushed it aside and looked up at Rachel, who was watching her with curiosity. "Yes, of course. Let me know what you need."

"Will do. I should get going. I won't make it to the gym tonight, but I'll aim for tomorrow, okay?" Rachel started backing away, as if itching to get at the next task. She never stopped.

"Sounds good. And don't forget to plan your birthday date with Adam. We've got the kids that night."

Rachel smiled for the first time. "You have no idea how much I need something to look forward to."

Jordan wandered through the conference space until she found Cay outside leaning up against the building, having a smoke.

"We done? Can we get back to the office now?"

"We're done," Jordan confirmed. "And I could use the walk."

Cay took a last drag of her cigarette and stubbed it out against a garbage can. "That's my one ciggie for the month. Seemed like a good day for it."

They began the fifteen-minute walk to their office. The day was grey, the roads and sidewalks still wet from the morning's drizzle. Damp wind pushed around the buildings, forcing Jordan to acknowledge the cold and zip up her jacket.

"Did Rachel have any more information?"

Jordan filled her in about the note. "They're pulling together statements and video footage. And they're creating a task force. Rachel wants me on it as some kind of community representation."

"You'll have to check with Campbell."

"That's the plan," Jordan said evenly.

Cay let out a huff. "Sorry, I know you know how to do this job."

"It's okay. I think this whole thing has everyone rattled."

"A task force," Cay said. "I wonder to what end. Are you a member of the community being protested or the community under investigation?"

There it was. That was Jordan's uncertainty. The line of us and them. The line of protection and advocacy. Fighting for and fighting against. Her whole life had been fighting. Jordan suddenly felt tired.

"Let's leave it, shall we?" Cay said sympathetically. "For now. Let's let today be today. We can circle back around and look at it again tomorrow."

Wise words. Advice she'd given more than once. Advice she obviously needed to hear.

"I think that's what I need. Thanks."

They turned a street corner, narrowly avoiding a crowd of tourists who were just getting off a massive tour bus, likely on their way back from Peggy's Cove. Cay and Jordan wound their way through and around the crowd until they were back on the street, a block from their office.

"How are things with Madigan and the mentoring program?"

"They're good," Jordan said. "Madi seems really good. Steady. She's taken to Ali much faster than I would have thought, actually."

"I think you have a lot to do with that."

"What do you mean?"

"Ali was pre-vetted by you. My guess is Ali jumped over a few of Madigan's initial suspicions because she is someone you like and trust. Your opinion holds great weight with Madi."

Jordan considered this angle. It made sense, she supposed.

"She's got a performance this week," Jordan said. "I'm wondering if she's going to tell Ali about it."

"Ah, yes. That will be a real test for them, won't it?"

It would be. Madi had taken a long time to tell Jordan she was a spoken word poet. Jordan had always known writing was an outlet for Madi, but she hadn't known she'd started to perform at small poetry slams. Jordan had been nearly destroyed by the power of Madi's voice the first time she'd heard her. Madi had a gift. She hoped she shared it with Ali.

"I'm not going to say anything to Ali about it," Jordan said. "I'll leave that up to Madi. But I'll be there on Thursday."

"Me, too," Cay said as they arrived at the community centre. She smiled up at Jordan as she pulled open the glass doors. "It's good to see the fledglings launch, isn't it?"

"Yes," Jordan said as she smiled. "It's good to see them fly."

Chapter Six

Jordan—Fifteen

Steven has been taken to hospital, and Jordan's fear is a flame inside her chest. The police come to the house, a knock on the shredded screen door. The officer's voice is low and tries to be gentle. Jordan, standing behind her mom, can only look at the cruiser parked at the curb, lights off and siren silent. She stares at the coat of arms on the side of the cruiser and tries not to hear the words. A fight at the bar, Steven intervening and getting pushed. A bad landing, an awkward angle. Ambulance. Hospital. Need to get down there.

She's fifteen, too young to drive her mom to the hospital. The wait for Jake to get there is long, and her fear flame leaps higher and burns hotter when Jordan's mom tells her she has to stay home with her dad. They argue, Jordan following her mom around the house as she packs seemingly random things into her purse. A clementine, a pen, packets of sugar. For no reason she can understand, this makes Jordan furious and she yells, a long list of hurts and accusations that burn their way up her throat. Jordan's mom is silent as she pulls individual tissues from the box and folds them into a pile before tucking them into her purse next to the clementine.

And just as silently, her mother leaves when Jake arrives. They drive away, and Jordan sits on the porch and listens to the TV in the background, hoping her dad doesn't move. She prays and hurts and squeezes her head in her hands when the rage and fear get too big. She plans her route to the hospital six different ways, argues with her mom in her head as to why she should be there. She shies away from the emptiness in her chest, holds on to the flame instead. It's safer.

The phone rings. The heat of the house is oppressive as Jordan walks back inside. The presence of her father is a burden, the sound of the comedy reruns an awful backdrop as she answers the phone.

Then Jordan is only cold. She is glacial and immovable, and the cold is so deep it seems warmth has never existed inside her before. Steven is gone. She hears Jake's voice, shaking like it never has, saying Steven died of his injuries. Steven is gone and Jake is shaky and in that moment, Jordan extends the tendrils of ice even deeper, anchoring herself to the immovable cold.

❖

Thursday afternoon, and Madi was pissed.

Jordan worked with two kids who were new to the program, but she kept an eye on Madi, who stalked around the gym in her street clothes, drawing kids away from their workouts and warm-ups, making some of the teens laugh and others scowl. Ali had tried to engage her when she'd first come in, but Jordan had watched as Ali had obviously taken the temperature of the situation and given Madi some space. Madi had been completely ignoring Ali now for close to an hour.

Ali had paired up with Rupert and Sierra, taking pointers from the two boxers on how to use the heavy bag that hung from a stand. Madi noticed. Jordan could tell she noticed. Madi hadn't behaved like this in a long time. When a fight nearly broke out near the ring, Madi laughing in the middle of it, Jordan decided she had to step in. As she walked over, hands in the pockets of her loose shorts, Jordan reminded herself to keep her frustration in check. Madi was looking for a fight. She absolutely would not get it from Jordan.

"Hey, Madi. You got a second?"

Madi looked up from where she was kneading the shoulders of one of the boxers waiting for their turn to spar. Raya had short, dark hair and had been a regular at the gym for the last year. Madi had referred to her as a fuck buddy once. But not someone you'd want to be in a relationship with.

"Let me finish getting Raya warmed up for the ring."

Raya grinned at Madi and shifted herself a little closer. Madi smiled back, but her smile was empty, devoid of any warmth or connection. Jordan wondered just what the hell Madi was doing.

"Come find me when you're ready," Jordan said, making sure her voice did not betray her irritation. Or her worry.

Jordan surveyed the gym and asked Sean to keep an eye on everything while she went up to get the post-workout snack from her apartment. She was juggling a tray of vegetables and an oversized bag of pretzels on her way down the narrow outside stairs when she saw Madi waiting for her at the bottom. Jordan silently handed her the bag of pretzels.

"You wanted something?" Madi said as they walked around the building and back into the gym.

"Just to check in," Jordan said. The music had switched to cool-down; a slow electronica beat now permeated the gym space. "You seem off today."

"You don't like my behaviour, is that what you're saying? Am I not focused enough for you?"

Jordan pushed the tray of vegetables onto the back table and removed the lid. Madi pulled a giant bowl off a shelf and poured the pretzels into it.

"No, that's not it. You just seem out of sorts. I wanted to know if you're okay."

Madi said nothing, folding the bag into half and then quarters. Then she tossed it into the garbage can and looked up at Jordan. Still the blankness, though maybe also a little bit of calm.

"It's just a day. Like any other fucking day."

Which meant it wasn't.

"You nervous about your performance tonight?"

"No."

"Something happen at work? With your aunt?"

Madi snorted. "I love twenty questions. No and no."

"Then what is it?"

"It's nothing, Jordan. Okay? Nothing."

Madi pissed was a sight to behold. Jordan had been on the receiving end too many times to be concerned by it.

"Last question, I swear. Which makes it only six, by my count."

Madi almost cracked a smile. She turned it into a grimace. "Fuck it. Go ahead."

"Is it nothing or nothing you want to talk about?"

Madi looked around the room, casually giving the finger to a group in the corner making rude gestures as they went through their cool-down routine.

"I'll take door number two, Professor McAddie. Now, should we feed these ingrates or what?"

"Ingrates, huh? It's like you've been to school or something, Professor Battiste."

This time Madi did smile. It vanished quickly, replaced by a look of pure vulnerability before Madi covered it with forced indifference. The change was so rapid, Jordan could barely keep up. Caring about Madi meant riding a roller coaster.

"You coming tonight?" Madi said, not meeting Jordan's eyes.

"Definitely. I'm planning to be there by nine. Cay is coming, too."

Madi blew out a breath and nodded. Jordan saw her glance over at Ali, then quickly away.

"We should move before the stampede begins," Madi said.

"I haven't said anything to Ali, you know."

"Oh."

"I can. I just thought you might want to invite her yourself."

Another quick glance at Ali.

"I..." Madi hesitated. Then she clamped her mouth shut.

"It's okay to care what she thinks."

Madi scowled. "Great. An impromptu therapy session."

Jordan threw up her hands. "Yeah, okay. I'll stop."

Madi fidgeted with the ends of her ponytail. Her body was agitated, unsure. A state that Jordan knew Madi hated.

"Fuck it."

Madi pushed away from the table and walked over to where Ali was stretching alongside Rupert and Sierra. Ali smiled as Madi approached, and Jordan's heart pounded just a little harder in her chest as Ali welcomed her into her space. No hint of defensiveness or concern at Madi's prickly behaviour. Just welcome and acceptance. Exactly what Madi needed.

Their conversation was short, and Madi's expression was only a little defensive as she spoke. Then her shoulders relaxed when Ali smiled again and pulled out her phone. They seemed to exchange information, then Madi turned and walked away. Ali searched for Jordan, and when she saw her looking, smiled and gave a discreet thumbs-up. Jordan smiled back, a happiness so complete she could not feel its edges.

"It's done," Madi said. "I've got you a date tonight. You can thank me later." She snagged some pretzels and kept walking. "I've got to go get ready. See you tonight."

Jordan laughed as Madi sauntered out. The world, for now, seemed to have righted itself.

❖

The entrance to the bar was long and narrow, but the crowd was happy and the music was loud as Jordan and Ali joined the loose lineup around the bar to order drinks. Once they had cold pint glasses in hand, they wound their way around the happy drinkers to the wider back room. It was quieter here, and the tables and chairs were all oriented around a very small stage. Ali was staring at the tall canvases that lined one of the walls, haunting silhouettes in poses of defiance, seduction, and sorrow. Jordan touched Ali's arm to get her attention, the backs of her fingers sliding along the soft folds of her black shirt just long enough for Jordan to feel the sensation in her stomach. Long enough for Ali to look down, too long for Jordan to pass it off as a casual touch. Jordan swallowed.

"I see Cay up near the front. We'll join her, if that's okay."

"Of course."

Jordan breathed a little easier as they sat at the small table with Cay. The addition of another person, especially one as outgoing as Cay, shifted the dynamic enough to give Jordan some space. As Cay and Ali talked about city life and Ali's favourite places to eat in Chicago, Jordan listened to the beating of her heart over the pulse of music and voices. It wasn't rapid or out of synch around Ali. Not always, anyway. It was simply noticeable, a function of her body she took for granted, a life dependency she relied on and gave so little thought to. Until Ali was around. What was her heart trying to tell her? A message about righting past wrongs, closing off a broken part of their history, maybe. Or, infinitely more frightening, a message to pay attention to the connection of today. And the possibilities for the future.

Jordan took a sip of her beer, the bright flavour saving her once again from her careening thoughts.

"But is it home?"

Cay's question to Ali caught Jordan off guard. She recognized the tone of her voice. Part curiosity, part pointed query. Aimed at the heart.

"It's home for now," Ali said. She sounded reflective but not uncomfortable, Jordan decided. Cay said nothing, and Jordan knew she was letting the silence prompt a deeper answer. "It's a home base more than a home, I guess. But it's not a place to put down roots, if that's what you're asking."

Cay nodded and waited, but Ali took a sip of her beer and glanced at Jordan, who simply smiled reassuringly. "I wonder what it means to put down roots." When Ali didn't answer, Cay spoke again quickly. "Forgive my intrusion. I guess I'm asking a broader question. It's something we think about with our youth. What home means, what connection means, what a solid foundation looks like. Many of them have a home base. Most of them are seeking home. Comfort and connection. Something that ties you to the people and the place around you."

Ali spun her beer slowly in a circle but kept her eyes on Cay.

"Are you trying to *be* that for your kids? Or are you trying to *find* that for your kids?"

Cay gave a shocked and delighted laugh at Ali's question.

"Jordan McAddie, where have you been hiding this treasure? She's been here one week and can ask the question no Ministry rep with their heads shoved up their funding formulas would ever think to ask. An excellent question. The answer is both. For some people, it is the finding. For some, it is the giving. Jordan and I have always worked for both."

"I can see that," Ali said. "At the gym. I can see that…influence."

Ali shook her head, like that wasn't the word she wanted. But the rest of their conversation was halted as a large man in dark jeans, a bright white shirt, and a rainbow bow tie took the mic and welcomed everyone to the October poetry slam. The light dimmed in the room and the chatter died along with it. The sound of the revelers in the bar area made them seem somehow secreted away. The spotlight drew everyone's attention as the MC introduced the first performer.

Jordan had known nothing of spoken word poetry before Madi. But from the first time she'd heard it, she'd loved how the words and the voice gave power to each other. Tonight was no different. The performers spoke hard truths along with gut-wrenching confessions and comedy on the fallacies of the human condition. Some of the poets were young, some old, some nervous, some defiant. None were gentle.

Jordan stole glances at Ali, wondering what she thought of all this. Her eyes were riveted to the stage. She laughed and looked thoughtful and calculating as she listened and drank her beer. When the MC introduced Madi, Ali looked at Jordan. She seemed nervous. Jordan loved her for it in that instant.

"There's our girl," Cay muttered. They were a table of nervous wrecks. Jordan turned more fully in her chair as the MC helped Madi adjust the mic to her small height. Madi looked calm, and her pale face took on a surreal glow in the spotlight. As the MC walked off stage, Madi shook her arms out in a gesture Jordan recognized as one of her own. Then she approached the mic and started to speak.

"It's my turn. No one has used those words, but I can feel the pressure of them. I can feel their expectation, the congratulatory looks they give each other when they think I am not looking. I could be their best success story. I have the chance to make my way through the adult world with the tools they've worked so hard to give me. I have the chance to make them all proud.

"But I am no different than yesterday or three years ago. I am not convinced I have learned more. I'm stunted, maybe—like my growth. A childhood of neglect. So, I feel no different than when I was ten and argued with my foster mom so relentlessly she backhanded me hard enough to see stars. Stars like the best part of overnight camp they sent me to every year. Stars like the meds they gave me at twelve that turned my day into a galaxy. Stars like the pinpoints of light in the boxing ring when I fight.

"My nineteenth birthday stripped away every soft place to land, every harness and tether they attached to me as a Crown ward. Every safety line I once fought against, feeling leashed, a feral dog snapping at its rescuers. I would laugh now at the irony, but I might start crying. I might never stop.

"What kind of inefficiency is it to spend hours and years and resources making me understand and trust the system only to yank it away on my nineteenth birthday? What kind of cruelty? The people are there, and that hasn't changed. But I see their caseload, I feel the weight of their jobs with an empathy and guilt I can't admit. They have to turn me over. It's someone else's turn to benefit from their strength and love. My bitterness is big enough to consume me. I pretend it isn't. But in the quiet moments inside a head that is never quiet, I nurture my demons of bitterness and abandonment."

Jordan ached, a hurt so profound she felt heavy and brittle all at once. She had never understood how Madi carried her pain, her uncertainty, the depth to which she felt everything. The poetry helped, the therapy helped, the stability of home with her aunt helped. Jordan and Cay helped. But none of it seemed like enough.

"You two okay?" Ali said.

Jordan heard the noise as patrons stood to grab another drink during the intermission. She looked over at Cay, who was staring at the now empty stage, evidence of tears on her cheeks.

"Cay?" Jordan needed to see what Cay was feeling, to know how to process this.

Cay finally glanced back at Jordan, a shock of sorrow blended into the lines of her face. She seemed haunted. Ali gently touched first Cay's arm, then Jordan's.

"I'm going to leave you two to talk for a moment. I'll get us some more drinks. Cay? What are you having?"

Cay blinked, then touched a tissue to the tears on her cheeks.

"Just a club soda. Thanks, love."

Ali gave Jordan a sympathetic smile and stood, squeezing Jordan's shoulder lightly on the way by.

Jordan wasn't sure what to say.

"I can't tell if we've succeeded or failed," Cay said. "There seems to be no middle ground."

"There rarely is with Madi," Jordan said.

Cay smiled at that. "That is a truth to remember."

"I think," Jordan hesitated and tried to order her thoughts, "I think that was her fear talking. She uses poetry to talk about being scared."

"Madi hates being scared."

"Exactly."

Neither of them seemed to want to circle back to Cay's original thought. Success or failure? To celebrate or cry?

"May I sit for a moment?"

Jordan barely recognized Helena in dark jeans and a purple sweater. She'd never seen her outside of work hours. And Helena always seemed to have work hours.

"Yes, of course," Cay said.

Helena pulled back Ali's chair and sat. Jordan thought she saw evidence of tears. Her heart ached a little more. Pain on pain, a long line of worry, never-ending doubt.

"You make a difference in her life," Helena said. Her voice was light, and Jordan had to strain to hear. "You have centred Madigan in your fight for Madigan. You have built her voice and her advocacy. She has more tools, as she called them, than most of the young adults I see in my service. She has been fortunate."

Jordan felt the tears in her throat. She wanted so badly to believe she had done right by Madi. By all her kids. But especially Madigan Battiste.

Cay cleared her throat. "Thank you, Helena. We were just sitting here wondering if Madi's performance meant we had succeeded or failed."

Helena took Cay's hand and reached for Jordan's. They sat linked like that until Helena spoke again, her eyes shining with fervour. "The system fails. Those that prop up the system are failing. But you two, I have always felt a kinship—"

Ali returned just then. She walked to the front of the table with the three drinks clutched in her hands. She smiled at Helena, open and inviting. Jordan watched as Helena's face went from passionate to blank in a heartbeat. Helena pushed back her chair and stood.

"I did not realize I was intruding."

"You're not," Ali said. "It looks like I am. But we can grab another chair."

Helena stood in her spot, the awkwardness of the moment obviously overwhelming her. She seemed to be in two places at once, and Jordan felt the need to rescue her. Jordan stood.

"Helena, this is Ali Clarke."

Ali gave that same warm smile and stuck out her hand. Helena shook it.

"Madi's my mentor," Ali said.

Jordan winced and waited for Helena to bring up the same concerns she'd had earlier this week about the uncaring and greedy nature of corporations. But Helena simply gave her a professional smile.

"Yes, it is good to meet you. I've heard it has been a successful partnership." She pushed her chair back and looked over her shoulder as if checking for someone. She nodded once to whoever it was and turned back to the group. "It's nice to meet you. I think I will head out and get some work done. I just wanted to see Madigan's performance. I'm happy I did."

Helena left then, the noise of the returning crowd covering the awkwardness of her exit.

"Did I mess up?" Ali said, coming around the table and taking her original seat.

"No, not at all," Cay answered. "That's Helena. Most comfortable talking about the homeless and the failings of social services. Least comfortable talking about…anything else really."

Jordan gave a short laugh. "Very true. She's incredibly dedicated."

"As are the two of you, obviously," Ali said gently.

Cay and Jordan smiled at each other. "Christ on a cod boat, we try," Cay said.

"God, I've missed Maritime speak," Ali said, laughing. She passed around the fresh drinks, then raised her glass. "To friends. And home. And success."

That lump lodged in Jordan's throat again as she raised her glass with Ali and Cay.

The house lights dimmed, and Jordan retreated into the solitude of darkness as the next poet took the stage. Her head and heart rebounded with warmth and worry, love and connection, pride and fear. She realized she'd missed half the performer's poem and forced herself to listen again. As the young poet took their applause and left the stage, Jordan felt a light touch at her elbow. Madi was crouching down by the table. Her pale face looked flushed, her eyes bright as she still rode the high of her performance.

"You're all here!" Madi whispered. "Fucking aces. What did you think?" Before anyone could respond, Madi waved them away. "Don't tell me. You're here and you were crying and I think you liked it." Madi closed her eyes and seemed to take a deep breath. She looked so vulnerable in that moment, talking herself into believing they loved her.

Madi opened her eyes as the MC came on stage to introduce the next poet. "I have to go. But I'll see you around. Bye."

And she was gone again, all darkness and light, shadow and blinding sun. The complexities of Madigan Battiste.

Jordan half listened to the final poets, allowing herself to recognize her exhaustion from the day as the words fell around her, pushing to be heard and felt. When the final poet had closed with a fisted salute to the sky, Jordan felt nearly bruised. She'd left other poetry slams feeling like this. It was both risk and reward.

The house lights came back on, the audience blinking back into the real world.

"I've never experienced anything like that," Ali said.

"It's powerful, isn't it?" Cay said as she stood and put on her long, wool sweater that wrapped like a cape.

Ali and Jordan stood as well. "Will we see Madi again?" Ali said.

Jordan and Cay looked at each other. "No, likely not tonight. Tomorrow."

The three women followed the crowd out of the bar into the cold night air of the city street. Jordan and Ali walked Cay around the block to where her car was parked.

"I am happy we experienced this together, my friend," Cay said as she gave Jordan a hug. "And I'm happy you were here as well," Cay said to Ali. "You are part of Madi's story now."

Ali looked taken aback both at Cay's statement and the hug that followed it.

"Thank you," Ali said. "I really do value that. I've never met anyone like Madi."

Jordan and Cay exchanged grins. "Neither have we," Jordan said.

Cay smiled and then sighed. "Madi is a soul that was meant to be young. But her soul was weathered and chafed and crushed until her newness disappeared. There is nothing as sad as a soul turned old before it's meant to."

Tears again down the back of Jordan's throat. This night was nearly too much.

"You're a poet yourself, Cay," Jordan said, stepping in for one more hug. "I wonder where she gets it from."

Cay laughed and wiped away fresh tears.

"Enough. Go. Be well."

Once Cay had driven off with a honk of her horn and a wave out the window, Jordan and Ali looked at each other.

"Walk me home?" Ali said.

Jordan smiled. "I'd love to."

They turned toward the waterfront, angling down and across the hill to Ali's hotel. Jordan pushed her hands into her pockets, thinking how very much she'd like to take Ali's hands in hers and walk through the city, just like they used to.

"You walked me home from school sometimes," Ali said, apparently thinking similar thoughts. "When I didn't have practice and you weren't heading straight to the gym."

"Which was most of the time," Jordan said.

"True. Jesus, we were ripped back then."

Jordan laughed. "And never tired."

"Except when Ms. Laurens was back together with her girlfriend. Then she made our lives hell."

Jordan laughed as she remembered their gym teacher, a former hockey player who was always fighting with her girlfriend and spent most of their gym classes in the office either crying or yelling on the phone. As a result, most of their gym classes were self-directed. But when Ms. Laurens was happy, she was a gym teacher who pushed her students to their very limits.

"You talked to me for the first time in gym class," Jordan said.

"I did," Ali said with a smile. "You were showing off your abs. Upside down."

"I was doing crunches on the bar," Jordan clarified. "My shirt wouldn't stay tucked in."

"Mm-hmm. You were making half the class envious. And sending at least half that many into lustful fantasies." Ali nudged Jordan in the ribs with her elbow, and Jordan stumbled a few steps.

"Hey, I was just trying to follow the workout routine on the board. I was the new kid, remember?"

"I remember," Ali said quietly. "New and angry."

Jordan had been angry. Steven dead, Jake a new dad, her mom sober but shaky. After a final fight with her father, everyone agreed some time away would be best. Jordan was lucky Constable Mike and his wife had taken her in. She hadn't felt lucky at the time.

"Seems like so long ago," Jordan said.

"I remember talking to you while you were still upside down on that bar. I remember demanding you help me do the workout." Ali laughed. "I couldn't decide if I was acting on attraction or envy."

"I think envy was the true motivator. You're a wee bit competitive."

"True."

They were quiet as they left the busier main strip of downtown. They passed closed-up shops displaying tartans, outdoor gear, and used books. The silence stretched until Jordan wanted to ask if Ali was okay. If she'd said something she shouldn't, if the trip back in time had caused more hurt than happiness. Then Jordan felt Ali take her hand, with a warmth and a strength and a connection so new and so achingly familiar that Jordan's heart rocketed around in her chest. She looked at Ali, her eyes bright in the glow of the streetlights. Ali was smiling.

"This okay?"

Too many questions layered in one, an unintentional trap. Jordan answered the only way she could.

"Yes."

They were on a side street less than a block from Ali's hotel, surrounded by apartment buildings and municipal garages and empty lots. A lone figure walked up the hill toward them. Jordan had just registered his presence when she heard and felt footsteps behind them. She immediately stepped into the empty street, not wanting to be trapped against the stone wall of the condo beside them. The man approaching them did the same. Jordan looked quickly over her shoulder and saw two more behind them, angling out to block their retreat back up the street. All of them wore dark clothing, and all were hooded.

"Jordan?"

Jordan had Ali's hand in a death grip. She loosened it slightly. "Get ready to run."

Jordan had lived on the streets of Halifax, and she'd been rolled more than once. She'd fought back every time. But it had been a long time since she was in this position. She wasn't ready for a street fight, not with Ali beside her.

"I'm not going anywhere," Ali said, dropping Jordan's hand. Of course Ali thought she could fight. Stubborn.

Jordan stopped in the middle of the street, right in the centre of the streetlights. They were highly visible, and it was still early enough she could count on some traffic coming by. A police cruiser would be even better.

"Just a message, Jordan. You and your girlfriend don't need to look so scared."

Jordan said nothing. She didn't recognize the man's voice. It was rough, like he was a smoker. His clothes were nondescript, and he kept the light angled so most of his face was in shadow.

"Just lay low, stop talking to the police, and reap the benefits of the movement. Stay out of the way, that's all you have to do."

He stepped closer and Jordan and Ali took a step backwards until she felt hands holding them there.

"Fuck off, all of you," Jordan said, shaking the hands off her shoulders. When she heard one of the guys behind her laugh and felt his grip tighten, she smashed an elbow back, catching him in the gut. His breath rushed out as he doubled over.

"Bitch," the other said, grabbing Ali.

In a move so fast Jordan wasn't even really sure what she was seeing, Ali trapped the man's hand over her shoulder, crouched down, and threw him over her head onto his back on the street. Jordan, distracted by the throw, barely registered the fist heading for her stomach, but she had just enough time to spin away from the powerful but not well-aimed punch. It glanced off her side as a car turned down the street behind them, lighting up this bizarre scene in the glow of its headlights. The guys scattered, the man Ali had laid out on the street scrambling to his feet and disappearing into the empty lot.

Jordan grabbed Ali's hand again and pulled her back toward the sidewalk.

"You okay? Hurt?" Jordan said. Her heart pounded, and she was breathing hard. So was Ali.

"No. Just shaken up. And pissed. You hurt?"

"Barely touched me." Jordan could feel the muscles in her side clench. Nothing seemed too damaged. Ali was pissed but not hurt, that's all that mattered.

"You ladies okay?"

The car had pulled over with its four-way flashers on. A middle-aged man with a bushy beard and a vaporizer in his hand leaned out the passenger window.

"We're okay, thanks. Your arrival was well-timed, though."

"Can I call someone for you? Give you a ride?"

Jordan waved away his offer. "We're not too far from where we need to go. But thanks."

The man raised his vaporizer in a salute. "You two take care. And keep kicking ass."

Ali gave a short laugh as the car carried on down the hill. "The dichotomies of Halifax. Maritime hospitality and street thugs in the same minute."

Ali sounded rattled. Jordan took her hand and tugged gently. "Come on. I'm going to call Rachel as we walk."

Jordan awkwardly pulled out her phone. Texting with her left hand was a pain in the ass, but she refused to let Ali go. She sent a short text, starting with the fact that she and Ali were fine. Rachel's answer was immediate. *Call the police, I'm coming over.*

"Rachel says to call the police," Jordan said.

"Obviously," Ali muttered. She pulled her hand away. Jordan wondered what she'd done wrong.

"I want to make sure Cay and Madi are okay. I want to text them first."

"You do that. I'll call the police."

Adrenaline still pumped its way through Jordan's body. Her heart rate was too high, and she needed to breathe and calm. They were off the side street, in sight of people and lights and the hotel. The fight had been a brief moment, threats and anger and the edges of violence. All seemingly purposeful. All thwarted.

Jordan texted Cay and Madi the same message: *You safe?* Neither of them would be particularly concerned to receive that text from Jordan. They both knew she worried. Cay's answer was immediate; she was home and in her pyjamas. Nothing from Madi, which wasn't really surprising.

The wide stone steps, tall glass doors, and overlit brilliance of the hotel entrance was a jarring but welcome respite from the dark street.

"They're sending someone to the hotel," Ali said as she hung up. "Guess I should warn the front desk."

Jordan watched Ali walk to the front desk and give a brief report to the manager, whose eyes widened as he anxiously asked questions. Ali answered them calmly, indicated Jordan over her shoulder, and then ended the conversation.

"I don't think I made his night," Ali said. She wouldn't quite meet Jordan's eyes. She looked down the hallway toward the loud hotel bar. "Want a drink?"

Concern wormed its way through Jordan's belly.

"No, thanks."

"Suit yourself. I'm going to grab something."

Jordan sat on one of the oddly shaped leather couches in the lobby. The light and warmth of the hotel had been inviting a moment ago, but now the bright space felt oppressive. Jordan wanted to hide out, make herself a smaller target, retreat from the threat. She breathed. This was not a fight. Danger was not immediate. The police were on their way. Rachel had her back. Her family was safe. And Ali? She would figure out what was going on with Ali.

Ali walked back into the lobby carrying two steaming mugs. She handed one to Jordan and sat.

"Decaf coffee is shit, but it seemed like the better choice. Okay, fine. Mine's an Irish coffee but whatever. That was messed up."

Still rattled, then. Jordan gratefully wrapped her hand around the warm mug. The adrenaline had left her body, leaving her tired and cold. Ali must be feeling the same way.

"Thanks, this is perfect."

Ali nodded and sipped her coffee, staring at the glass coffee table in front of them.

"So…you know self-defense?"

Ali finally looked at Jordan. The distance receded just a fraction as her expression softened. "I dated a woman in my senior year who taught self-defense classes. The relationship lasted less than six months, but I really liked the class. Even moved on to judo for a couple of years." Ali stared down into her milky coffee. Jordan could smell the Baileys. "But then life happened. Work was too busy to keep up the judo."

"You obviously remembered enough. That was an impressive move."

"Yeah," Ali said thoughtfully. "I've practiced that move a hundred times. It was really weird to use it for real."

Ali still wasn't entirely present, and Jordan wondered where she was. With the woman who taught her the course? Kitted out for judo practice on soft mats? Or still back on the street with someone's hands on her neck, ready to hurt her?

Jordan nudged Ali gently with her knee. Ali looked up, eyes haunted. "Play it out in your head. Remember we chased them off. Remember we're safe. That's the only ending here. Okay?"

Ali nodded and was about to speak when Rachel walked in with a uniformed officer.

"Jordan, hey. You're okay?" Rachel gave her a quick hug. Jordan nodded, and Rachel turned to Ali. "Hi, again. How about you? Are you okay?"

Ali stood with squared shoulders. "Yes, I'm fine. Thank you."

Stiff and polite. Jordan guessed they were seeing Ali's boardroom demeanour. She was all toughness and control, self-assured even in the face of crisis.

The officer introduced herself as Constable Lewis, and the four of them sat in the uncomfortable chairs. Ali and Jordan answered questions while the officer took notes, and Rachel sat listening intently and interjecting occasionally. Jordan tried to ignore the stares of the bar patrons and other hotel guests. She hated being a spectacle.

"Is there anything else you think might be relevant?" Constable Lewis said after they'd recounted their night.

Jordan and Ali looked at each other for reference, then both turned back to the officer and shook their heads.

"Okay, then. We have your contact information, and an officer will be calling in the next couple of days to follow up."

"I'll be out of town middle of the week," Ali said suddenly. "But available by phone."

This was news to Jordan. The disappointment didn't sit comfortably, but Ali did not owe Jordan her schedule.

Constable Lewis took a note and checked with Rachel before taking her leave.

"I'm worried you were targeted, Jordan," Rachel said once the three of them were alone.

Jordan was, too. Especially because she was with Ali. And especially because she hadn't heard back from Madi. Who else was being targeted?

"If this is a protest, some sort of…" Jordan searched for the right word and heard the rough voice of the man on the street. "Movement, an underground movement. I don't think I'm a target. The threat was for me to stay quiet and stay out of the way. Like this is going to benefit me in some way."

Rachel tucked her hair behind her ear. "I know. I see that, too. But this warning turned violent pretty quickly. Just be safe, okay? Be smart about where you go on your own." Rachel turned to Ali, who had been quiet. "And you, too. It sounds like you kicked some ass tonight, but we'd like you to stay safe while you're visiting."

Visiting. Going out of town. Violence on the streets. Any connection Jordan had been feeling was fading fast. Had they really been holding hands an hour ago? It was already a fragmented memory.

"Yes, thank you, Constable Shreve. I will be careful."

Rachel glanced at Jordan. "Need a ride home?"

Jordan turned to Ali. She wanted to stay, to walk Ali up to her room. She wanted to feel Ali's arms around her, to hold on to her and give comfort. To receive it.

Ali stood abruptly. "That's a good idea," she said with no inflection in her tone. "Thank you for your time, Constable Shreve. Good night, Jordan. I'll see you tomorrow."

Ali met Jordan's eyes, but her expression gave away very little. It was the closure of a board meeting, ending on strength. Jordan watched her walk away, no hint of vulnerability or concern. No hint of connection.

"I messed up, didn't I?" Rachel said, looking contrite.

"No, not at all."

"You were going to stay and I just—"

Jordan held up a hand to stop her. That potential future felt like fiction. Ali was tough and capable, self-assured and confident. She had a condo and a life in Chicago. Degrees on her wall, conference calls to Southeast Asia, frequent flyer miles. Jordan had a run-down gym that permanently smelled like sweat. Volatile street kids. A barely mended family. She had nothing to offer Ali except an apology for their past, and she'd already given her that.

Jordan put the hurt aside until she could be in her own space. She looked away from the empty hallway, then back at Rachel.

"I'll take that drive home now, please."

Chapter Seven

The streets had gone quiet; the movement or protest or whatever it was had gone farther underground. Jordan kept an eye out, but Halifax seemed as busy and unconcerned as usual. Nothing about her gym or her routes to the university and work seemed out of place or threatening. Oddly, the kids had gone quiet, too. The gym was still loud, music reverberating from the cross-hatched metal rafters, but the kids seemed wary.

A few had approached her the day after the incident on the street. Their concern warmed Jordan's heart. But their sidelong glances at each other, the cursed mutterings and whispered threats made Jordan uneasy. She reassured them she was okay, tried to convince them she was not in danger and they had no need to worry. They looked unconvinced as they drifted off to their circuits. She had hoped the weekend would settle things. It didn't. Concern and quiet seemed to permeate their space.

Work demanded her presence, school demanded her focus, and the kids demanded her heart and time. Ali demanded nothing. They texted every day, just a few words, checking in after their shared dark night on the street. Their conversation was stilted and polite at the gym. Jordan could find no fault with it. They were friendly, but it felt like Ali had drawn a line, and Jordan would respect that. She could not pretend it didn't hurt.

Jordan was opening up the gym after work on Wednesday afternoon when a text came through from Madi.

She's gone?

Ali had left the day before for Chicago. Business, Ali had said in a text. Jordan sensed she'd needed to escape. She couldn't blame her.

Ali back Friday, Jordan texted back as she entered the gym. She opened the electrical panel inside the door and flipped the four switches. Overhead lights buzzed and hummed as they came on. The sound was familiar, but Jordan felt like something was off. She held still and listened. The gym was cold and the air was a little stale. Nothing seemed out of place, though. She shook off the feeling and walked through the gym.

The change rooms were empty, the floor still showing rusted squares where the old lockers had been. Jordan had torn out those lockers not long after she'd started the program, replacing them with open cubbies her brother Jake had made. She'd discovered a small group of kids were dealing marijuana out of her gym. Police had been called, they'd been banned from the program, the lockers had been removed, and now every few months Jordan had the K-9 drug unit use her gym for training. She always made sure the kids were around for that.

Jordan pushed open as many of the old windows as she could in the building, hoping to get some of the cold, late October air in before the kids arrived. She still had the feeling something wasn't quite right but she had no evidence to support it. Her phone chimed again.

U okay?

Madi hadn't taken the news that Jordan and Ali had been targeted after her poetry reading very well. She'd paled and cursed, demanded answers, and then gone quiet.

All is well, grasshopper, Jordan texted. *Get your butt down here and help me set up. Five minute bouts tonight.*

Jordan wanted to shake things up a little tonight. She was tired of silence. The lack of news from Rachel, the uneasy quiet of her kids, Madi's flatness, all made Jordan want to scream. Worst of all was not hearing from Ali. Fourteen years of silence, and now all Jordan wanted was a text. She felt pathetic.

Jordan heard the metal door scrape open as Madi walked in. She looked the same, dark jeans and a black hoodie. Black boots laced up over her calves. She was all toughness, her Madi.

"Five-minute bouts?" Madi said by way of greeting. Her eyes looked brighter than they had recently. "Aces."

"You want to fight?"

"Hell, yeah. I'm in."

"Good," Jordan said. "Grab the markers from the office, we'll set up a fight schedule." Madi pulled her key from her pocket and headed up the metal steps. Only Jordan and Sean had keys to the outside doors, but she'd gifted Madi with her own key to the equipment room and office. It was a symbol of trust, a symbol of partnership as she mentored Madi as a boxing manager. Madi was excelling at the role. She had always looked out for her friends, but the manager's job gave her a focus for her worry.

Jordan began getting equipment from the back room. The kids always wanted bouts and matches, but Jordan had been relentless in her training schedule. You practiced, you ran circuits, you worked out. Most of fighting was training. Glory was in conditioning your body and preparing your mind, not swinging wildly at an opponent when you weren't ready.

Tonight felt like a good night to shake things up. Pull the kids out of their mood. Force them to focus, build them up, pump them up.

Kids started trickling in, and the noise increased as they took in the long tables of gear and Madi on a step stool creating the fight schedule. Jordan had to yell at them to change and get warmed up. No one was going in the ring without warming up. But she was smiling. Things were feeling back to normal.

"Hey, stranger."

Jordan was pulling out the bin of mouthguards and antibacterial mouthwash when Sean walked in.

"Hey yourself. You sure you don't mind coming in tonight?"

"Macy's home tonight, and I've been studying all day. I need a break, man. It's this or go for a swim in the harbour."

Jordan laughed. Sean worked part-time, studied part-time, and parented full-time. "Well, I appreciate it. It's five-minute bout night. You can keep an eye on the main ring, and I'll set up the second. We'll start off with a demonstration. That work?"

"Aye, boss. It does." Sean grinned and walked off.

Once most of the kids had arrived, Rupert led the group through a high-energy and very odd workout set to Michael Jackson's "Thriller." The kids were laughing and rolling their eyes, most at least half-heartedly participating with the warm-up. Seamus was here tonight, obviously dragged along by some friends. He seemed no worse for wear from his run-in with the police at the recycling bin tower incident. She made a mental note to try and check in with him tonight, if she had a chance.

It was a ridiculously busy night for Jordan. She had a second, smaller ring set up on the far side of the gym so the kids wouldn't have to wait so long for their turn. After her demonstration fight with Sean, Jordan bounded between the two rings, ensuring the fights were fair and, above all, safe.

Nearing the end of the night, the train derailed. Most kids had already had their matches. Jordan was trying to corral them into cheering or running circuits, but she had a losing battle on her hands as kids milled about, waiting for the last few fights to be over and the food to come out. Jordan was focused on the fight in the front of her, calling out instructions to the girls in the centre of the ring, when she heard a shout from the ring behind her.

The anger in the tone alerted her, not cheerful jibes or victorious yells. She turned quickly, thinking maybe one of the fights had gotten out of hand, but the two boxers in Sean's ring were standing with their gloved hands down by their sides, watching something in the crowd. Sean was already getting out of the ring, and Jordan jumped down from the mats, dodging through the teenagers who were pushing in toward the centre of the action.

Jordan finally broke through the crowd in time to see Madi yelling in someone's face. Jordan recognized Philip, someone Madi had dated a few years ago. He was scowling down at Madi, not touching her but not backing away either. Sean inserted himself into the space between them, putting a hand to each of their shoulders and forcing them back. He'd refereed enough fights to know separating only one fighter almost always led to an escalation. Philip and Madi both resisted and Jordan stepped into the small, cleared circle.

"Hey! Both of you take a step back."

Philip smirked and Madi swore, but they both eased back. Sean stayed where he was, looking to Jordan for direction.

"What just happened here?" Jordan said.

"She's fucking crazy."

"Fuck you."

That had accomplished all of nothing. Jordan took a breath.

"Philip, try again. This time without insults."

Philip threw up his hands. "I was just watching the fight and talking to my friends and this—" Philip seemed to catch the look from Jordan and switched tactics. "And suddenly Madi's all up in my face yelling. For nothing."

Jordan doubted that.

"Madi? What's up?"

"He was talking shit. I told him to stop. He didn't."

"Facts are facts, shorty," Philip said in the pumped-up teenage boy tone that always grated on Jordan's nerves.

"Like the fact that you're a tiny-pricked asshole," Madi said, her voice low and menacing.

The crowd around them reacted with laughter and jeers. Trusting Sean to keep them separated, Jordan turned and addressed the other teens.

"Enough, guys. Back off and be quiet. Give them a chance to work this out."

Before Jordan had time to try and help the two furious teens in front of her do exactly that, Philip took his last shot.

"You don't even fight for yourself. You just latch on to people who fight for you. Jordan, Sierra, your dad, Helena and the—"

Jordan was ready to jump in and shut Philip down with his targeted barbs when Madi cut him off.

"Fuck you, Philip. You're incapable of opening your mouth without shit coming out. I'm done."

Madi turned and left, her face stony. Jordan wished she could stop Madi so they could get to the bottom of what had prompted this fight and find a resolution. But she needed to allow Madi to retreat and save face. With these kids, social currency and influence was paramount.

The crowd was buzzing, and Philip was beginning to strut, like he'd just won an argument. Jordan needed to bring this under control, fast. She stepped in toward Philip and lowered her voice so only the teen could hear.

"Targeting weakness in the ring makes you a winner. But make it personal outside of the ring and you run the very real risk of becoming an asshole."

Philip snorted and shook his head. Jordan couldn't expect contriteness this soon after a confrontation. She'd just have to hope he'd hear it eventually.

Jordan eased back and addressed the large group. "Who wants to read out the shit rule?"

Some kids laughed and a few rolled their eyes as Jordan walked toward the crooked list of painted words above the equipment room door. She wanted to draw everyone's attention away from whatever had happened with Madi and Philip, and she needed to remind them she was here, whatever else was going on.

"Come on, it's the favourite rule. Someone read it out for me."

A handful of kids called out the rule in sing-song voices. "Don't bring your shit into the ring. Find someone to talk to."

"Right," Jordan said. "You've all got shit going on, I know. Bring it to the gym and sweat it out, bring it to me and talk it out. But before you get in the ring, before you take on a fight, you have to put it away." The group was quiet. They looked at Jordan but also stole glances at each other. Something was definitely up. "Anything you guys want to tell me?"

More silence and Jordan waited it out, covering her impatience and concern with the illusion of calm.

"Does being hungry count?" Rupert said, breaking the silence as well as the tension. Jordan recognized that whatever was going on, they weren't going to let her know what it was now.

"If I'm not mistaken, there's only one bout left in each ring. Then food. Boxers, go prepare yourselves." Jordan tossed her keys to Rupert. "Go grab the food from the fridge. And there's a grocery bag with cookies. That comes directly to me."

The teens whooped and hollered at the mention of cookies. Jordan tried to drown out the noise, tried to push away her exhaustion and the feeling of having failed. She wanted to find Madi. She wanted quiet. She wanted to sink into her couch and hide from a world that was too much off-centre. But she didn't. She carried the energy for these kids, pushing them forward, keeping their focus, maintaining this connection. When things broke down, Jordan wanted them to walk away remembering how it was repaired. Every single time.

The last two bouts finished up with no incident. Jordan kept her eyes on the kids, kept her ears tuned to the crowd, and kept her senses open to the shifts in mood. Things finally seemed calmer. As the kids descended on the food table, Jordan caught sight of Madi. She was having an intense conversation with Raya at the door. Raya looked upset; Madi looked glacial. Jordan watched as Raya reached for Madi. Madi took Raya's hand, held it, then stepped back. This was Madi in retreat. Quieter maybe than it would have been in years past. Calmer. But definite. Madi looked up once before she left and searched the crowd. She found Jordan, nodded once, and left.

Jordan was spent by the time the gym was cleaned up and the kids were gone. She dragged herself up to her apartment and collapsed on her couch, burying her face in a soft pillow she kept exactly for these days. Eyes squeezed shut in a sad attempt to keep the hurts of the world at bay, Jordan's stress brought every worry to the surface. Jordan knew she should text someone, journal, find something to eat. Anything to prevent herself from sinking any lower. But she just couldn't.

Her phone signaled a text. Jordan grabbed it off the coffee table. It was Ali.

Hey, Jordan.

Jordan flipped onto her back and texted back.

Hey. How's Chicago?

Exactly the same. How's Halifax?

Jordan wondered what to say. She wanted Ali to be the one she talked to tonight. Lay everything out and sort through the contents of her thoughts and her heart. But she and Ali weren't quite there yet. Maybe they never would be.

Dunno, Jordan texted back. *I moved to Fiji. Much warmer.*

Ali texted back a laughing emoji and Jordan grinned at her phone, her mood lifting. She waited as Ali texted more.

I owe you an apology.

What for?

Running away.

Jordan didn't quite know what to say to that. She aimed for a neutral response.

Is that what you did?

Basically. I did need to be at the office a few days. But my departure was abrupt and I'm sorry for that.

Would they ever stop apologizing to each other? It didn't seem possible.

I think you've got a few more abrupt departures before you make up for mine. So you're good.

Jordan sent the last text with her heart pounding. It was an agonizing wait for Ali's response.

Ha! I'll remember that.

Jordan grinned at her phone, alone in her apartment, as she and Ali said goodnight. A shitty day made better by a few texts with Ali. Jordan knew what this meant. She was falling for Ali again. Maybe it wasn't just their past. It was Ali's ability to really see Jordan's kids. The way she saw Madi's heart. The way she allowed Jordan to see Ali's uncertainty about herself.

Jordan lay on her couch looking up at the ceiling and smiling foolishly. She wanted to name the frisson of happiness that pulsed through her body. Or she could just let it be, knowing Ali was coming home in a few days. Jordan could look into the future and maybe, just maybe, see happiness.

Chapter Eight

Jordan—Eighteen

Eighteen and Jordan is convinced her heart cannot possibly contain everything it wants to feel for Ali. They are lying in Ali's bed, the huge house quiet and empty. Their breathing has finally slowed, from the nearly frantic gasps for air as they had touched and kissed, both demanding and claiming release, to the easing, gentle laughter as they'd smiled and shifted to hold each other. Now Ali is asleep and Jordan nearly there. Their foreheads are touching, and they're breathing the same pocket of air, fingers entwined. Sex with Ali is a joy Jordan is not sure she can contain. But this unexpected peace afterward, the trust of Ali falling asleep in her arms for the first time, makes Jordan feel as if there's a possibility warm times could last forever.

They wake early, still wrapped around each other. Dawn sunlight in Ali's hair makes Jordan want to find the words to describe how beautiful she is. But there's a shyness in this morning light, an awareness this huge bedroom with the long window seats, posters covering the striped wallpaper, gym bag and cleats thrown into a corner is very much Ali's space. Ali wants nothing to do with shyness as she pushes back the cover and jumps out of bed, her naked body glorious and strong. She pulls Jordan with her, excitement in her smile and voice, in the way she teases Jordan as they stumble down the stairs into the kitchen.

Jordan can feel the tug of fantasy, pretending to be adults in this huge house on a Saturday morning with the sun so bright it makes every surface in the kitchen gleam. Ali seems to feel it, too, and they grin and pour cereal into matching bowls and sit side by side on stools at the breakfast bar. Ali pours Jordan a tall glass of freshly squeezed orange juice. The bright sweetness matches the morning, and Jordan laughs into the sunshine and holds her girlfriend's hand.

The fantasy lasts until after they have said their goodbyes, drawn out with kissing in the hallway, against the front door, and on the front step. The smile lingers as Jordan walks away in a haze of lust and love and laughter, the combination so potent Jordan is barely aware of her surroundings until a neighbour walks by with his dog and nods and smiles hello at Jordan.

The fantasy is broken. She's an eighteen-year-old kid in the wrong neighbourhood, and the feeling of belonging is sucked out of her so fast that Jordan has to close her eyes against the pain of it. She keeps walking, ignoring the play of light and shadow through the tall trees overhead. She licks her lips, searching for a taste of Ali's kisses, the brightness of the orange juice. But she feels nothing, and Jordan swallows and presses on until she can see the harbour and the cranes in the distance, reminding herself this is where she came from.

❖

Jordan and Ali started their run in darkness, turning on their headlamps the moment they left the glow of the empty parking lot behind. Dawn was still at least fifteen minutes away, and they had timed this run to see the sunrise as Ali had requested. Ali had been subdued and hesitant, as if seeking permission for something she didn't have the right to ask. Jordan couldn't understand the hesitation, but she'd wanted very much to give her this. So she'd found a second headlamp and arranged to pick Ali up at her hotel at quarter after six.

They'd discussed the route up to Point Pleasant in the hushed tones of a Sunday morning in church. They were quiet now, just the synchronicity of breath and movement, the crunch and smesh of gravel beneath their feet, and the wind in the dark trees overhead.

They had run together often as teenagers, jostling and laughing and competitive. There had been nothing but light then, the focus of training and conditioning goals, the sweetness of attainment and success. It was the first time Jordan had ever been able to look beyond an individual goal, to lift her head and look into the future without a crushing sense of fear. It was a bubble of time, lasting only as long as she'd been at Saint Sebastian's High School. As long as she'd been with Ali.

Jordan shook her arms out, unconsciously trying to reset her thoughts. It helped her blink back into the present and remind herself that she'd learned to lift her head up. She was done boxing shadows. The last kilometre of gravel path before the top was steeper. The gloom and grey of pre-dawn light began making shapes of the trees and rocks around them. Jordan looked up briefly, hoping they had a clear sky for Ali's sunrise, but the old pines were unyielding in their cover, swaying their heavy branches with the breeze off the water.

Ali pulled ahead in the last turn as they entered the clearing that lead up to the Prince of Wales Tower. The old stone battery was massive and round and squat, built by the British to defend Halifax against the French in the days before colonized Canada was more than a breath of a nation. Ali slowed and finally walked and Jordan did the same, breathing as her body instantly began to cool. The stones at the base of the tower were dark and covered in the moss and lichen of the damp forest. Ali approached and ran her hand over the stone as she walked. Jordan followed, curious about what was going on in Ali's head but content to follow her lead. Ali had been subdued since Jordan had picked her up from the airport. Something was obviously weighing on her mind.

Ali moved away from the tower toward the fenced edge of the forest. She looked back just then and Jordan could see the glint of mischief in her smile before Ali jumped over the fence.

Jordan cursed and grabbed a piece of fencing, struggling to find a foothold against the wet wood before she got over, dropping down to a narrow stretch of weeds below. The horizon was grey, the sky mostly clear of clouds as Jordan searched for Ali's headlamp in the gloom of forest ahead.

Still muttering about safety and municipal laws, Jordan picked her way between trees and thorny bushes in the dark, keeping her headlamp trained on the lack of path ahead of her. Intent on not breaking anything, Jordan nearly tripped over Ali, who had stopped on a rocky outcrop with only a few trees and shrubs between them and a view of the distant horizon over the Atlantic Ocean.

Ali had taken off her headlamp, and Jordan quickly did the same. The breeze smelled of brine, fish, pine, and damp soil. Jordan closed her eyes briefly, waiting for the wind to shift. When it did, a second later, Jordan breathed in the scent of Ali standing so close. She had no words for it, nothing tangible she could associate with that scent, but it was Ali. Jordan *knew* her, a deep knowing, embedded in her memory, in her very core. Jordan shivered at the thought and opened her eyes. Ali was watching her, but Jordan couldn't read anything in her eyes before she turned back to the horizon.

Grey dominated the sky but then orange and yellow pushed their way through in lines and streaks. The sunrise was a battle this morning. Ali seemed to be watching intently, as if waiting for a message or a sign, as the sun stubbornly struggled against an invisible force. Orange turned to pink as the sun broke the horizon, reflecting against the waves, twin balls of light that would follow each other in their daily arc over the ocean.

Jordan turned as Ali sighed. It seemed to be a sigh of loss rather than contentment, and Jordan wondered what Ali had been looking for this morning. She wasn't sure she should ask. Not with their history or their tenuous present.

"Okay?" she said. Jordan's voice was dampened by the forest and the moment.

Ali looked up and smiled sadly. "Yeah, I think so."

"You were looking for something."

"Yes."

"Did you find it?"

Ali's gaze went back to the water. "No."

Jordan let the quiet envelop them again. They still had a few hours until the park was filled with joggers and cyclists and families with strollers. Jordan took the solitude for the gift it was.

"I see a lot of sunrises," Ali said. She looked up at Jordan. "You'd think I wouldn't with the amount I work and travel, but I make it a priority. Wherever I am, I make sure to see at least one sunrise. It… grounds me, I guess."

Jordan nodded. She understood the importance of finding ways to stay grounded.

"You wanted something different from this one."

Ali looked briefly disconcerted, then laughed quietly before breaking eye contact. "I guess. But I'm not sure what."

Ali's uncertainty contrasted with everything Jordan knew about her.

"I wanted you with me for this one," Ali said, smiling. "So I got that from this morning."

Jordan smiled back, the warmth of the sun and Ali's smile heating her outside and in. As Ali turned to her and stepped closer, Jordan's heart thudded against her ribcage. Warmth flared to heat as Ali took the last step until the distance between them was only past and present, memory and want.

"Ali." Jordan had no other words.

Jordan held still, her mind empty of thought, and then Ali reached up and kissed Jordan so gently and softly that Jordan's eyes fluttered closed. Jordan kissed her back with the resonance of past and the reverence of now. Longing and happiness and desire flooded Jordan's system as Ali pulled her closer.

They surfaced from the kiss as a gust of wind brought the cry of a gull and the smell of the ocean. Jordan knew Ali had broken contact but Jordan kept her eyes closed. She was afraid. What if she opened her eyes and saw disappointment? That she wasn't who she had been, that she wasn't what Ali wanted now. What if she saw hope and possibility?

"Open your eyes, Jordan."

"No."

Jordan felt the breath of Ali's laughter.

"Chicken shit."

Jordan opened her eyes. Ali was smiling. Jordan so desperately wanted to echo it.

"Is this why you wanted to come here this morning?"

Ali's smile dimmed a little and she moved away. Jordan let her go.

"Not exactly."

It had been the wrong question, obviously. But Jordan knew she shouldn't ask the question she wanted the answer to. *What do you want from me?*

"You're going to tell me this isn't a good idea," Ali finally said, taking another step back and turning once again to the view over the water.

"It's not," Jordan said gently.

"Because we're not the same as when we were eighteen? Because we're too different? Because of that bullshit story you told me fourteen years ago about not being good enough?"

That last one was truer than Jordan wanted to admit, but she focused on the angry edge of Ali's questions. Her anger was the heart of this.

"How long are you here for, Ali?"

"Another four or five months," she said, her tone still angry. "You know that."

"And after that?"

Ali's shoulders slumped. She took a long time to answer, and the snap was gone from her voice when she did. "I don't know."

Jordan nodded. "I know where I'll be. I came home to Halifax for a reason. I know where I want to be, and I'm working at getting there. With school and my career. Taking steps with my family. Being there for my kids. I'm home. And what I don't want…I don't want a relationship that is temporary. That's just not how I work."

Ali didn't react to the last statement. She continued to stare out at the water, and eventually Jordan did the same. The sun had risen farther in the sky, enough that Jordan was beginning to sweat in her running jacket by the time Ali spoke.

"I owe you another apology."

Jordan felt a little sick. "For the kiss?"

Ali gave her a fleeting smile. "No way. You're a damn good kisser, McAddie."

Jordan laughed lightly. "So are you, Clarke."

"Now shut up and let me finish." Ali said. Her smile faltered. "I'm a little lost. Fuck it. I'm a *lot* lost. I went to law school because I was angry about corporate loopholes, and I wanted to win a fight with our legal department. Who does that?" She ran a hand through her hair distractedly. "The truth is I can collect degrees, seniority, clients, and yearly bonuses all I want. Really, that's all I've been doing for the last decade. And it doesn't mean a thing. That's what I see whenever I stop to see the sunrise. I see my own emptiness, and I hate it. It's not a ladder I know how to climb, it's not a battle I know how to prepare for." She blew out a short breath. "So I came here today looking for clarity. I came here with you hoping you'd provide me with an answer. And that wasn't fair."

I gave you an answer, Jordan thought. *I never said I don't want you. I said I don't want you temporarily.* "Regrets?" Jordan said. She left the subject of the question open on purpose.

"No," Ali said, almost immediately. She smiled up at Jordan, some of her power returning in that moment. "And not just because I don't believe in them."

They'd argued about regrets a lot in high school, as only teenagers with grand convictions can. Ali had always said regrets were limiting, likely unconsciously imitating her father, a man she'd always looked up to. Jordan had argued for regrets as a way of learning, doing better.

"You?" Ali said, bringing Jordan back. "Regrets?"

"Some," Jordan answered. "I'm still working at learning from them."

Silence descended again as they both seemed to silently acknowledge the day that had begun and the movement they'd taken this morning in their relationship. At once stalled and restarted. Jordan tried to find contentment in the path but found only disappointment and the residual heat from their kiss. She let a sigh escape.

"Ready to head back?" Ali said.

Jordan looked into the face of the woman she had loved more than anything. And still could not have. Then she stepped back, preparing to let her heart break and mend.

"I'm ready."

❖

Jordan's days had a new rhythm as October gave way to the grey dampness of November. Work was still a flurry of meetings and phone calls, of feeling pulled in eighteen directions and constantly running to keep up. The gym was in a state of flux with new kids coming in and some regulars dropping out. This happened sometimes, especially in the winter as lack of light weighed on the minds of kids already struggling with mental health issues. Jordan arranged car pickups, bought bus passes, and extended her hours, knowing getting to the gym, working out, staying connected could maybe make a difference.

Jordan and Ali talked almost every day. These moments—a text, a coffee, leaning against the door frame of the gym and talking forever after the kids left—were the beats of the rhythm that carried a new cadence. Jordan thought about how she'd told Ali the kiss hadn't been a good idea. But their connection was stronger every day, and seeing Ali at her gym three or four times a week only confirmed it.

Madi was the discordant note. She and Jordan had cleared the air about the fight at the gym, though Jordan never felt satisfied by Madi's explanation that Philip was just trying to get under her skin. Madi was still hesitant and distant. She showed up every day, helped run the program, connected with the teens as she ran her circuits, but then she just left. She gravitated toward Ali, seeming more relaxed when it was just the two of them. Jordan tried not to be hurt by this. She knew the more people who surrounded Madi with stability and love, the better.

The streets had gone quiet, too. No new messages or protests had appeared, so Jordan was surprised when she was invited to the first meeting of the newly formed task force. Regional Police Headquarters was only a few blocks from Jordan's office. In the middle of the week, Jordan put on her raincoat against the drizzle and hiked up the hill past the Citadel. She signed into the Halifax Police Regional Headquarters and was escorted to a boardroom lined with fake wood paneling and pictures of men in uniform. Rachel waved her over to an empty seat.

"Hey. Glad you could make it."

"No problem," Jordan said. She recognized a few officers, a harm reduction worker from a downtown clinic, and Helena Cavio. She nodded her acknowledgement to each just as Rachel's sergeant brought the meeting to order.

"Hello, everyone, and thank you for coming. My name is Staff Sergeant Matthew Buck, and we've brought you all together to get some community insight and input into this situation." Buck fiddled with a remote, and a slideshow popped up on one of the walls. "Constable Shreve put this timeline together as we're trying to get a sense of commonalities, time frames, and locations." He pressed the button again and read out the information, each slide accompanied by a picture.

"October fourth, graffiti on public and private property across the city and letters with the same symbol sent to the mayor and regional councilors. October ninth, the recycling bin tower in the Heights. October tenth, letter deliveries to local community agencies. October nineteenth, needles at the Ministry meeting." Sergeant Buck paused and looked over at Jordan. "We have noted that Jordan McAddie and an acquaintance were approached the evening of October twenty-first with a warning to stay out of the way, but since we cannot definitively link it to these street protesters, we have kept it out of the timeline for now."

Jordan nodded her acknowledgement of the statement. She and Rachel both believed the attack on the street was rooted in the group, but she understood the need to move forward on facts, not instinct.

"We're still looking into it," Rachel whispered as Buck continued. "But you should know that extra patrols around your neighbourhood have been stopped."

"It's okay, Rach," Jordan whispered back.

"We've got a new development to add to the timeline," Buck said, drawing Jordan's attention back. "Since it involves social media and we can't keep it under wraps, we'll be making a statement later today." He clicked to the next slide. It looked like a screenshot of an email. "What you're seeing here is an email from UnHaRMGroup@gmail.com to *Interior Heights*, a successful online and traditional print magazine on interior decorating." Buck raised his hand as laughter broke out in the room. "I know, but stay with me for a second. *Interior Heights* is running a contest to find Canada's Ugliest Bedroom. Prize is a complete makeover. Unharm, as this group seems to be calling itself, has apparently entered the streets of Halifax as a contender."

Jordan could feel discomfort replacing laughter in the room. She could feel it in herself, in her bones. There was a history of hurt here. Jordan also had to sit with the discomfort of knowing this group was right. She couldn't agree with their methods, but what did it say about her that she agreed with their message?

Without thinking, Jordan sought out the one person in the room she knew would understand. Helena was already looking at Jordan with an expression of sympathy and connection.

"We're following up with this email address, obviously," Buck continued. "You'll note the capital letters *H*, *R*, and *M*."

"Halifax Regional Municipality," one of the officers added. It was a common enough term to comprise Halifax and Dartmouth across the bridge.

"Right," Buck acknowledged. "We haven't heard of any other cities dealing with this same issue, but this confirms that this group is unique to our fair city."

"Lucky us," the same officer muttered.

"Moving on," Buck said pointedly. "*Interior Heights* contacted us two days ago when the email came through. They are complying with our requests not to respond and to forward any more correspondence to us. Since *Interior Heights* is a Toronto-based company, our counterparts at the RCMP have now become involved as well. The investigation is ongoing."

"Staff Sergeant Buck, what is it that you're looking for from us?" Helena said. "I'd like to offer what I can, but I'm not entirely sure what the goal is here."

The other community members of the task force looked interested as well.

"Thank you for the question, Ms. Cavio. As officers, our main priority is to maintain peace. We need to find out who is behind this, what their motivation is, and try to predict and prevent any escalation in unwanted and destructive behaviour." The sergeant paused to look around the room. Everyone was quiet. "So, we've established what we know, now we have to find out what we don't know and what we need to know. That's where you all come in."

Jordan still wasn't sure what Sergeant Buck was asking, and it was obvious none of the other community members did, either. Rachel jumped in.

"Let's shift from who the protesters are, maybe. Given the content of the events, who do you think is being targeted?"

"That's what I'm struggling with in all this," a woman from across the room said.

"Please continue, Ms. Cormac," Rachel said. Jordan finally remembered the woman's name. Kelly Cormac. "We'd like this to be a dialogue."

"I just can't figure it out," Kelly went on. "Are we, social services supporting the vulnerable populations of Halifax, the intended targets or the intended recipients of these protests?"

"Are they helping us or hurting us?" Jordan said, more to herself than anyone else. But she'd drawn the attention of the crowd. "Sorry, it's the question that's been on my mind since I was approached the other night."

"What was that about, anyway?" Kelly said.

Jordan glanced at Sergeant Buck, who waved his permission for her to continue.

"I was told to stop talking to the police and to sit back and to reap the benefits of the movement."

"The movement? That is the word that was used?" Helena spoke up for the first time.

"Yes, I remember them using that word."

"Movement is an interesting word, I think," Helena said. "It suggests progress, change, future." Helena shrugged. "I recognize that does not help your investigation. But it may have some significance in the motivation of this group."

"That jibes pretty well with their message sent to the mayor and councilors," Rachel added. "'Lighting the dark to help you see.'"

Jordan saw Helena nod approvingly, as if Rachel had connected some pieces of a puzzle. Jordan still wasn't sure they were really coming to any conclusions.

"You were jumped that night?" Kelly said to Jordan. "Did I hear that right?"

"I don't think that was the original intent. But I took issue with three guys approaching us in the dark. They tried to rough us up. It didn't work."

"Right on," Kelly said, grinning.

Helena didn't look very happy. Neither did Sergeant Buck.

"If anyone is approached in this manner, give us a call," Sergeant Buck said. "Whether you are the target or the recipient, and to my way of thinking it's both, we're here to protect you. It's our job."

"And the vulnerable persons of this city," Helena said. Jordan recognized the insistence in her voice. Helena would never leave the perspective and the plight of the people they supported out of the conversation. "I would hate for this task force to forget those we support are not the enemy. They face risk. Their voices should be heard. In fact, I move to bring a community member onto this task force."

Rachel leaned back in her seat, a clear signal to Jordan she was uncomfortable with this suggestion. Sergeant Buck fiddled with the data projector remote in his hand, though he never took his eyes off Helena.

"I understand and respect your opinion, Helena. It's why we asked you all here today, to have those voices represented—"

"No," Helena interrupted. "We are representatives of social

services. We are connected to this group, but we are not their voice. They have their own voices, and that should be respected."

Jordan could admire Helena's stubbornness even as she recognized the tension created by her request.

"Here's the problem," Sergeant Buck said. His voice had noticeably cooled, though his posture remained open. This was a man used to confrontation. "We have reason to believe this protest group, Unharm, is made up of members of the vulnerable population of the Regional Municipality of Halifax. In fact, it's an established pattern. So to invite a member of the group we are currently investigating to this team is more than a little problematic."

Helena leaned forward in her chair, her diminutive stature not diminishing the power of her words. "We should not all be painted with the same brush," Helena said. She seemed to catch the aggressiveness of her tone and posture. "We should all be seen as complex beings with a multitude of facets, identities, and values. If we lose the perspective of those we are trying to protect and support, we have lost. Regardless of what this movement does next."

Us and them, Jordan thought. Always us and them, push and pull, protect and persecute. Hand up or hand out.

"Thank you for your perspective, Helena," Sergeant Buck said. He looked around the room. "Thanks to all of you for being here today. I'd like for us all to keep an eye out. Please contact us if you hear anything or if you are approached. We'll be contacting you for another meeting date in the near future."

The meeting wrapped up with a lack of sense of progression. Like so many other meetings Jordan attended, they'd spun around in circles, never leaving the starting gate or even knowing where they were headed. She sighed and rubbed at her temples. A coffee was definitely needed on the way back to the office. Maybe even a donut.

"Okay there, Jordan?"

Rachel was looking at her with concern.

"Yeah, Rach. Up too late reading textbooks. Nothing a coffee can't solve."

"If you say so. I've got to run, I'm already late for my next meeting. But I'll see you tonight at the gym?"

"Sounds good. And don't forget we're babysitting on Friday."

Rachel flashed her a real grin, full of her characteristic energy. "I haven't forgotten. I've been looking forward to it for weeks."

Jordan waved as Rachel ran off. She put on her damp raincoat and waved goodbye to the group before heading back out onto the street.

Clouds hung low in the sky and cold rain soaked through at Jordan's shoulders within half a block. It was a miserable kind of day, heavy and hurtful. Jordan spun quietly in her own head, thinking of the meeting, of where she fit in the paradigm of us and them.

A figure huddled between the brick building of the coffee shop Jordan was aiming for and the neighbouring record store. His head was bowed, and the dirty, lined denim jacket was doing nothing to keep out the wet misery of the day.

"Excuse me," Jordan said. The man lifted his head. He looked about Jordan's age, his face red from the cold. "I'm grabbing a coffee. Can I get you something to eat?"

Jordan never knew how her offer would be received. She could get a fuck you or a thank you.

"I'd rather some money, to be honest wit' you." The rhythmic blending of his words suggested a Cape Breton accent.

Jordan dug into her pocket. "I've only got a five. Maybe also a sandwich? Coffee?"

The folded-up blue five-dollar bill disappeared quickly into the man's pocket. "I'll thank you for both."

Standing in line at the coffee shop, allowing her body to heat from the outside in, Jordan reflected on her morning. She'd keep her eyes out and her ears open for whatever was happening on the street. She'd keep a closer eye on her kids, find out if the recent flux in dynamics and mood had anything to do with what was happening with the Unharm movement. It would be so easy for her kids to get drawn in, so easy to convince them they should join and fight. But Jordan couldn't accuse them. Instead, she'd focus on what she could do, and for now, that would be enough.

CHAPTER NINE

"We're supposed to grease the pan. Who has grease? Can you even buy grease?"

"It means, like, butter or oil, you idiot."

"Shit. Can someone else crack the eggs? I think I just cut my finger on a shell."

Jordan leaned against the doorway of the kitchen at the community centre, watching half a dozen of her kids try to make a cake. It was a sweet scene, except for the swearing. They'd insisted on making a cake from scratch, though none of them had ever done it before. But Constable Shreve deserved a real birthday cake, vanilla with chocolate icing. So Jordan had bought the ingredients and booked out the community kitchen after school. Word had gone out at the boxing gym that everyone was invited to help out. Rupert and five girls, including Madi, had shown up.

"Mix on high for two minutes," Madi called out, peering at the recipe on her phone.

"Am I high? Is that how this recipe is going down?"

Jordan raised an eyebrow as the kids laughed. The girl who'd made the joke pretended to look apologetic but at least she seemed to get the message about the drug humour.

"Hand mixer is in the drawer to your right, Rupert," Jordan called out.

A scuffle broke out getting the beaters into the hand mixer. They were mostly laughing, though a fair bit of their constant fight was for dominance. Jordan found the most exhausting thing about working with these kids was their unquenchable need for power, respect, and control. Even in a simple task like baking a birthday cake.

The door to the kitchen opened and Ali walked in. She was wearing dark jeans, a button-up shirt, and a blazer, and she had a beat-up but expensive leather bag slung over one shoulder. She was smiling but was obviously tired.

"Hey, JP."

"Hey. What are you doing here?" Jordan indicated the mild chaos of the kitchen. "Coming to help bake?"

Ali gave a short laugh. "I wish. I've got to try and catch the last flight out to Toronto tonight. Central office is having a panic about an investor application…" Ali ran her hand distractedly through her hair and blew out a breath. "Blah, blah investment and corporate policy shit."

"Sounds like a lot of fun," Jordan said sympathetically. "Need a ride to the airport? I can try and find someone to supervise the crew."

Ali waved away the offer. "No, but thanks. I've called a cab. I just wanted to tell you I was leaving this time. I'm not running away."

Ali was nearly babbling, completely uncharacteristic. Jordan put a hand on Ali's arm, just a light touch, the brush of her thumb over Ali's bicep before she dropped her hand again.

"Hey, it's fine. You don't owe me your schedule. But thanks for letting me know." Ali swallowed, like she wanted to say something else. Jordan waited but nothing else materialized. "You look beat."

"I am. It's been a long week. And I'll be up most of tonight trying to get up to speed for the conference call tomorrow. But it's just an overnight. I'll be back tomorrow."

Jordan's heart gave a sharp thud. Her instinct to protect and heal and comfort was so incredibly strong. She wanted to tell Ali she'd get her from the airport, to make her a meal, run her a bath, bring her a glass of wine. Girlfriend things. That was space taken up by a partner. Jordan didn't occupy that space in Ali's life. But Jesus, did she want to.

"Tell me you're going somewhere lit." Madi's ball of ferocious energy broke the quiet tension between Ali and Jordan.

"Hey, half-pint," Ali said, her eyes brightening. "I'm heading to Toronto, so I'm going to miss our workout tonight."

"You are running scared. One tiny threat that I'm going to run you into the ground, and you take off."

"Trust me, I'll take one of your brutal workouts over a late-night flight, reports, and fighting corporations any day."

Madi tilted her head to the side, observing Ali through hooded eyes.

"You mean that."

"Yep."

"You're a freak."

"You know it."

Ali and Madi grinned at each other. They had their own language, these two. It made Jordan's heart happy even as it made her the tiniest bit jealous. Jordan couldn't help thinking she was the common denominator. Maybe she brought tension to all the relationships in her life. Her parents, Ali, even Rachel and Madi.

"Jordan?"

Ali was looking at her curiously. Madi seemed vaguely annoyed.

"Sorry, drifted."

"I think you're needed in the kitchen," Ali said.

Jordan followed Ali's gaze. Rupert was holding the mixer, dripping with cake batter, above his head while at least two girls jumped to get at it.

"Jesus," Jordan muttered, pushing away from the door. She glanced back at Ali. "Good luck in Toronto. Text me if you want a lift from the airport tomorrow."

Jordan didn't get a chance to see Ali leave as she refereed the final steps and saw the three round cake tins safely into the preheated oven. Once the clean-up was done and the excitement over, most of the kids drifted out or sat on the counters on their phones, occasionally showing each other a funny meme or video before lapsing back into silence.

Jordan checked the time on the oven and pulled a textbook from her backpack, thinking she could catch up on her reading before tonight. They were scheduled for a short workout at the gym, and then Jordan and the kids had offered to look after Rachel's two little ones while she went on a date with her husband. It meant a double amount of babysitting for Jordan. She was tired already.

"Hey, JMac."

Jordan smiled as Madi jumped up onto the counter beside her.

"That's a new one."

"I'm trying it out. Do you like it?"

Jordan shrugged. "It's not bad."

Madi thumped her heels lightly against the painted pine cabinets.

"I heard you're part of some sort of task force or committee or something. With the cops."

Street information wasn't always accurate, but it was fast.

"I am."

Madi's feet thumped a little faster.

"You sure that's a good idea?"

"Yes. I want to help if I can." Jordan caught Madi as she rolled her eyes. "What was that for?"

"Nothing."

"Okay, then."

They sat in silence. Jordan wished she knew what bridge she needed to cross with Madi to make things better between them.

Madi suddenly stopped thumping the cabinets with her feet.

"It's just, you're not a fucking superhero, you know? No cape or anything."

"I know that," Jordan said, trying and failing not to feel the sting of Madi's words.

"I don't think you do."

Jordan said nothing. When Madi was in one of these moods, it was best to let her spin it out without providing any fuel for her fire. Jordan steeled herself for the onslaught. She didn't have long to wait.

"You should have been a fucking firefighter or something. Running into burning buildings and rescuing babies and comforting sobbing moms. I bet you'd go home feeling like a million bucks every goddamn day."

A few of the kids looked up as Madi raised her voice. When they looked to Jordan for direction, Jordan gave a quick shake of her head. They went back to their phones, used to the occasional explosion and apparently trusting Jordan to handle it.

"So, this task force or whatever. You get that you're not rescuing anyone, right? But you can't fucking help it, can you? Doesn't matter three guys tried to take you and Ali out. That they told you explicitly to back down and shut up. Doesn't matter you could just sit back and let someone else deal with it. No, you're right there on your fucking high horse."

Madi jumped down off the counter and stood in front of Jordan. She was shaking with a barely checked rage. Jordan wished she could ease the stress for Madi, but she couldn't. Not as the target.

"Did you ever think, just for one second, that you're not a part of this?" Madi hissed the question, her voice lowered but seething. "You're not on the street, you were never on the street. This has nothing to do with you. So just leave it the fuck alone."

Madi left then, grabbing her backpack off the counter and stalking out of the kitchen. Jordan wanted to call her back and sort this out, but she would preserve Madi's dignity and her clear need to end this conversation on her own terms. The kids all looked up from their phones as the door to the kitchen closed. They looked at Jordan with curiosity and embarrassment.

"It's all good," Jordan said with a calmness she didn't really feel. "We'll work it out when we're ready."

Sometimes it was exhausting being a model of good self-regulation.

The kids all stole glances at each other.

"What is it, guys?" Jordan said.

"She's kinda right," Rupert said.

One of the girls hissed at him to shut up. Jordan felt sick. She wasn't sure she had the energy for this.

"What do you mean?"

Rupert looked uncertainly at the girls in the room and shrugged.

"Rupert didn't mean anything," one of the girls said, without looking up from her phone. "Just sometimes Madi has a point about things. But don't tell her that. She already walks around like she knows what's best for everyone."

The timer on the stove beeped loudly, and the kids all jumped off the counters and crowded around, fighting over oven mitts and someone yelling about finding the recipe since Madi had it on her phone. Jordan let the fight with Madi and the strange fallout with the other teens fade into the background. She'd have to figure it out, but right now a birthday cake needed attending to.

❖

Madi didn't show for the workout, the babysitting, or the presentation of the cake to Rachel. Jordan was disappointed but not surprised.

Rachel's two kids were adorable and fun, loving the attention of the handful of teens who stayed after the workout to babysit. It was good for Jordan's heart to see her tough, bruised, and sometimes raging kids sitting on the floor calling out for baby Gracie to pull herself up to a shaky stand and toddle her way across the floor. Hannah, three years old and a dynamic bundle of energy like her mom, ran excited laps around the gym, commanding the teenagers running with her to gallop like a horse or snort like a pig, then collapsing into a giggling heap before starting all over again.

Cay and Jordan kept an eye on all the kids, large and small. They passed out pizza when it arrived and helped one of the guys in his attempt to feed Gracie her oatmeal and sweet potato mixture while on the move. Jordan brought the energy down a few notches with a Disney movie on her laptop, as Ariel sang about hopes and dreams. The teens hummed the tune and Hannah swayed in time to the music.

"They're magical, sometimes, these kids," Cay said as she gathered greasy paper plates.

"The littles or the bigs?"

"Rachel's two are sweeties, but I meant ours. These big tough guys show all their heart around the little kids."

"It is pretty great."

"We should do this more often," Cay mused. "Maybe make some community connections, offer it up as a resource or a support. That way we could tap into some of that funding…"

Jordan laughed. "You never quit, do you?"

Cay looked abashed, then grinned. "Nope, and neither do you."

Jordan thought about these words, hurled at her as an accusation earlier. Cay looked at her curiously.

"Want to tell me what's bugging you? I'm noticing your shadow isn't here tonight."

Jordan flattened a few more empty pizza boxes for the recycling before answering.

"Madi's mad at me for joining the task force."

Cay tilted her head to the side. "Worried about you?"

"No, that's not it. Or not entirely. She…"

Jordan didn't really want to share what Madi had said. It shamed her.

"Say it, my friend. Whatever it is, it's poison. Might as well get it out."

Jordan sighed. "She accused me of acting like a superhero all the time. Told me I didn't belong and to stay out of it."

"I have a couple thoughts, if you'd like to hear them," Cay said.

"I would."

"First, I think you're wrong. I think Madi is showing her worry for you." Jordan made a sound of protest, but Cay held up her hand. "Let me finish. Did you not hear her speak the other night? At her poetry performance."

"Yes, I did."

"Tell me what message you heard."

Jordan shifted uncomfortably. Suddenly she felt like she'd missed something important. "That she's feeling unprepared for being an adult, and she's angry at the system for not being able to protect her. And for kicking her out. But I'm not kicking her out. I wouldn't."

"I know that, Jordan. And most of the time Madi does, too. But that's not the part of her poem that I'm thinking about. Remember when she said, 'I feel the weight of their caseload with an empathy I cannot admit I have'? Or something to that effect. She *worries* about you. She worries she's a burden. She worries you take on too much. She worries not enough people are worrying about you."

"Oh."

Jordan wasn't sure what else to say. She watched one of the kids wipe pizza sauce off Hannah's face as she sang along with the dancing lobster on the screen.

Cay sighed. "Jordan McAddie, you live your life for everyone else, which is noble as shit. But don't think for a second we aren't aware you're not living for yourself."

Jordan closed her eyes against the onslaught of emotions that welled up in her chest. She felt seen and exposed, as if she'd been hiding this part of her, not knowing all along she was utterly transparent to those who loved her.

"I don't want people to worry about me," Jordan managed to say.

"It's uncomfortable, isn't it?"

Jordan let out a long breath. "Yes. Jesus, yes."

"Well, get used to it," Cay said bluntly, smiling when Jordan gave a short laugh. "Madi had to get used to it. Hell, most of the kids who come through your program have to get used to it. I think you are up for the challenge."

"Thanks. I needed a little perspective."

"That's what I'm here for," Cay said and winked. "Also cake."

When Rachel and Adam arrived ten minutes later, pizza had been consumed and the movie abandoned in favour of rolling around on the floor in a made-up game that seemed to have no rules. Rachel gave a huge smile as the girls squealed and ran into her outstretched arms, nearly knocking her over as she laughed.

The teens hung back shyly, either unsure how to interact with Rachel when she wasn't in uniform or workout wear, or unsure where they fit in the sweet family scene. With a quiet prompt from Jordan, they ran to the back room to get the cake and candles while Jordan tried to fill in the necessary details of the girls' night. Moments later, the front lights went out with a clang as someone tripped the breaker and the three-layer chocolate cake was brought out with a sparkler in the middle as the teens sang a raucous happy birthday.

Rachel's eyes teared up as the teens approached, and Jordan allowed herself to feel the happiness of this moment. For her kids, for Rachel, and even for herself.

Laughter filled the gym as Hannah blew and blew on the sparkler with no effect. Then they all cheered when it finally sputtered out on its own, and the three-year-old raised her arms in victory. The cake was sliced and passed around on small paper plates. Rachel pretended to hesitate before she took her first bite.

"Who made the cake?" she said suspiciously.

"We did," the teens said around mouthfuls of chocolate icing.

"But Jordan supervised," Rupert added.

"Well, okay, then," Rachel said, her eyes dancing as she took a giant bite of cake. "I trust you with the lives of my kids but maybe not so much in the kitchen."

Rachel's comment was met with stunned silence.

"Really?" one of the girls said.

Rachel offered her next bite of cake to baby Gracie, who opened her mouth to receive it like a chubby baby bird.

"Other than Adam's parents, you guys are the only ones who have ever babysat these two. So, yes."

"That's crazy cool," someone said.

Jordan couldn't have summarized the sentiment any better.

The party wrapped up quickly after Hannah's good mood turned to tears when Rachel refused her third slice of birthday cake. Adam whisked her away as Rachel, with baby Gracie falling asleep in her arms, hugged each of the kids.

"Happy birthday, Rach," Jordan said when it was her turn for a hug.

"You're the best," Rachel said into Jordan's ear. "Now go get some sleep."

When the kids scattered and the gym was cleaned up, Jordan sent one final text to Madi before following Rachel's advice.

CHAPTER TEN

Jordan spent Saturday morning cleaning her apartment. She brought up the speaker from the gym and blasted music through the small space as she scrubbed the floors, dusted shelves, and vacuumed the furniture. One of the advantages of living in an area mostly zoned as business industrial was no neighbours to complain about the AC/DC ripping through the walls before eight o'clock on a Saturday morning.

Two things made the day even better. Madi sent a picture of her X-large Timmy's and the caption "power of wakey juice." Jordan took it as an olive branch, if not an apology. And her brother Jake called to ask if he could stop by the gym mid-afternoon.

Jordan was showered and halfway through a paper on consultation and counseling theories when she got a text that Jake was waiting downstairs. She pulled on a hoodie and banged her way down the metal staircase, rounding the building to see Jake pulling the tarp off a wooden structure in the bed of his beloved F-150 truck.

"What's this?" Jordan said, checking out the unfinished pine frame, maybe four feet by four feet. Narrow slots ran along each shelf and a piece of white wainscoting backed the whole thing.

Jake leaned the frame against his boot and tilted it back to look at it as he spoke. "It's for cell phones. For your guys to put their phones while they're working out." He looked embarrassed. "You mentioned it a few months ago, and I looked up some designs. Had a few scrap pieces around the shop, so..."

"Jake, that's amazing. Thank you."

They'd never been very good at talking. With twelve years between them, they didn't have much in common. Jordan had always felt a little like she was a burden to Jake, incapable of looking after herself. Even after he'd moved out, he'd still bring food to the house, take out the garbage, or fix the constant neglect. But he was always angry about it. It had taken Jordan a long time to understand the anger wasn't directed at her, and his constant presence and his ability to *do* for Steven and Jordan was the only way he could show love.

"Kim says I should have finished it," Jake said, referring to his wife. "But I figured it was fine as is." Jake shrugged again.

"It's perfect. Bring it in, we'll set it up."

Jake pulled a toolbox from the bed of the truck. "There's a bag in the cab with a power bar and some cords. Grab it."

Jordan held the door as Jake maneuvered the frame into the gym. As they chose a spot and Jordan steadied the frame while Jake set up his drill, Jordan felt like she was going to cry. She'd mentioned this four or five months ago in passing, not even directly to Jake. The sound of the drill was loud in the gym, making it impossible to talk while they worked. Jake was clearly more comfortable this way. Jordan would have to be careful in her thanks.

Once the frame was installed, Jake began threading various charging cords through the small gaps, attaching them underneath to the two power bars he'd secured to the wall of the gym.

"Where did those come from?" Jordan asked about the phone cords.

Jake didn't look up from his task as he answered. "We had a bunch at home. I asked the guys at work to bring some in if they had extra. It's a random assortment, but there should be something for everyone."

Jake stepped back as he finished securing the last cord. He and Jordan looked at the newly installed phone charging station.

"This will mean a lot to the kids. Thanks," Jordan said.

Jake grunted and started packing up his tools. "Not a problem."

Sensing he wanted to escape the praise or any personal talk, Jordan said nothing else as they cleaned up and walked back into the sun.

Jake stopped and looked at Jordan after he'd loaded his toolbox in the truck. He had his hands shoved into the pockets of his jeans. In the sunlight, Jordan could see he had more grey hair around his temples than last time she'd seen him. He was in his mid-forties now. Steven would have been thirty-eight, and Jordan wondered if he'd also be growing grey like his older brother.

"Mom told Kim you guys had a nice weekend a while back," Jake said.

"We did. Mom was happy to get out of the house. And to have people to cook for."

Jake grunted and dug his keys out of his pocket.

"Kim wants..." Jake cleared his throat. "Jesus," he muttered and started again. "Kim wants me to find out if you've got someone special in your life. I told her it was none of our business. But she wants to invite you...and whoever...over for dinner."

Jake's discomfort was almost comical.

"Tell Kim thanks. And I'll call her."

Jake's shoulders relaxed a little when it was clear Jordan wasn't going to get into the details.

"Yeah, I'll do that." Jake opened the driver side door.

"Jake?"

"Yeah?"

"Thanks for everything."

A tiny, crooked smile from her big brother. The most she'd get out of him. Then the truck door slammed, and Jake backed onto the street.

Jordan walked into the gym to sweep up the sawdust left over from their small construction project. She thought about family, about providing, about forgiveness. Then, without giving herself a moment to back down, Jordan pulled out her phone and texted Ali. She invited her over for a home-cooked meal and a movie tonight, if she was up for it. Or another time, if she wasn't.

Ali's response was immediate.

Christ on a cod boat, yes. YES.

Jordan laughed in the empty gym and tucked away her phone. She had a date to get ready for.

❖

Jordan checked the clock on her phone one more time. Ali had texted twenty minutes ago to say she'd landed but not to worry about picking her up because her car service was arranged. Jordan had said to come right over if she was still up for it. Ali had given a short, neutral response. Now Jordan was worried. Her apartment was clean and the meatloaf smelled good warming in the oven. Jordan had bought wine and beer and had even rinsed off the wine glasses she rarely used. Everything seemed perfect. Except now she was worried Ali wasn't expecting a date.

Jordan heard a car door slam, and then the clang of the metal steps outside her apartment. She quickly blew out the candle on a bookshelf, as if its soft glow could reveal the intent of her heart. She waved her hand above the wispy trail of black smoke before crossing to the front door.

Ali was dressed in a simple suit, her bag slung over one shoulder. She looked tired, but she smiled when Jordan met her at the top of the stairs and held the door open.

"Hey. Come on in," Jordan said. It felt like a moment for a hug. But also maybe it didn't.

"Thanks," Ali said, brushing by Jordan on the way into her apartment. Ali stood just inside the door as Jordan closed it behind them. She surveyed the apartment, trying to see it from Ali's perspective. Sparse and small, with a few pictures and one painting, a gift from an artistically inclined teen a long time ago. The smell of the candle lingered.

"Sweet apartment," Ali said as she dropped her bag and took off her shoes.

Jordan wanted to shrink under Ali's assessment. She tried to fall back on humour.

"It's got a killer view of the back parking lot and the woodworking shop next door."

Ali laughed and looked at Jordan, who still hung back by the door. "Are you going to invite me in or stand there and worry that I'm judging you all night?"

Jordan blew out a breath and ran a hand through her short hair. "Ah, be nice. I'm stressing out, here."

Ali squeezed Jordan's hand, the pressure brief and warm. "I know. Thanks for having me over. I've had nothing but sandwiches, protein shakes, and coffee for two days. Whatever you are cooking smells delicious."

"It's meatloaf and mashed potatoes." As the words left her mouth, she heard their lack of polish. But Ali's eyes grew wide.

"Seriously? You cooked my favourite home meal?" Ali seemed stunned.

"Yeah."

Ali groaned and Jordan instantly felt better. She'd done something right. "Why are we still standing here? Let's eat."

"Do you have something to change into?" Jordan asked. "I'm not sure you're allowed to eat mashed potatoes in a suit. It's a Maritime law you've clearly forgotten."

Ali punched her lightly on the shoulder. "I have a suit, wrinkled jeans, or pyjamas."

"Dude, pyjamas," Jordan said, finally feeling like she was finding her groove. "You can change in my room just down the hall."

Ali grabbed her bag and disappeared down the short hallway. Jordan went into the kitchen and started serving dinner. She heard a noise behind her and turned to see Ali leaning against the counter of her small kitchen. She wore red plaid pants and a faded Chicago Cubs hoodie. Her feet were bare, and she'd tucked her hair behind her ears. She looked for a moment like the teenager Jordan remembered. But then she smiled at Jordan, and she was all present Ali. Jordan silently handed her a glass of wine, then turned back to her task.

"I made broccoli. I don't remember how you feel about broccoli. But the plate seemed incomplete without a vegetable."

"Potato is a vegetable," Ali countered, taking the plate Jordan handed her. "And I love broccoli. Thanks, JP."

Jordan grabbed her own plate off the counter. "We can sit in the kitchen," she said, indicating the bar stools on the far side of the counter. "Or we can eat in the living room. Pretty much the only space I've got." She tried not to sound like she was apologizing. Which she was.

"Living room, definitely."

They settled on the couch beside each other, plates balanced on their laps.

"We did this a few times in high school," Ali said. "Saturday nights if you didn't have a bout, and I didn't have a match."

"So, only a few Saturday nights, then," Jordan said. "We never did have very much time."

Ali made that groaning sound again as she took her first bite of meatloaf and mashed potatoes. Jordan wished she wouldn't make that sound. She wished she would make it again.

"This is so good. Perfect." Ali took another bite, and Jordan tried not to feel too pleased.

They ate in silence for a few minutes, and she started to relax. Having Ali here felt entirely right. Eating together, the nearness of her, the easiness of occupying space and time.

"You're right," Ali said, after she'd cleared nearly half her plate. She stopped to take a sip of wine. "We never did have very much time."

Jordan also sipped at her wine. Her words were truer than she'd intended. "Then I'm grateful we get some now."

"Me too."

"How was Toronto?"

Ali's expression fell, a disappointment and worry that seemed out of place. Though Jordan was coming to recognize how often she saw it on Ali's face.

"Fine," Ali responded. "I mean, we got the issue sorted and Centera Corp has broadened its reach for contracts on the eastern seaboard. But I realized how much of my time is spent managing grown-ass adults who bluster and push their weight around without a fucking clue what they're doing. I feel like a damn kindergarten teacher except my 'kids' are grown men with MBAs, and they wear expensive suits instead of jumpers."

Jordan laughed, and Ali smiled before the light left her eyes again. "You're thinking of moving on, aren't you?" Jordan said. She regretted it instantly. Ali looked at her plate before taking another sip of wine. Just because she could read Ali so clearly, she didn't have to announce it.

The silence stretched as Ali finished eating her dinner and put her plate on the coffee table. For one moment, Jordan thought she was going to get up and leave. Instead, Ali tucked her feet up and curled herself on the couch, hugging her knees to her chest. Jordan angled herself toward Ali, still keeping some distance because she felt like Ali needed it.

"I've been thinking about leaving for a while. Tom knows, so it won't come as a surprise. It's one of the reasons he pushed for me to take on this mentorship back home. Here."

"He thinks you should come home?"

Ali blinked at the word but didn't comment. "He thinks I need to reevaluate where I want to be."

"Where do you want to be?"

"I don't know," Ali said.

Jordan knew Ali was uncomfortable saying that. She waited for her to follow it up with a declarative statement that she was going to find out, investigate, uncover, or demand an answer from the world. That was how Ali Clarke lived her life, but even the sunrise couldn't provide an answer.

Ali sighed and pulled the bottom of her pyjama pants over her bare toes. Jordan hesitated before leaning back and reaching for a small bag beside the couch. She pulled out a pair of fuzzy blue socks with green polka dots and presented them to Ali.

"Ahh!" Ali squealed, a delighted sound that made Jordan laugh. "I used to love those socks," she said, grabbing them and pulling off the tag before slipping them over her feet. They clashed horrendously with Ali's pyjama pants but Ali wiggled her toes, her expression one of bliss. Jordan's heart swelled. She'd helped Ali feel better. Ali looked up at Jordan. "You're the best. Thanks."

"You're welcome."

Jordan didn't know where to look. Ali was all kinds of adorable, staring down at her feet. Jordan wanted to put her feet on her lap like they used to. Sprawl on the couch together, legs entwined, hands resting on thighs or held possessively against a stomach. Joined and connected. But Jordan had already drawn the line.

Jordan grabbed their empty plates and stood up. "You can check out Netflix if you want to watch a movie."

"Should we stay with the nostalgia theme we seem to have going?" Ali called out as Jordan cleaned up the dishes in the kitchen.

"Sure. I flagged a few in My List, see what looks good."

Jordan portioned out the rest of the leftovers, thinking she'd give some to Madi next time she saw her. She put the rest of the dishes in the sink to soak.

"*Ten Things I Hate about You*!" Ali called excitedly as Jordan joined her back in the living room. "I had such a crush on Julia Stiles."

"I remember. I was only a little jealous."

"Bullshit," Ali said without taking her eyes from the screen. "You said you'd fight her for me."

"And you punched me and told me stop acting like a patriarchal asshole."

Ali grinned and looked back to the list of movies scrolling past. "Ooh, I found it. *Tomb Raider.* I wanted to be Lara Croft, you wanted to date Lara Croft." Jordan laughed as Ali selected the movie and dropped the remote back on the table. Then she curled herself back on the couch as the opening scene rolled.

They watched in easy, warm silence. Jordan had forgotten how absorbed Ali would get in a movie. They couldn't talk because movie watching was serious business. After a few minutes, Ali stretched out, leaning back against the armrest of the couch. Jordan gave up on boundaries as she lifted Ali's feet onto her lap. Ali sighed, settled herself more comfortably, and grew still again.

Jordan watched the movie and tried to hold still. She held Ali's feet trapped against her thighs, but she wanted to explore. She did, in her mind. She inched her fingers under the hem of Ali's pyjama pants, tracing lines against the smooth skin above Ali's ankle. Following the hard line of her femur, she dropped down to spread the span of her hand over Ali's calf, sweeping her thumb over the muscle once and then twice. She explored the hollow at the back of Ali's knee, maybe inciting a shiver from Ali as her skin warmed under Jordan's touch.

With no warning, the lights and TV in Jordan's apartment died. The sound of a distant but distinct clang through the wall she shared with the gym made Jordan's pulse spike. The only way the power could be shut off was manually, from inside the gym.

"What the hell?" Ali said as she pulled away from Jordan and sat up.

"Shh," Jordan said quietly. She reached for her phone but didn't attempt to wake it up and provide any light. She was listening intently, trying to hear any other sounds of a threat. The lights outside on the street meant this wasn't a grid issue. She tried to remember if she'd locked the door when Ali came in.

"Jordan?"

Ali had reached for her phone as well, but Jordan grabbed her hand and held it, shaking her head silently. She was about to whisper an explanation when crashing and loud thumps on the other side of the wall made them both duck and flinch. Fear and anger clawed their way up Jordan's chest into her throat. Someone was in the office, on the other side of the concrete wall. Jordan blindly accessed the emergency dial on her phone.

"911 dispatch, what is your emergency."

"Someone has broken into my place. They're still here. I need the police."

Jordan tugged Ali to the far wall. She felt trapped in the dark, unsure where the danger was coming from or what was going to happen next.

"Ma'am, I'm going to need your address."

Jordan whispered it and gave a brief description of the layout of the building with the gym and her apartment. Ali left her side and reached for the door. Jordan wanted to snatch her back. She was afraid someone was waiting on the other side of the door, on the stairs. But Ali was just checking the lock. She met Jordan's eyes in the faint glow of the streetlight and nodded. Then she slowly pulled back the dark curtain covering the window to try and peek out.

A crash broke the silence, as broken glass and a rock the size of Jordan's fist flew through the air. Ali launched herself back and away from the window with a yell.

"Ali!" Jordan dropped the phone and leapt between the broken window and Ali. She heard the sound of banging on the metal stairs outside, and a distant, angry yell. The voice sounded high and feminine. Jordan concentrated on the intensity of the sound, and her fear spiked until she realized the steps were going down, not up.

"I'm okay. I'm okay," Ali said as Jordan dragged her around the counter in the kitchen and tugged her down on the floor.

They squeezed into the space between the counter and fridge as Jordan strained to hear any more sounds, her whole body taut and ready to run or fight. But the apartment was quiet, no more clanging on the stairs, no sounds from the gym. The curtains swayed gently in the small breeze as wind quietly whistled through the hole in the window. Quiet. Stillness. Jordan wanted so badly to breathe. Wanted so badly to actually turn and look at Ali beside her.

"Anything?" Ali whispered.

Jordan shook her head. She wished Ali was anywhere but here. That Ali had never come home. That she'd had never invited Ali in, shown her her life, cooked her a meal. Touched her. Wanted her. Loved her.

"You okay?" Another whisper as Ali edged a little closer. Jordan could feel Ali's warmth along her whole side. She closed her eyes and nodded.

A slice of light arced around the edges of the curtain just as Jordan heard the sound of car tires and the faint protest of brakes.

"That might be the police," Jordan said. She crouched and kept her head low as she edged around the counter. Her phone was still by the front door, its face now dark. She heard the slow, steady tread of boots on the stairs, and then more powerful lights swept up and around. Low murmurings accompanied the steady progress up the stairs and now Jordan was sure it was the police. A knock sounded on the door.

"Police. We got a 911 call."

Jordan finally glanced back at Ali. She was crouched by the wall, her face pale. Small pieces of glass glistened in her hair. She looked fierce and determined and ready to fight. Jordan swallowed a wave of nausea and fought back self-hatred. There would be time for that later.

Jordan stood and walked the long way to the front door, avoiding the glass on the floor. She quickly looked through the far window, just enough to see the bulk of a police jacket before unlocking the door. She opened it a crack, ready to body slam it shut again.

"Jordan? It's Constable Frederickson. I've got Constable Alfie with me as well. Looks like you've had a little excitement."

Relief swamped Jordan's system at the sound of the familiar voice. She opened the door all the way, then pressed her hands together in an effort to stop them from shaking.

"We did a quick circuit of the building, and we're not seeing anything." He leaned back and looked at the window. "Except this, of course. Anyone hurt?"

"No, no one was hurt."

"How many of you are in the residence?"

"Two," Jordan said. She could see Ali picking her way through the living room.

A distant thump on the other side of the wall made them both freeze. Jordan locked eyes with Ali.

"Sorry, folks. We've got another patrol unit going through the gym. Shoulda told you that right off."

Jordan breathed again. Ali silently continued her way to Jordan's side. She picked up Jordan's boots and handed them to her before putting on Jordan's runners. Jordan followed the silent prompt and stole a quick look at Ali's face. Composed and calm. A little off balance but totally in control.

"A few more questions," Frederickson said. "Should anyone be in the gym this time of night? No late-night workouts or classes?"

"No."

"Who has keys to the main doors?"

"Me and my gym manager, Sean Murphy. A friend has a backup set."

Constable Alfie looked interested and pulled out a notebook.

"We'll need the contact information for your gym manager. And the name of that friend."

"My friend's name is Constable Rachel Shreve," Jordan said as she scrolled through her phone to find Sean's details.

Alfie snorted quietly and Frederickson laughed. "Looks like we've got our suspect."

Jordan tried to smile, she really did.

The short-wave radio attached to Alfie's shoulder crackled to life. They all listened as the second unit gave the all-clear for the gym. No suspects, no signs of life.

"Looks like it's safe. I'm going to leave Alfie here to take some pictures of the apartment and the window. We'll get a statement from…"

Constable Frederickson paused, eyebrows raised.

"Alison Clarke," Ali said, reaching out to shake Frederickson's hand.

"Clarke. You related to Edwin Clarke, by any chance?"

Ali smiled. "Edwin Senior was my grandfather. Edwin Junior's my father's youngest brother."

"Ah, well then." Frederickson seemed pleased at having made a connection. "Haven't heard from any of the Clarkes since they moved down the coast. Used to be real involved in the annual fundraisers."

"Yes, sir, they were."

Jordan watched with surreal detachment as Ali confidently navigated her way through yet another situation. Her ease should have been a balm to Jordan's anxiety, but it made her feel incompetent by contrast.

"Okay, then," Frederickson said and clapped his hands together. Jordan gave a small start. "Jordan, you come with me down to the gym, and we'll see if there's any damage or lost property."

Jordan glanced at Ali, who answered her silent question with a nod, then she grabbed a jacket off the hook behind the door and put it on as she followed Constable Frederickson to the gym.

Two officers were shining flashlights on a side door that led to a storage area.

"We've got signs of forced entry here, Chief," one of the younger officers said to Frederickson.

Jordan stepped closer and peered at the gouges in the wood around the door handle and lock.

"This is the only wooden door on the place," Jordan said. "The rest are steel. I haven't gotten around to replacing it yet."

"Now's looking like a good time," Frederickson said easily. "You two find anything inside?"

Both officers shook their heads.

"Nothing looks disturbed on first inspection."

"Let's have the owner go through."

Jordan followed the officers inside her own gym, feeling an odd sense of disconnection. The air was cold and stale. Jordan took a moment and breathed it in. She felt disoriented, catapulted backwards in time. She was standing outside the gym in the winter, her coat too big and too thin. A toque was down over her ears and her hoodie pulled up. She jumped up and down in the pre-dawn light, snow and icy slush crunching and squishing under her frozen feet. The coldest of cold times. Steven gone, her father drunk, her mother not able to get off the couch, and Jake wrapped up with his own family. All Jordan wanted was to get into the gym and punch the hanging bag until her muscles warmed and skin poured sweat. Even if her heart never thawed.

"Jordan?"

Jordan blinked in the dark, but nothing became clearer.

"I'm here."

But she wasn't, not really. Jordan followed the officers through each room in the gym. Nothing seemed disturbed. All that stood out to Jordan was that the main power switch to the whole building had been tripped, and the door to the office was unlocked. Nothing was missing from the office as far as she could see, but she did notice scuff marks on the concrete wall where it had been kicked.

"Looks like someone wanted to scare you," Constable Alfie said as Jordan, Ali, and all the officers met outside the gym ten minutes later.

Jordan was coming to the same conclusion as the young officer.

She was carefully not thinking about who had keys to the office. Anyone could have picked that lock easily. It meant nothing.

"Is this linked to the protest group?" Ali asked the officers. She looked cold in just her hoodie, arms wrapped around her body.

"Hard to say," Frederickson answered. He scratched at the scruff on his face. "That Unharm group has been pretty loud about laying claim to their antics. They've got that sun symbol attached to everything."

"True," Alfie said. "And we've found no evidence of it here."

Jordan stayed silent, wishing suddenly that she was alone. The calm, casual banter of the officers had made her feel secure in the absence of danger, but she still wanted everyone gone.

"Got somewhere you can stay tonight?" Frederickson said to Jordan.

"What? Oh, no. I'm fine."

The officers were all looking at her. So was Ali. The silence was awkward. Jordan stood up a little taller.

"Thanks for taking the time, guys. Really. I've got this handled."

The officers shuffled their feet and waited for the senior officer to close the call. Frederickson, for all his bumbling hometown bluster, was a shrewd man and a careful officer.

"Okay then, young lady. You know where to find us."

"I do. Thanks again."

The officers walked back to their cruisers, ambling in the way of men content with a job completed.

Jordan and Ali stood alone in the halo of the outdoor security light outside the gym. Jordan shivered with a combination of cold and unease. She started walking back to the apartment and Ali followed.

"You can grab your stuff, I'll take you back to your hotel."

"Don't be ridiculous. I'll help you clean up the glass. I hope you've got a vacuum."

"No, really. Don't worry about it." Jordan was nearly panicked, wanting Ali out of here. Spending the next hour alone in the cold of her apartment as she picked shards of glass seemed like the perfect punishment. For what exactly, she wasn't sure.

Ali said nothing and Jordan was relieved. And the smallest bit disappointed. They took the stairs back up to the apartment, and Jordan picked up Ali's bag from behind the couch. Ali stood surveying the window and the glass on the floor. She pushed back the curtains to reveal the jagged edges of the hole, not much bigger than the rock that had broken through.

"Have you got some plastic and tape to cover this up until tomorrow?" Ali looked over her shoulder at Jordan. "Maybe even Monday? It doesn't make sense to have someone come out tonight."

Jordan stood in silence, Ali's bag still in her hand. Ali's voice was all calm sureness. Jordan knew from the set of her shoulders and the tightness of her eyes that Ali was digging in for a fight. Jordan had never won against Ali's stubbornness. Not once. Instead, she'd run away. The impulse to do the exact same thing in this moment was so strong, Jordan felt the muscles in her legs twitch.

"Stop being an ass," Ali said, keeping her eyes on Jordan. "Whatever monologue you've got going on in your head about how I'd be better off somewhere else or with someone else is just going to piss me off."

Jordan blinked. "I'm not sure I like you," Jordan said.

Ali laughed. "You do."

They worked into the night together with an easiness Jordan didn't have the strength to question. They carefully picked up the biggest pieces of glass and dropped them into an old shoebox. Ali vacuumed up the smaller shards in the carpet and around the windowsill while Jordan cut layers of thick plastic bags to cover the hole. They taped it together, carefully pressing the duct tape over the splintered and fractured edges of the glass before they stepped back and surveyed the results, congratulating themselves on the final product and the low injury count. They only needed one bandage for a small slice to Jordan's finger.

"Now will you let me take you home?"

Ali looked less certain than she had before. She glanced at the couch where they'd been sitting hours before, curled and quiet and happy.

"I'd like to stay," she said quietly. "I'd like to finish the movie and fall asleep on the couch and complain about the crick in my neck in the morning while you make me coffee before we walk down to the bakery for cinnamon buns."

Jordan could not have prevented her smile if she'd tried. As they settled back on the couch, Ali's feet nestled in Jordan's lap, Jordan acknowledged to herself that, at least for tonight, she was done trying.

Chapter Eleven

Jordan—Seventeen

Seventeen and Jordan doesn't care about warm time or cold time. Home is a place to land, sleep, and change clothes. It's a burden and an embarrassment; her father in his chair watching TV or pacing the scruff of yard out back, her mother stretched and pulled taut. Sometimes she's cooking when Jordan comes home, a mark of her sobriety. But it's too late to play family. Jordan's friends are waiting, boxing is waiting, life and light and the cute girl who just moved in down the block. All waiting. School drags, feeling like another burden. And she's starting to get angry at the teachers who try to talk to her about her slipping marks, her absenteeism. They don't know. Not one of them knows hunger and hurt like a stitch in your side.

"You'll stay tonight, Jordan? Just an hour. Please."

Jordan wished the warmth in her mom's voice didn't tug at her so much.

"I'm not really interested in celebrating," Jordan mumbled. Her dad has been sober for six months. The first time since Steven died.

"An hour," she pleads.

Jordan hates that tone. Hates the strength and vulnerability it takes her mom to ask. Jordan hates so much these days.

"Is Jake coming?" Jordan slouches into a kitchen chair. Her mom smiles, knowing Jordan is staying.

"No, Kim is really sick this pregnancy."

Jordan is going to have another niece soon. She barely knows the first. Kim is protective of their young family.

Dinner is quiet and strained, and Jordan can't remember the last time they were all at the table together. Her dad concentrates on his food, though he perks up when Jordan, at her mom's prompting, starts talking about boxing.

"Shoulda been Steven," her dad mumbles. "He would have been a great fighter."

Rage is a cold thing in her chest. She can't leave it alone. She should.

"Steven is dead."

Her dad slams his open hand on the table.

"Alfred, stop it." Jordan's mom's voice is mad but also trembles. "Jordan, enough. We're meant to be celebrating."

"Celebrating what?" Jordan said. "That Dad can only say Steven's name in the few hours he's sober?"

"He was the best of us," her dad shouts.

Jordan wants to cry, but the cold rage strangles tears. He's right and she's so angry.

"And you couldn't say that when he was alive."

Three years of boxing should have prepared her for the backhand, but her dad had never hit her before. Jordan wasn't looking for it. The blow caught her on the side of her face, the force knocking her out of her chair onto the floor. Her mom was shrieking and Jordan held on to her face, dazed and aching. Her father sat so still at the table, the shock of his expression the first real emotion she'd seen on his face in years. Then he slowly stood and left the table.

Only then did tears surface as Jordan's cheek began to swell, heated blood rushing to the injury. She wiped angrily at her tears as her mom found an icepack and laid it gently against Jordan's rapidly swelling eye. Heat and cold didn't matter. Tears didn't matter. Jordan wasn't ever coming home again.

❖

November was Greek for grey.

It wasn't true, but one of the dock men her dad worked with used to say it, and it stuck with Jordan. She pulled her toque down over her ears and buried her chin into the zipped collar of her jacket as the cold, damp wind rushed across the Dalhousie University campus. She had always liked this campus with its austere old brick buildings. The ivy that clung to their sides was now browning and half frozen, which was exactly how Jordan felt. She had an hour between classes, and she ducked her head against another blast of icy wind, headed for the warmth of the more modern glass and concrete building that threw its light across the open quad.

Jordan shook back her hood as the moist heat of the student centre slammed against her cold cheeks, the smell of Subway buns and meatball sauce pervading every space. This wasn't her favourite place to be on campus, but it was warm and she could almost always find a table near an outlet this time of night. It was never empty. Someone was always studying, sleeping, or hiding.

Jordan plugged in her laptop and got out her textbooks. She might be able to get ahead of next week's reading if she focused. Jordan was finding her groove, highlighting passages in her text and taking notes for her upcoming assignment when Madi texted and broke her concentration. It was a check-in text, really all Jordan had been receiving since Madi had yelled at her in the community kitchen about being a superhero.

Jordan texted back immediately, hoping today they'd finally get past this odd disconnection. The polite dance of communicating but not. Madi always checked in but she also dropped the conversation as quickly as possible. Jordan didn't understand. She figured all she could do was keep being available for the next battle in their war of constancy.

Distracted from her reading, Jordan surveyed the wide open space of the student centre. A few people were waiting for subs, most people sitting by themselves with their earbuds in, staring at a device. It wasn't what Jordan had imagined when she started university. Everything was so ordinary, even the fact that she was almost twice the age of some of the students here. Jordan had fought the feeling of being a fraud in this establishment of higher learning a long time ago.

A familiar face caught Jordan's eye as she was about to turn back to her reading. Helena sat on the other side of the student centre, a book in one hand and a takeout coffee in the other. Jordan hesitated for a moment, wondering if Helena wanted time on her own. But selfishly, Jordan knew Helena was one of the people who could help her with the Madi conundrum. Maybe she could seek some reassurance her current wait and watch plan with Madi was the best way to go.

Jordan gathered her things and dumped them into her backpack before weaving her way through tables and chairs to the other side of the hall.

"Helena?"

Helena looked up, startled.

"Oh, Jordan. Hi."

"I scared you, I'm sorry."

"No, not at all. I..." Helena cleared her throat and gave a small smile. "I get easily absorbed when I'm reading."

Jordan laughed quietly, trying to put Helena at ease. "I understand. Are you taking a class here?"

"Not exactly, no. I started auditing courses a few years ago. I guess it became something of a habit."

Jordan had heard of people auditing courses, sitting in and participating but without getting any credit or working toward a degree. Jordan had to wonder where Helena found the time. She never seemed to stop working.

"A habit of learning," Jordan said. "I wish the kids would pick that up."

Helena smiled, as if the mention of the kids re-established why she and Jordan were speaking. Then she pushed the chair out beside her and gestured for Jordan to sit. "Please. Join me. I'm being rude."

Jordan sat. "Thanks. What courses are you auditing?"

Helena looked down at the takeout cup clutched in her hands and began pulling at the cardboard sleeve that covered it.

"A psychology course. Neuroscience of Addictions."

Jordan sat back and whistled. "Awesome. I'd love to take that, but I'm all out of electives. You thinking of getting the mental health and addictions certificate? I hear it's a great post-grad program."

Instead of sharing the connection Jordan felt like they were establishing, Helena seemed to be shrinking from Jordan's enthusiasm. Her shoulders became more hunched, and she leaned back in her chair, eyes focused on her hands as they ripped and shredded the cardboard.

"Sorry," Jordan said. "I've been a student too long, I guess. I start to get a little nerdy about course selection."

Helena met her eyes briefly and gave her a thin smile. Jordan wished she'd just left Helena alone. She shifted to grab her backpack, ready to make her apologies and leave.

"Stay, please," Helena said. She looked contrite, with a sheen of desperation. Jordan wondered how many friends she had. Helena Cavio seemed like the consummate loner. "There are a few reasons I audit courses instead of registering and pursuing a degree. It just never seems like the right time to go back to school."

Jordan read between the lines. As hard as Helena would fight for Ministry funding to support programs and services and their clients, discussing personal finances was clearly another matter entirely. She considered asking if Helena knew about the payment scale options, bursaries, and provincial government grants, all of which helped Jordan pay for her master's degree. But Jordan also wanted to allow Helena a way to exit this conversation with dignity.

"I actually wanted to ask you some advice," Jordan said. "It's why I came over when I saw you here."

"Okay," Helena said hesitantly.

"It's Madi. She's going through…" Jordan hesitated then shook her head. "No, we're going through a rough patch. Ups and downs. I feel like she's retreating from me, and I can't figure out if this is just the natural progression of Madi transitioning from youth to adult and I should just let her go. I'm worried. What if I'm creating or nurturing this dependency? What if I'm making it more about me than I am about her?"

Jordan laid out all her deepest fears. She wanted to do what was best for Madi, and she needed to know that was what drove her every decision.

"I have always believed if you are reflective enough to ask the question, you have very nearly answered it," Helena said.

Jordan wanted to believe it, she really did.

"So, you think if I'm aware of needing to allow Madi to grow and move on, then likely my actions are already following that path?"

"I believe so, yes."

Jordan sat back in her chair, considering Helena's words. Wondering if it was enough. She sighed. "I guess I'll just have to keep finding ways to remind her I'm here without tying her to me. Thanks, Helena."

"Madi is very protective of you as well, you know."

"Protective?"

"Yes. She worries about you. The break-in the other night? She was very angry about it when she came to group the next day."

Jordan tried to catch up with the information. Madi had only texted once to ask if everything was okay before dropping it. "I didn't know. I don't want to worry her."

Helena shrugged and picked up her coat, obviously ready to head out. "It's part of being Madi's foundation, I think. She needs that."

Jordan stayed seated as Helena pulled on her pea coat and buttoned it up.

"I needed that as a kid," Jordan said, wondering if it was okay to reveal this. "I was lucky to find it in a few people."

Helena picked up her book and her coffee cup. "I needed it, too."

But you didn't have it. Jordan let the words stay unspoken. It confirmed what Jordan had always suspected.

A man approached the table, and Helena smiled and gestured that she'd just be a moment. He was middle-aged, and Jordan didn't recognize him. He wore nondescript clothes and was a little rough around the edges. He seemed content to wait for Helena as she finished up her conversation.

"It was nice talking to you tonight, Helena."

Before Helena could respond, Jordan's phone chimed and a text alert popped up with a picture.

"Speak of the devil," Jordan muttered, pulling up the picture. Helena wound her scarf around her neck, eyes darting to the man waiting for her but also looking mildly curious. Jordan laughed at the picture of Madi and Ali with whipped cream mustaches, sticking out their tongues. She turned to show it to Helena. "I think Madi's doing okay. Maybe the lesson here is that I should worry less."

Helena had gone still, staring at the picture. Jordan had thought it would reassure Helena the way it had reassured her. Madi was okay. Maybe going through some ups and downs, but she was okay. Helena looked angry, though.

"An eight-dollar Starbucks is not what Madi needs in any scenario." Helena's voice had gone almost cold. "She would do better with you as her mentor, in my opinion. Realistic, hardworking. You *know* Madi, Jordan. You *were* Madi. Never forget that."

Helena turned and left, the man trailing behind her.

❖

Jordan ducked, and the right hook whistled by her ear in a rush of air. Sean grunted as his glove landed squarely in the space Jordan had created between her head and shoulder. He'd overextended, just a little too confident in landing that punch. She made him pay, taking the opening to his ribs in a three-punch combination that would have won her the bout if they'd been fighting for real. But they weren't, and Sean pushed Jordan off before she could do any more damage, swearing around his mouthguard.

Jordan grinned and stepped back before signaling the end to their match. She was covered in sweat, her muscles were loose, and her energy was high. She didn't get to spar very often with someone who had fought at her level, but occasionally her schedule lined up with Sean's.

Sean spst out his mouthguard in his corner and began undoing his gloves with his teeth.

"Good fight, boss," Sean said, shaking his hands out of the sparring gloves. "I was sure I had you in that last clinch."

"You were wrong, Murphy boy," Jordan said.

Sean grunted and toweled off the sweat around his head and neck. It really had been a good fight.

"I'm working on a fight weekend in the spring," he said. "Mind if I email you what I've got so far?"

Jordan took a long drink from her water bottle before she answered. "Sure, I'd love to see it. Make sure you put in the costs for what we'd need to buy or rent."

"On it, boss," Sean said.

Jordan shoved his shoulder good-naturedly. "Get out, next match is coming up."

Sean glanced at the two fighters waiting to enter the ring. They couldn't, not until Jordan and Sean tapped out. House rules. "We've got enough refs tonight if you want to take off. Study or whatever."

Jordan considered the offer as she and Sean jumped off the mat.

She'd wanted to be here tonight, to stay connected to this part of her gym. But now that her fight was done, Jordan wanted to be somewhere else.

"Thanks, man. Text me if you need anything."

"I always do, boss."

Which meant he never did. Sean was capable. Jordan reminded herself to lean on others. It still wasn't something she did well.

In the shower, Jordan acknowledged her agitation. Something was under her skin, a thought or worry that irritated her. She absent-mindedly ran a hand over the tattoo on her arm, the picture of her past. She wondered how past predicted future. Stories told and retold. As she pulled on jeans and an extra sweater for warmth, Jordan considered her thoughts like scars, like scabs. Memories that coursed through her veins and rose to the surface like blooms of a rash. The evidence of something deeper.

Outside, Jordan turned on her car and let the engine warm itself against the cold night air. She tucked her hands under her thighs for warmth and listened to the blasting air vent and the faint backdrop of heavy bass from the gym. She stared blankly up at her apartment. The window had been fixed, a three-hundred-dollar repair she had not been expecting. Jordan had made sure Ali wasn't around for that. She wasn't sure how she would have handled it if Ali had offered to pay.

The engine warm but her fingers nowhere close, Jordan put her car in gear and eased out of the parking lot. She knew where she was headed. Terminal Road was long, brightly lit, and nearly empty. The parking lots and industrial buildings were shut down for the day. A cruise ship, huge and white and overlit, gleamed against the dark backdrop of the harbour. It was a beacon Jordan felt no need to follow. It didn't fit with the picture of the port in her head. A map of childhood, a horizon that remained fixed and unchanging.

Jordan realized that was what she was seeking. The unchanged. But was it a point in time she was wishing for? A person, maybe. Or a feeling? Rightness, contentment, safety. That was what she itched to find. Jordan shook her head as she parked illegally in the corner of an industrial parking lot, halfway between the public seaport and the working port. She slammed her door and tucked her hands inside her coat pockets, pulling her hood up against the wind coming off the water. The salt air was heavy. She tasted it, thick and cold against the back of her throat. She swallowed its familiarity and walked to the edge of the light, looking for the spots of darkness she could hide in and order her disordered thoughts.

After going around the concrete barriers meant to keep her out, Jordan sat with her back against a port piling, looking out at the container berths and the dark, invisible sea beyond. Cranes reached far up into the inky blackness of the sky, the clanging and banging of their cargo muffled and oddly dispersed by the water and distance. Jordan was soothed and agitated by the sight all at once.

This had once been her future. It was certainly her past. How to reconcile the two? Her head was firmly convinced it was past, but how could she convince her heart? She struggled constantly to stay one step ahead of the whispering in her head that she was only one wrong decision, one mistake to tripping back into the scared, angry child she had been. Even worse, someone would call her out as an imposter any second. One mistake. One slip. One person to see beneath the surface, and her façade would crack. All her gains would vanish.

Jordan blanked her thoughts. The tightness in her chest was a warning. She paid attention to it, breathing in and out until the muscles in her shoulders and chest eased. She didn't need to spin this out. Jordan didn't need to give the negativity any more space. It would never be anchored in fact, and Jordan needed to remember that.

Pressing her hands against her eyes, Jordan tripped her thoughts back. Her life was a constant flux of contentment and disappointment. Failure and success. Warmth and cold. But maybe she could create a patchwork, stitching and binding the pieces together until they held tight.

Jordan breathed. The concrete seeped cold through her jeans, the wind tugged at her jacket and her hood. The tip of her nose was cold, and her eyes watered. She looked up one more time, the lights of the port cranes blurring into blazing stars in the night sky. The agitation slowly left her body, replaced by a resolve that felt familiar. Only the faintest voice asked how many more times she would have to go through this before she believed herself.

Jordan walked back to her car, feeling calmer as she got in and turned her back on the cranes. The phone she'd wedged into the console rang as Jordan was just about to leave the parking lot. She shifted back into park and checked the display. Ali.

"Hey. Thought you were working tonight," Jordan said.

"I am. I was." Ali's voice sounded clipped and flustered.

"What's going on?"

"It's Madi," Ali said. Jordan's heart dropped. "I think she needs help, and I don't know what to do."

Fear spiked. "Where is she?"

"I don't know exactly. I don't think she's in danger."

Ali sounded unsure. It didn't make Jordan feel any better.

"I'm on my way over."

Jordan hung up the phone and put her car back into gear, careening around the curves of the empty Terminal Road faster than she should. She hated not knowing where Madi was. Physically, yes. But more mentally. She'd been so used to having a read on Madi's emotional state, knowing when she needed space, presence, a lift up to higher ground. This absence was making Jordan crazy. And knowing Ali had some of that information but hadn't acted in the way Madi needed made Jordan angry.

She pulled up to the front of the hotel, ignoring the tension in her body, the signal that she needed to gain perspective. Right now Jordan didn't want perspective. She wanted answers.

The passenger door opened before Jordan had time to send a text to say she'd arrived. Ali dropped into the seat and Jordan immediately began peppering her with questions.

"Where are we heading? Any more info?"

"Hang on, JP. Let me just talk this out. I don't know that we need to go racing off just yet."

The old nickname rankled, but Jordan tried to quash it.

"Maybe you should start at the beginning."

"I don't really know where the start is. Madi and I have been texting, getting together for coffee every now and then."

"Yes, I know that."

Ali blinked at Jordan's short response but kept going. "Madi's been off the last week or so. It's like she wants to talk but doesn't. She wants me around but doesn't want to answer any questions."

Jordan was familiar with this version of Madi. Except right now, Madi didn't seem to want Jordan around. Hurt stoked the flame just a little higher.

"So, why do you think she's in trouble tonight? Right now."

Ali pulled out her phone and scrolled through the messages. "I guess just a weird sequence of messages. Saying she's heading down. Can feel her brain getting hijacked and she hates it. But then saying she's fine and handling it." Ali was silent as she scrolled through her messages. Jordan wanted to snatch the phone out of Ali's hand.

"May I see?" Jordan could not tell if her question was calm or threatening.

Ali closed the message app on her phone. "I don't think that's a good idea, JP."

"Stop calling me that."

Ali's eyes widened. "Okay."

Jordan took a breath in and let it out. "I'd like to use the message to evaluate Madi's mental state for myself. I can tell a lot about how she's feeling from the words she's choosing. I've got a longer track record than you."

Now she sounded petulant, not the position of strength she was aiming for.

Ali's features had hardened. "I know that. It's why I called you. But I'm imagining what Madi would think if I showed you our messages. She'd see it as a betrayal of trust. For both of us. And I don't want her to shut down or cut us off."

Ali was right. She had read Madi with complete accuracy. It calmed some of Jordan's agitation, taking off just a fraction of the unease.

"Am I wrong? I'm working blind here with Madi." Ali was showing her uncertainty, easing Jordan's anxiety even more. And it made her feel like a complete shit for being so hard on her.

"No, you're not wrong." Jordan rubbed a hand across her eyes and blew out a short breath. "Okay, from what you told me, there's cause for concern. But I know from experience that it's way worse when Madi stops communicating altogether."

"So what should we do?"

"I say we tell her the truth." Jordan tried a small smile. "With a little bit of lie."

"Okay, tell me what you mean."

"Tell her we were hanging out, and you mentioned she seemed to be struggling. And tell her I flipped out, and I'm being unreasonable. The only way I'll calm down is if I see her."

"She'll believe that?" Ali was obviously skeptical of this plan. So was Jordan, but she was grasping.

"No, not really. Maybe tell her I have no food in my fridge, and I'm refusing to go out for pizza until she's found?"

Ali finally smiled. "Yes, that she'll believe."

Jordan sat with forced patience while Ali typed. Ali finally dropped her phone in her lap and looked up.

"Now what?"

Jordan felt like she was coming out of her skin. "Let's drive. I can't just sit here anymore."

Jordan headed in the general direction of the apartment Madi shared with her aunt. It was the other side of downtown, which was the next likely place Madi could be.

"I'm sorry," Ali said.

"This isn't your fault," Jordan said. "I'm annoyed because I'm feeling completely ineffective. Literally driving in circles. Sometimes that's all it feels like with these kids, my entire damn job. I'm sorry if I'm taking it out on you. I shouldn't."

"I really hope I haven't screwed up here. I've only known Madi for a month, but she's already important to me."

"Madi can have that effect on people. And, if it helps, I think she feels the same way."

Ali sighed and slumped her shoulders. Jordan reached across and squeezed Ali's hand.

"Thanks, JP." Jordan felt Ali tense. She tried to think of something to say, but Ali's phone chimed and she picked it up. "Madi. She says she's at a meeting downtown and she's fine."

Jordan sped up and took the next left, angling toward downtown. They didn't speak until Jordan parked outside the community centre with her four-way flashers on in a tow-away zone. She pulled out her phone.

"It's been a weird few days," Jordan said out loud as she typed. "And a weird night. Ali and I outside the community centre. Would be great to see your face and know everything okay."

Jordan hit Send. The slow click-a-click-a of the hazard lights wore the very ends of Jordan's patience. Ali was silent, her eyes fixed on the glass doors.

Madi came out about two minutes later. As Jordan and Ali both climbed out of the car to meet her on the sidewalk, Jordan took stock. Madi was tense, agitated. And maybe a little scared.

"Might be easier to implant me with a GPS tracker, Jordan," Madi said, shoving her hands into her pockets. It was a weak volley, none of Madi's usual snap.

"Maybe for your next birthday," Jordan said.

Ali just looked between them, as if sensing the struggle they were having to engage in a real conversation, not this stilted awkwardness with too many things left unsaid.

"Well, I'm here," Madi said, throwing up her hands. "And I'm fine. See?" Madi turned a slow circle. "Why don't you two try a movie for your date night? This is pathetic."

Madi seemed okay. But she was hiding something.

"Maybe you're right. Thanks for putting up with us."

Madi blinked, like she was expecting an argument. "It's fine," she said. "Whatever."

Jordan caught Ali's eye and gestured to the car. "We can head out. Maybe grab a coffee somewhere."

"Sure," Ali said, obviously unsure but willing to follow Jordan's lead. If Madi needed them, she'd call. If she didn't, Jordan had to respect her boundaries.

"Great," Madi said.

"Great," Jordan echoed as she took a few steps back on the sidewalk.

Helen Cavio came out of the glass door of the community centre. She smiled at Jordan and focused on Madi, completely ignoring Ali.

"Madi, I was wondering where you'd disappeared to."

Madi looked uncomfortable, but she covered it quickly with forced nonchalance.

"Jordan was just checking up on me," Madi said, keeping her eyes on Jordan. "But she and Ali have decided they have better things to do with their night."

Helena looked between Madi and Jordan, still smiling. "I think you should invite them in. Share what we've been working on this evening."

Madi turned and stared openly at Helena as if she'd just said something ridiculous. Jordan wasn't sure what was happening. Madi looked nervous and Helena was nearly beaming. It was discordant.

"Madi?" Jordan said.

"Sure," Madi said, looking back at Jordan. "Come on in."

Jordan, Madi, and Ali followed Helena into the mostly empty community centre. She led them to a back conference room which had most of the tables and chairs pushed to one side. Fifteen or twenty men and women were in the room, which smelled of coffee, cookies, soap, and stale cigarette smoke.

Jordan recognized a number of people in the group, most of whom smiled and called out a welcome. A few looked like they didn't care, and a few seemed somewhere between disgruntled and suspicious.

Helena went to the front of the room and Madi squeezed herself into a space in the corner. Jordan was used to seeing Madi at the gym where she was often front and centre, commanding and cajoling. She was always a presence.

"We have a few guests with us. Some of you know Jordan McAddie, my counterpart in youth services. And her friend…is it Alison?"

Madi jumped in before Ali had a chance to reply. "Alison Clarke. We work out together at the gym."

Jordan thought it seemed like an odd way to characterize their relationship, but Ali just smiled. "That's right. Madi usually kicks my ass." A few people laughed, and one person elbowed Madi, who smiled shyly.

"Yes. Well, welcome," Helena said. She looked briefly discomfited by Ali's easygoing response, but she gestured at the wall where three large maps were clipped. "We're discussing what it means to have a home, to be home. We have a world map, a map of North America, and a map of Halifax. The white pins are places we've lived. The red pins are places we have considered home."

Jordan looked at the pins on all maps, most of them congregated on the map of Halifax but a few spread across Canada and some into the US. Only three white pins had made it to the wider world.

"There aren't as many red," Jordan said, taking in the maps all at once. "Is that what you've been talking about?"

Helena's eyes lit up again and she nodded approvingly. "Yes, exactly." She picked up a tray of pins. "Would you like to add to our map?"

"Sure," Jordan said, stepping forward. She took white pins and put one in Halifax, one in Montreal, and one in upper New York State, both places she'd trained. Then she took a red and put it next to the white pin in Halifax.

"Very good. You're welcome to speak to your choices, but you don't need to."

"I was born in Halifax, but it didn't feel like home until I left and came back. That's why a white and red pin."

Jordan looked at Madi, who was now tucked up into the chair with her arms wrapped around her legs.

"Thank you," Helena said. She too, glanced at Madi. "Madigan, did you want to make a connection?"

Madi looked like she wasn't going to speak at first. "I did the same," she said quietly. Then she spoke a little louder. "I put a white and red pin in Halifax because I've lived in so many foster homes here, but none of them felt like home."

"But you searched for it and never gave up," Helena said. "You never settled. You never let someone else tell you what it meant to have a home. Well done, Madigan."

Madi looked like she wanted to be pleased by the attention, but she wouldn't let herself. Madi looked around at the men and women, some of whom clapped her on the back and smiled encouragingly. Madi's answering smile seemed pained. Jordan wondered why Madi was so conflicted in receiving this acknowledgement.

"Alison?" Helena said, drawing Jordan's attention back. "You are welcome to add to our map."

Ali stepped forward without hesitation and took a few white pins. She put one somewhere in Connecticut, one in Chicago, one in New York. Then she took a red pin and put it in Halifax.

Ali retreated to her spot beside Jordan, but she kept her eyes on the maps, as if searching for an answer she'd just given.

"Did you want to tell your story?" Helena asked.

"No, but thank you," Ali said. Her voice was quiet and reflective.

Helena nodded and addressed the group. "I think the next time we are all together, we should talk about wants and needs of home. What all homes should have in common, regardless of income, background, history." Helena closed her eyes and took a deep breath. "As always, I thank every one of you for sharing your strength. This connection makes your voice stronger. Never forget that."

The meeting broke up, and Madi was swallowed up by the bustle of the large group. Jordan steered Ali to the exit, and they walked silently through the empty community centre, both obviously reflecting on what they'd just witnessed. Jordan held two thoughts in her head as they got in the car and drove through the quiet, dark streets. The first was that she felt relieved, to know she wasn't the only one struggling with the understanding of home. And two, Madi was struggling with the attention from her peers and Helena. Something made her uncomfortable. Maybe this meant they were all wrestling with the effort of belonging.

Chapter Twelve

Jordan was still thinking about the map activity from the night before when Madi showed up early the next day at the gym, which she hadn't done in a long time. Jordan welcomed her the usual way, and they worked through the set-up routine like a hundred times before. Conversation was stilted at first, but they found their rhythm, with the gentle verbal jabs and jokes that said "I know you" and "I love you" without having to bring those words to the surface.

Kids began to trickle in, and Madi kept up a near-continuous yell for them to leave their shoes on the mat so they didn't track muddy rainwater into the gym. This was Madi in command, tiny and dynamic and caring and commanding. So different from the more subdued and hesitant young woman Jordan had seen at the group the night before. Maybe she just needed time to feel comfortable there, Jordan thought. Or maybe she was uncomfortable with the obvious zeal with which Helena lead the group. Jordan thought she should find a way to ask that wouldn't embarrass Madi. It would be tricky.

Ali showed up in loose track pants and a T-shirt, greeting most of the teens by name. With Madi's silent approval, other kids had gravitated toward Ali over the last few weeks. Some approached her shyly, some with the bluster of teenage awkwardness, and some curious and distrusting of someone so completely outside their circle of understanding. They didn't expect Ali's continued presence and her calm interest in their lives. Watching Ali joke around with her kids about the warm-up music, Jordan had to admit to herself she knew exactly how those kids felt.

It was a good turnout for a Monday. Groups doubled up at circuits, and Ali warmed up with Sierra and Madi while Jordan kept an eye on the number of kids. This many people meant more energy and more history and more potential for drama, but most of the kids seemed focused and chill as Jordan wound her way back to Madi and Sierra.

Madi was in the middle of trying to convince Sierra to register for a fight the following spring as Ali held the target punch pads for Sierra. Jordan and Madi had agreed Sierra was ready for a competitive bout, but as Sierra's manager, Madi had to convince her. Jordan wasn't sure the conversation was going well since Sierra was worrying the skin on her lips with her teeth, her doubt palpable.

"I don't know, Madi. I don't feel ready."

"That's why you have me. I hold all the details as well as your worry. You focus on the conditioning and training. I've got the rest."

Jordan's heart swelled with pride even as she caught Ali's mirrored smile. This was why she'd chosen to mentor Madi as a manager. She had the right combination of tough and gentle. She used it with all the teens in the program, friends or not.

"Maybe," Sierra said again. "How does it look to the courts, though, Jordan? Are the judges going to think I'm a bad mom if I take up competitive fighting?"

Jordan registered Ali's blink of surprise at Sierra's question before Ali adjusted her stance with the pads and indicated Sierra should start another combination. Sierra smoothly executed it, pivoting and flexing, advancing and retreating with the instinct of a fighter. Jordan waited until they'd finished to answer Sierra's question.

"Your connection to boxing looks like you're setting goals and achieving them. You're dedicating yourself to a routine and a regimen. As long as you're keeping out of fights outside the ring, I think you're good."

Sierra stole a glance at Madi.

"You're not in a fight. You're good," Madi said evenly and, to Jordan's mind, very deliberately. Jordan looked up at Ali, who was removing the pads from around her forearms. She hadn't seemed to find the statement odd in any way. Jordan tried to do the same.

Sierra continued to worry at her dry lips. "Maybe," she said finally. "Ask me next week, and I'll tell you."

Madi's face lit up with this tiny step forward. "Aces. I'll find out everything I can about the fight. Time commitment and travel and all that shit. So you'll know exactly what you're signing up for when you say yes."

Sierra laughed at Madi's enthusiasm, but she still looked unsure. As Madi tossed her arm around Sierra's shoulder and they went to the next station, Jordan silently congratulated herself for pairing these two up. Sierra needed Madi's confidence, and Madi needed to see she had something to offer. Every now and then, these kids reminded Jordan she knew what she was doing.

"Madi has talked her into it already, hasn't she?" Ali said, wiping down the pads with the spray bottle and a towel.

"Likely. Sierra's pretty determined, but she's got a long history of self-sabotage. I'm hopeful Madi can keep an eye out for the signs and intervene if she needs to."

Ali tossed the towel into one of the bins scattered around the room. Her expression was thoughtful, and Jordan waited for the questions she could sense forming. Jordan had always loved Ali's curiosity, her desire to *know*.

The cool-down music signaled the end of another gym night. Jordan and Ali stood together and watched the teenagers drop and stretch, groaning about the low and slow music or the stupidity of the routine. Jordan was just about to comment when an odd buzzing and jangling sound emanated from the front of the gym. Everyone stopped and looked up. The sound was coming from the phone rack, where twenty or so stacked and charging phones were all signaling and chiming and buzzing and blaring at the same time. Then they petered out and stopped, the softly drifting cool-down music the only sound in the gym.

"Leave it alone, guys," Madi called from the far side of the gym. "Five more minutes of cool-down. Don't make Jordan threaten to take away the ranch dip again."

A few kids laughed as they followed Madi's lead and continued the cool-down. But every one of them stole glances at one another, muttering in low whispers. A few glanced up at Jordan and Ali, then quickly away.

"What the hell just happened?" Ali said.

"I'm not entirely sure," Jordan said. Her tone was detached, not calm. Now was not the time for calm.

Ali looked at Jordan sharply, but Jordan continued to stare at the kids.

"Later?" Ali said. "Can we talk about this later?"

"Yes, please."

Ali touched her fingers to the inside of Jordan's wrist. It was a quiet, comforting touch, but it was also an intimacy of knowing. Jordan could find no room in her heart to reject it, and her senses flooded with the want for more.

"God," Jordan gasped quietly. She touched Ali lightly on the shoulder even as she stepped away, the conflict of closeness. "Let me get these guys sorted," she said.

The kids crowded around the food as usual, some leaving as soon as they'd grabbed handfuls of crackers and apple slices. As Jordan set up for the evening class coming in, she noticed the kids leaving in small groups, with furtive glances at their phones and glares for silence. Something organized, Jordan thought. Those had been Rachel's words weeks ago. That's what this felt like.

By the time the last kid had left, shepherded out by an overly cheerful Madi, anger and fear had built a wall in Jordan's chest. Every muscle was tight, and she wanted to question the kids until she had answers. But she couldn't, not yet. Secrets needed somewhere safe to surface. The kids needed reminders that Jordan was safety and would not reject them for anything. As the anger and fear and confusion chased each other through her head, Jordan knew with absolute certainty she could not provide that today.

"Come on. Let's get out of here."

Jordan looked up to meet Ali's calm, blue-grey eyes. Ali was certainty, Ali was calm and a safe place to surface.

"Yes. Okay."

They walked outside in silence, the cold night air heavy with the threat of more rain. Jordan felt Ali's nearness, her physical proximity matching her presence in Jordan's head. *In my life*, Jordan thought. She did not allow the thought to scare her.

"Where to?" Jordan said as they rounded the corner of the building.

"Wherever you find it easiest to talk."

Jordan looked up at the stairs to her apartment for a moment, then indicated they'd go in her car. They were quiet as they got in, and Jordan retraced her route to the harbour.

Ali looked up at the cranes as soon as she got out of the car. "I should have known," she murmured, her words nearly lost to Jordan in the wind.

"I'm predictable, I guess," Jordan tried to joke. She didn't feel like joking. Everything was too heavy.

"No. You're grounded. There's a difference. As someone's who has been feeling lost lately, grounded is good."

Jordan led Ali to the corner of the building, climbing over the barriers and edging along the narrow strip of concrete along the harbour wall. Ali held on to one of the moorings and leaned over the water farther than Jordan would have liked.

"Easy there, Clarke," Jordan said. "Cold night for a swim."

Ali looked back and grinned, the wind whipping her hair around her face, her eyes dancing. But she pulled herself back and sat with her legs dangling over the edge, far above the dark waterline. Jordan sat beside her, tucking her hands between her thighs for warmth.

"Tell me what's going on."

The dam burst, a torrent of words and fear. "Part of me is convinced the kids are involved in this Unharm protest group. I'm thinking that's what the simultaneous texts were about, some kind of message. They're connected to it somehow, caught up in it." Ali nodded and Jordan was reassured that Ali had come to the same conclusion. "I'm worried Madi is involved."

"Why do you think that? What's your evidence?"

"She lied the other night about the meeting. She's angry about me being on the task force. Things have just been…weird between us."

"For how long?"

Jordan tried to remember when tension didn't exist for them. She couldn't, really. But she could measure this new intensity of silence.

"Six weeks maybe? Two months, tops."

Ali shifted until she was sitting on her hands. Jordan wished she'd brought a blanket.

"Do you think it has anything to do with me showing up?"

Jordan wanted to reassure Ali and say no, but Ali would hate being placated. "I think that's part of it. I don't think Madi was expecting to like you so much. She wasn't expecting to have you matter."

Jordan checked Ali's expression. She was nodding slowly and staring off across the dark harbour.

"So maybe some of her behaviour is about that?" Ali said. "Whatever she finds difficult about our mentorship."

"Friendship," Jordan corrected gently. "If it was just a mentorship, she wouldn't be struggling."

"I don't want Madi to struggle because of me."

"Productive struggle," Jordan said. "Sometimes valuable learning only comes through discomfort and failure."

Ali's gaze was sharp and questioning. "Huh. I'm going to have to think about that. But we're off topic. Madi, the kids, street protest group."

Jordan sighed. "I don't have any evidence, I guess. A gut feeling."

"Do you think your kids are behind it? The whole thing. The graffiti, the needles, the notes."

Jordan was shaking her head before Ali had finished speaking. "No. It's bigger than that. It's deeper." She let out a short breath and ran her fingers through her short hair. "I'm not trying to diminish my kids or their intelligence or their drive. But this protest group seems…" Jordan growled, frustrated she couldn't find the words.

"It's got a wider field of view," Ali said, her voice reflective. "It reaches beyond the scope of their influence."

"Yes. Exactly. What's happening with this group has more history than a bunch of teenagers could possibly bring to the table. I'm not thinking they're leading it, but Jesus I'm scared they're tangled up in it."

"Have you talked to Rachel about it?"

"No. Not yet." Was she protecting her kids by talking to Rachel? Or putting them in danger?

"I think you know your next step," Ali said.

"Yeah, you're right." Talk to Rachel, talk to the kids. Pay attention to the feeling in her gut, the pressure on her chest.

The wind shifted suddenly, gusting with a surprising strength.

"It's going to rain soon," Ali said.

"You can take the girl out of the Maritimes, but you can't take the Maritimes out of the girl," Jordan murmured.

Ali shoved Jordan with her shoulder. Jordan laughed and was about to respond when the sound of rain on water made them both peer into the dark harbour. The rain hit seconds later, and they both scrambled to their feet, Ali laughing as Jordan vaulted the concrete barrier, unlocking the car as they ran.

They slammed the car doors as the rain beat down in a heavy, pervasive staccato. Their breath was fogging the windows, so Jordan turned on the car, angling the vents to clear the windshield.

"Well, I was right," Ali said, wiping rain from her face on the inside of her shirt. Wet hair clung to the side of Ali's neck. Jordan could almost feel the heat of Ali's skin, the iciness of her own fingers against the skin of Ali's neck as she imagined lifting that lock of hair and tucking it back behind Ali's ear. The rain ratcheted up another impossible notch, the sound drowning out thought and reason. Jordan's fingers burned with imagined heat. She held still, transfixed and conflicted.

It took Jordan a moment to understand Ali was speaking. Her words were drowned out by the rain and the hazy warmth of Jordan's desire to touch Ali. She didn't know what had been said, and she blinked in confusion as Ali faced Jordan. Then Ali ran her hand along the side of Jordan's neck. Jordan shivered as Ali mirrored the movement in her imagination. Heat and cold merged in a chaos of sensation as Ali curled her fingers into Jordan's hair and tugged her closer.

Their kiss was heat and ice. Jordan tasted rainwater and Ali, faint saltiness on her tongue as Jordan sank into their kiss. She brought her hand up to rest against Ali's collarbone and felt the vibration of Ali's groan through her palm. Jordan shivered as Ali pulled back just enough to break the kiss. The rain began to ease.

"God, Ali."

Jordan didn't know what else to say. She didn't have the words or the courage to say what she wanted.

"Before you tell me this is a bad idea again, hear me out," Ali said.

Jordan nodded. The nearness of Ali made it hard to think.

"I want to be in your life again. No matter what happens, I want to be in your life. For you to be in mine."

Ali had always shone golden, the strength and bravery of a lion. Jordan swallowed the words that struggled to the surface, the ones that would reveal she was still not good enough for Ali Clarke.

"Jordan?"

"Yes."

"You've forgotten how to talk."

"You kissed away all my words."

Jordan felt Ali laugh through her fingertips. Instead of answering, she kissed Ali's smile. In that moment, they were all the words she needed.

Jordan eventually surfaced from the kiss into the hazy damp warmth of the car and their closeness. Ali smiled, and happiness seeped through Jordan's pores and swept through her chest.

"The rain has stopped," Jordan said, without looking away from Ali.

"The snow has started." The temperature had dropped enough that snow had replaced rain—nearly silent flakes danced and whipped their away around the car. The harbour was invisible through a wall of white.

"Maybe that's our sign we should stop making out in the car like teenagers," Jordan said and Ali laughed as they leaned back in their seats. "I'll take you back to your hotel."

"Sure," Ali said, reaching back to pull on her seat belt. "But only if you come in with me."

Jordan froze with her hand on the stick shift.

"You sure?"

"Yes."

Jordan drove through the quiet squall of snow, the flurries whipping around her car. As she shifted gears, she reached out and touched Ali's leg. Ali stroked the back of Jordan's hand, comforting and exciting. Connected.

The squall was furious by the time Jordan had parked, but she and Ali laughed as they ran through the snow, both covered in melting flakes by the time they hit the warm hotel lobby. The front desk staff welcomed Ali by name, and the murmur of laughter and voices and music intruded from the bar down the hall. Jordan wanted everyone and everything to go away. She wanted to be alone with Ali, wanted her touch, wanted that look in Ali's eyes to be just for her. The way it had been once before. The way it could be again.

Jordan's stomach dropped as the elevator doors closed, and the ground shifted beneath her feet.

"Okay?" Ali said, facing Jordan.

"Yes," Jordan breathed out. She wasn't, not really. They were racing toward something, either an ending or a beginning. Whatever it was, it was long awaited.

"Jordan, stop thinking," Ali whispered, running her lips along Jordan's jawline.

Jordan shivered and closed her eyes. "I can't," Jordan whispered back.

Ali stepped away as the elevator dinged their arrival on the eleventh floor and the doors opened. Jordan followed Ali down the short, ornate hallway to her door. Jordan didn't notice anything about Ali's hotel room other than a large space, opulent furniture, and a view through the window of the harbour. Then Ali's nearness, tugging at the zipper of Jordan's jacket, melted snow on their hands, in their hair. Heat surfacing in Jordan's core, in her cheeks.

Then everything stopped. Ali had stepped back, standing in front of Jordan with her hands in her back pockets. Her body language—hip cocked, chin up, eyes bright—was a challenge. Jordan understood this dance, this fight. Hers was the next move.

"I want you," Jordan said.

"Yes." Ali accepted the rules of this match. There was more.

"I never stopped."

Ali made a strangled sound. Jordan needed to confess, but Ali clearly didn't know how to take it. Jordan stepped into Ali's space and ducked her head to kiss along Ali's jaw. She tugged Ali's earlobe gently with her teeth. She needed Ali to accept this before anything else.

"I said, I never stopped wanting you."

Jordan traced her fingers along one side of Ali's jaw even as she kissed her way up the other. Ali reached for her, hands on Jordan's hips, tugging her closer.

"I know. Jordan, I know. Please…"

Ali's words fueled Jordan's desire, heat that burned in her chest, her fingertips. Heat that tightened the muscles in her thighs as Ali took Jordan's mouth in a long kiss that threatened to pull them both under.

It nearly did. Jordan felt her knees start to buckle as Ali abruptly backed away. She pulled her sweater over her head, her undershirt framing the muscles of her shoulders and arms. Jordan fixed her eyes on the points of Ali's collarbone, which seemed to shine in the muted lamplight.

They tugged at each other's clothes, wrestling with zippers and snaps and buckles. All the barriers that kept them apart, the clothing and time and regret all fell away as Ali, naked and perfect and confident, flung the covers back on the bed, taking Jordan with her.

Heat, so much heat. Ali's skin against hers, warmed through to the blood and sinew. Warmed into her heart as Jordan kissed Ali's swollen lips, then lowered her head to lick the hard rise of her collarbone. Jordan could hear every expulsion of air as she explored the ridges and bones, then rubbed her cheek along Ali's breast, finally dragging her lips over Ali's nipple. Ali gave a cry and a command as she anchored Jordan's head there, her hand in Jordan's hair, her neck muscles straining. Jordan sucked Ali's warm, pebbled flesh into her mouth as Ali arched against her and groaned deep in her chest.

Ali only let her explore for so long. Jordan nearly smiled when Ali trapped Jordan between her legs, knees clamped around her hips. Jordan used the angle to thrust against Ali, slowly at first, then harder as the movement rocketed through her body. Ali cried out and loosened her grip as she lifted herself to meet each of Jordan's thrusts. This synchronicity of body and breath was nearly too much. It threatened to destroy her completely. Then Ali tightened her legs around Jordan's hips and whispered in her ear.

"Stop distracting me."

Jordan smiled, and Ali bit down on the muscle in Jordan's neck. She wanted to pull away from the pain and sink into it all at once. She hesitated long enough for Ali to make her move. Ali planted her feet, lifted her hips, and flipped Jordan onto her back. Jordan didn't even consider resisting. She couldn't. Her body was a series of live wires and frayed nerve endings that wanted nothing more than to coalesce into a burning, bright whole.

Jordan focused her eyes on Ali, smiling triumphantly above her. Ali's hair shone golden in the muted lamplight, her skin suffused with heated blood and victory. She was beautiful and strong and Jordan loved her. Jordan needed her.

"Ali..."

Ali's kiss silenced the rest of her words. Jordan closed her eyes and ran her hands up Ali's back, smooth skin over muscles and bone. Jordan opened her eyes as Ali sat up, straddling one of Jordan's thighs. Jordan heard a strangled sound escape her own throat as Ali ran her fingers up the inside of her thigh, but all she could do was look down between them as Ali teased her way higher until she found Jordan's very centre. Jordan sighed, closing her eyes in surrender as Ali took complete command of her body. Every sweet stroke broke a new wave of sensation deep in her core, and she could do nothing but take it.

As the waves built, as Ali pushed her toward the ultimate triumph of this sweet battle, Jordan felt a new desire take hold. She needed to know and claim Ali's body the way Ali was claiming hers. She pressed her leg up into Ali, feeling heat as Ali gasped and her eyes went hazy. Then Jordan reached up and cupped her hand around the back of Ali's neck, pulling her down and kissing her hard. Ali groaned into Jordan's mouth, and her touch faltered, the rhythm and connection briefly broken. Jordan let out a breath at the loss, then felt the shared sensation of entering Ali as Ali repositioned herself to take Jordan inside, then claimed Jordan again.

Nothing existed outside their joined bodies, breath synchronized with breath, thrust with thrust. Heat and an impossible agony of sensation drove them higher, Jordan swallowing the whispered curse on Ali's lips as her thighs tightened and she bore down on Ali's fingers. For one sweet, terrifying moment Jordan was sure she would die from this sensation, that she could not possibly survive the climax of this moment. Then Ali arched her back and cried out, and Jordan gloried in the vision of this beautiful woman above her as Ali drove her over the edge. Her orgasm obliterated all thought in a blinding, never-ending wave.

Jordan took a long time to surface. Ali lay sprawled across her body, completely limp, her head tucked into Jordan's neck. They breathed together and Jordan could feel the steady rise and fall of Ali's back. She blinked, the only movement she felt capable of in that moment. She felt the urge to tighten her grip, to possess Ali and anchor her to this time and place. To never let her go. But she also accepted the peace of this moment, her certainty that Ali was here with her. She remembered Ali's earlier words, that she wanted to be in Jordan's life again. Jordan found the energy to smile, then she closed her eyes and slept.

CHAPTER THIRTEEN

"You can't order room service eggs. It's an atrocity."

Jordan laughed at Ali's declaration and threw the fake leather-bound menu onto the white bedspread. She watched Ali towel-drying her dark blonde hair as she looked out the hotel window.

"An atrocity? That's a serious accusation. And a serious word before you've had coffee."

Ali threw her damp towel at Jordan, who was already fully dressed after their shared morning shower. The rest of their night and their morning together had been easy laughter and connection, kissing in the shower, returning to the twisted bed sheets. Jordan acknowledged that things were changed. She accepted her happiness, even though a question lodged in her chest. She tried to quiet it, convincing herself there was time to ask and hear the answer. Today she could allow joy.

"Jordan?"

Ali came to sit on the bed, where Jordan was leaning up against the headboard.

"Sorry, what did you say?"

Ali smiled and leaned in for a long, sweet kiss. Jordan thought she could melt, like snow caught on the tip of the tongue.

"Sex always did kind of make you stupid," Ali murmured against Jordan's lips.

Jordan answered by sucking Ali's bottom lip into her mouth and biting down lightly before releasing her. Ali laughed and leaned back.

"I asked if you wanted to go downstairs for breakfast or grab our coats and head out somewhere."

"Let's go out, if you don't mind. There's a diner across the bridge

I want to take you to. And since you woke us up at an ungodly hour, it shouldn't be busy."

Ali made a face and Jordan laughed. "You couldn't possibly be complaining, Jordan McAddie. Your brain isn't that scrambled, I hope."

Jordan ran her over Ali's hips, stroking her fingers up Ali's ribcage. "No, definitely not complaining."

Ali smiled but stayed silent. And she didn't move. Jordan saw a question in Ali's eyes and wondered if it was the same one in her chest.

"It wasn't like this before, was it? When we were younger. It wasn't this…intense."

So, Ali was still looking back while Jordan was looking forward.

"No, it wasn't quite like this."

Ali nodded once, obviously still thinking. Jordan kept running her hand up and down Ali's side, comforting them both.

"I think even then I knew it could be. But I had to…" Ali trailed off, breaking eye contact and looking down before meeting Jordan's eyes again. "I had to diminish it, I think. What we had then. I had to make it smaller and less significant. Because that was easier than admitting I'd lost my heart at seventeen."

"I did the same thing, if it helps at all." Ali said nothing, and Jordan took a breath and kept going. "I had to pretend your place in my heart was the one everyone keeps for their first love. But it was more than that. I always knew it was more than that."

Jordan wanted to hold her breath, but she'd been trained to keep breathing. She had enough experience in the ring to know that punches landed harder and hurt more if you held your breath.

Ali held Jordan's gaze, as if searching for something Jordan couldn't identify. Maybe she wasn't meant to. Then Ali leaned in for a quick kiss and stood.

"We need coffee. And food." Ali ran her hands through her damp hair then looked back at Jordan. "Let's go, McAddie."

Jordan grinned at Ali's commanding tone.

"On it, Clarke."

Dressed for the cold, Jordan and Ali took the elevator down to the lobby. It seemed busy for the early hour, a buzzing of background noise punctuated with sharp voices. Ali tucked her hand into Jordan's, and the simplicity of the movement struck a chord in Jordan's chest.

A harried-looking staff member in the hotel colours of grey and maroon walked up to them, a stack of papers in his hand.

"Ms. Clarke, good morning. We have a bit of a situation developing. If you could see the front desk before you head out, that would be most helpful."

Ali looked confused but thanked the man as he hurried away.

"I wonder what's up," Ali murmured.

None of the hotel staff looked happy, Jordan noted as Ali waited to speak to someone. The manager was on the phone in the corner, typing rapidly into the computer as she asked questions. She hit the keyboard with a final bang and Jordan watched her walk to the printer as it booted to life and began spitting out papers. It looked like a city planning map, from what Jordan could see. Jordan shadowed Ali as a front desk staff called her forward. A knot of unease wound itself tighter in Jordan's belly.

"Ms. Clarke, hello. We've just been informed by Halifax Regional Police that a threat has been made to the city water supply." Jordan's stomach bottomed out as her heart rate ratcheted up. "The police have not yet validated the threat, nor are they releasing details, but we are in the process of turning off the water as a precautionary measure. Word is going out to our guests right now."

"Jesus," Ali muttered. She looked up at Jordan who could do nothing but stare. "Is it affecting the whole city?"

The manager walked by, cordless phone still tucked between her shoulder and her ear, and handed a stack of the maps to the desk clerk.

"Ah, here. Okay, this is some of the information we've been waiting for." He turned the paper around so Jordan and Ali could see the map. Sections of the city were outlined and covered in grey. The hotel was right in the middle. "Not the whole city. It's possible we may be able to book you into another hotel once we find out if indeed our water supply is compromised."

"Okay, thanks. When will you know?"

"I'm sorry, ma'am. At this point, I'm really not sure. We just received this information in the last ten minutes."

Jordan pulled the map closer, tracing the lines with her finger. "My place isn't affected, according to this. You can stay with me."

The desk clerk kept silent as Ali looked up at Jordan. "You sure?"

"Yes. Of course."

Ali turned back to the desk clerk. "You have my cell number and email on file. I'd appreciate an update when you have one." The clerk nodded gratefully at Ali's easy tone. Jordan could not imagine any of the hotel staff were going to be having a very good day.

"Can I take this?" Jordan said, indicating the map.

"Yes, please do."

Jordan picked up the map and inclined her head to the front door. "Let's go eat, and we'll make a plan. We can always grab your stuff after."

They headed out into a city blanketed in snow. It was cold, but the wind was quiet, the light grey sky made lighter by the reflection off the snow. Jordan blinked until her eyes adjusted as they walked through the slush to her car.

Once they were inside, the engine warming in the quiet parking lot, Ali finally spoke.

"You think it's related to the protest group?"

"I'd be shocked if it wasn't." She took her phone out of her back pocket but hesitated.

"Calling Rachel?"

"I'm thinking about it. Feels a little like I'm pulling strings to get information just because we're friends."

"You were going to call her anyway," Ali pointed out. "You wanted to talk to her about Madi and the other kids. What you suspect. If things are escalating…"

Ali let the sentence hang, but even without the final words, Jordan felt the knot of anxiety in her stomach. She had a sense of danger, a need to fight back against an unseen opponent.

"Hey, take it easy," Ali said, slipping a cold hand around the back of Jordan's neck. The shock of her fingers snapped Jordan out of her spinning thoughts. "One step at a time. Send Rachel a message, be clear about what you know and what you suspect. Then let her make the professional decision as to when and how to follow up."

"Yes, okay." But Jordan continued to stare at the screen on her phone. She opened her text app and typed out a message to Rachel. Once that was sent, she sent out a query for Madi to check in when she could. Jordan really didn't know what to expect. She couldn't place Madi in space or time or mental mindset. And that scared her.

"When's the last time you texted with Madi?" Jordan said as she tucked her phone away and put her car in gear.

"Yesterday. Before getting to the gym."

Neither of them spoke as they drove through slushy side streets. The main roads were clear and wet, and traffic was light as they crossed the bridge. They still hadn't spoken by the time Jordan pulled into the nearly empty parking lot and killed the engine.

"Sorry," she said, not entirely sure what she was apologizing for but hating the distance she'd somehow created. She reached across the seats and touched the back of Ali's hand. Ali turned her palm and joined their hands together.

"Don't be," Ali said lightly. "I know there's a lot on your mind right now." Jordan squeezed Ali's fingers in acknowledgement. "Let me carry some of it. If you can."

Jordan let out a breath into the already cold air of the car. She'd been shouldering burdens on her own for so long, she didn't know if she was capable of sharing the way Ali was asking her to. "I'll try."

Ali smiled. "Good. Now feed me non-atrocious eggs. And buckets of coffee."

Jordan laughed. "Yes, ma'am."

They were stuffed, their plates almost clear and the stained beige carafe of coffee on their table nearly empty by the time Jordan's phone pinged with a response to her earlier queries. Ali was right. With food in her belly and caffeine careening through her synapses, Jordan felt calmer and more able to take on whatever was happening. She looked at her phone. It was a very short message from Rachel.

Jordan turned the phone around so Ali could see the message. All it said was, *Can you talk?*

"Yes," Ali said. "You go call Rachel, I'll take care of the bill."

Jordan hesitated, but the look in Ali's eye made her refrain from saying anything. "Okay, thanks."

"No problem. I'll be out shortly," Ali said as Jordan stood and put on her coat. "And points for not arguing."

Jordan laughed. "There are points?"

"There's *always* points." Ali grinned. "Go. I'm right behind you."

As Jordan left the now noisy diner, dialing Rachel as she hit the cold, damp air, she tried to stay connected to those words. Ali was right behind her.

"Jordan? Hey." Rachel sounded harried and was obviously at work, the sound of voices and phones in the background making it hard for Jordan to hear.

"Sorry to bother you, Rach," Jordan said.

"No, it's okay. I need to talk to you." She heard a shuffling sound, and then the phone was muted and Jordan could just hear the low tone of voices before Rachel came back. "Sorry, it's a zoo around here."

"The water thing?"

Rachel let out a short, frustrated breath. "You heard about that already, did you? Yes, the water thing. City officials are shitting bricks."

"I can only imagine. What can I do?"

"Any chance you could meet me at my office? This conversation might be quicker in person, and there's no way I'm getting away from my desk."

"Yeah, no problem. We're just over the bridge. I can be there in twenty or so."

The passenger door opened just then, and Ali looked in questioningly. Jordan gestured her into the car.

"We? Is Madi with you?"

"No, Ali. Do you mind if she's there?"

"Not at all, bring her. Police headquarters is a romantic place for a date."

Jordan heard someone in the background laugh, and then the phone was muted again before Rachel came back on the line.

"I've got to go. See you when you get here."

Jordan ended the call and stared for a moment at her phone before looking back up at Ali. "I have to go meet with Rachel. I can drop you off at my place if you want."

"I'll go with you."

Jordan dropped her phone into the console. "Okay, thanks."

The snow was melting rapidly across the city. Slush was now water, with shingled roofs and fence lines edged in white. Everything felt a little darker and grittier than it had in the beautiful morning light.

"I'm going to try and remember not to call you JP," Ali said, seemingly out of nowhere.

"No, don't. I was mad that night I told you to stop calling me that. I don't mind. Really."

"You were mad?"

Jordan waited at the traffic light at the foot of the bridge and glanced at Ali. "At myself and the situation. Not you."

Ali seemed to be thinking about this as the light changed and Jordan moved into the intersection, pushing the clutch to shift gears up the hill.

"I think you were mad at me. A little. For being there in the middle of it."

Jordan didn't know what to say. Admitting she could sometimes be an asshole didn't seem conducive to pursuing a relationship. Though lying was possibly worse.

"Worried," Jordan said. She gripped the steering wheel tighter and made herself try again. "Scared. I didn't like you seeing me scared. And the nickname reminds of a time I was so scared that I ran. Not my proudest moment."

Ali was silent, and Jordan concentrated on the slick streets. Then she felt Ali slip her hand onto her thigh and rest it there. Jordan covered it briefly with her own before placing her hand back on the stick shift.

The officer at the front desk of Halifax Police Department headquarters was particularly cheerful as she signed Jordan and Ali in with visitors' badges and called Rachel to let her know they were here. Rachel emerged from a locked metal door and waved them in a few minutes later. She looked alert and focused and stressed. Jordan wished she could do something to make this easier.

"You guys want a coffee?"

"No, thanks. We just came from breakfast."

Jordan watched a question and a smile surface in Rachel's eyes then drop away as an officer approached and handed Rachel a piece of paper. Rachel scanned it quickly and looked back up at the officer.

"Really?" She didn't sound impressed.

The officer shrugged. "They weren't kidding about 'all hands on deck,' apparently."

Rachel sighed and handed the document back to the officer. "Okay, thanks. I'll be in the mud room if anyone needs me."

Jordan glanced at Ali, who gave her an encouraging smile before following Rachel through a maze of desks and doors and short hallways. The smell of coffee grew stronger and stronger until Rachel finally stopped in a tiny nook with a potted fake palm tree underneath a thickly glassed diamond-shaped window. Four stools and a high table with magazines lined the walls.

"The mud room," Rachel announced, indicating Jordan and Ali should grab a seat. She threw a thumb over her shoulder at the wall. "Break room is on the other side, perpetual pot of coffee, so this place smells like coffee mud twenty-four seven."

"You cops are awfully fancy," Jordan said as she took Ali's coat and draped it along with hers across the spare chair. Then she pulled out a stool for Ali before taking a seat. Rachel watched the exchange with silent interest.

"What can you tell us?" Jordan said.

"What do you know?" Rachel responded.

"That there's been a threat made to a section of the city's water supply. That's pretty much it."

"My hotel is affected," Ali added. "That's how we heard about it."

"Ah, I wondered. Well, here's what's gone out to the press. At some point after midnight, the Halifax Regional Municipality Facebook page was hacked." Rachel pulled out her phone and searched briefly before turning the screen so Jordan and Ali could see. The main page had a stamp across it that said "we want clean water" with the stylized sun logo underneath. Rachel scrolled down the page, and the stamp stayed like a warning watermark.

"Nice," Jordan muttered.

"There's more," Rachel continued. "At six a.m., emails were sent out simultaneously to the mayor's office and the general manager of the Halifax Regional Water Commission. I can't show you that document, but the threat to the water supply is specific and alarming. Ten minutes later, a break-in was reported at the booster station for the Douglas Water Supply plant, which feeds parts of the city. The station itself was breached, and an empty drum was found inside the building. There are four technicians, two civil engineers, and a chemical engineer—all from different agencies—running tests right now. We've got officers and city officials and first responders going door to door in the affected areas."

"Jesus," Ali muttered. "Have they turned up anything?"

"Nothing so far. We should have results within an hour from the targeted water systems. But of course we can't give an all-clear until we check every water system from here to Cow Bay. That could take days."

"And you're dealing with public panic and pressure from the top to figure it out," Jordan said.

"You got it," Rachel said. "And the pressure has just intensified tenfold to root out the Unharm protest group. Even an unfounded threat to the city's water supply is a serious criminal act, and my supervisors want someone in custody yesterday."

Jordan glanced at Ali as her stomach rolled with unease. She was sitting at police headquarters talking arrests and criminal acts. And she was going to give her suspicions about her kids? This seemed wrong.

"It's okay," Ali said quietly. Jordan wasn't so sure.

"Your text said you have suspicions," Rachel said. Her tone sounded neutral. Jordan wasn't sure if that was better or worse.

Jordan opened her mouth to speak. The words were right there, but she couldn't find the breath to give them weight.

"Jordan is worried her kids are mixed up in this," Ali said.

Rachel nodded as if it wasn't odd that Ali was speaking for Jordan. "How long have you been concerned about this?" She spoke directly to Jordan.

"Since the needles," Jordan said, finding her voice. These were her kids, her concerns. The blame and guilt could belong to her as well. The words fell out as she stared down at her hands. "Whoever served those trays of needles were young and should have been in school, and I started thinking about it. Why would they be involved? Maybe they were hired to do it. Maybe that was it. Or it was fun, like the graffiti." Now that Jordan had started, she had a hard time stopping. "Seamus was involved in that recycling bin tower thing in the Heights. But I could pass that off as wrong place, wrong time. And the kids have been weird recently. Off, somehow. They keep checking in with each other, like there's a secret." She looked up at Rachel. "Those kids can't keep secrets, they're horrible at it. You know that."

Rachel nodded again. "I know them, Jordan. I'm not getting a lot of specifics, here."

Jordan sighed. "I know. I don't have any specifics, not really. Last night at the end of the workout, all their cell phones went off at once. Like someone was sending them all a message. It just made me think something was up. And maybe I should bring it to you."

Rachel's cop stare was unnerving, but Jordan expected no less. There was a lot riding on this. "Do you know who contacted the kids last night?"

"No, Madi redirected their attention back to the workout."

A long silence, tension, unease. Jordan really wanted to be out of here.

"I'd like to ask you about Madi."

Jordan sat up straight in her chair and swallowed her defensiveness. "Okay."

"Do you think she's involved?"

"I have no evidence that she is."

"I understand. The question is do you think she's involved."

How to answer this? Her instinct fought to protect Madi, keep her sheltered and close in a way she never had been. "I think she knows something, yes." The words made her sick.

"Can you tell me about that?"

"She's acting strangely. She's distant and not really talking to me. Everything I do makes her angry."

"I understand," Rachel said, though Jordan wasn't sure she was making sense. "Where has Madi been spending her time recently?"

"Same as always," Jordan said, trying to temper the defensiveness in her tone. "Work at the mall, the gym, group, and home with her aunt. She goes out with friends sometimes, but not much."

Rachel took a few notes, then looked up again. "You said group. Is that the one Helena Cavio runs?"

"That's right."

"You've been thinking for a while that your relationship has been changing. It's good for Madi to depend on other people. I think you even said you wanted to help her create that space in her life. To teach her it was okay."

Yes, all of those things were true, Jordan thought. Maybe that's all this was, the long drawn-out fading of supports and friendship as Madi found her own way into the adult world. Maybe Jordan had conflated the two things when in fact they weren't related at all.

"Madi wanted you off the task force," Ali said. She pressed her leg lightly against Jordan's. "She was pretty clear about that."

"Yes, but what does that really prove?"

Jordan didn't have an answer to that. After a moment, Rachel slapped her hand down on the small table.

"There's a pattern here, actually." She pointed at Jordan. "You're the pattern."

Jordan's stomach dropped, but Ali spoke.

"What do you mean?"

Rachel glanced at Ali, then spoke to Jordan. "You keep getting warned away. That's why you two were approached on Grafton Street by those three guys. I think the break-in at your gym was another warning to stay out of it. And I think Madi's behaviour is a way of keeping you distant."

"She has a key," Jordan mumbled, staring down at her hands.

"What was that?" Rachel said, leaning in.

Jordan sighed. "Madi has a key to the office at the gym." She waited for Rachel's admonishment at keeping this piece of information. But all she saw was understanding.

"It was your kids," Rachel said. "They were trying to scare you away. I can see Madi leading that charge."

Jordan shook her head. "She doesn't need to protect me."

Rachel gave a sad, tired smile. "I'm going to let you sit with the stupidity of that statement for a moment while I go talk to my supervisor. I'll be right back."

Then Rachel was gone, and Jordan and Ali sat alone in the tiny alcove that reeked of old coffee.

"Stupidity?" Jordan said finally, turning to Ali.

"It was a dumb thing to say."

"Not really? Madi doesn't need to protect me."

"You're looking at it the wrong way. If Madi knows something about this, knows you're on the task force, knows you've been approached...What are her thoughts about your involvement?" When Jordan still couldn't answer, Ali tried again. "Think about it from her perspective, not from yours."

"I don't know," Jordan said. She couldn't evaluate this.

"What would Cay say if she were here?"

Jordan cracked a smile. "She'd say I was being stupid. And blind."

Rachel returned just then. "I'm coming to the workout tonight. I'd like to question the kids. My supervisor wants to take any avenue of any lead. The kids might be the lead that breaks this open."

Before Jordan could work through why that didn't sit quite right with her, Ali jumped in.

"Not a good idea," Ali said reasonably, but the edge was back in her tone. "A lot of them are underage. You'd need a parent or guardian present to question them."

"Let me rephrase," Rachel said, her tone just as reasonable and just as edged. "I'd like to have a community forum, open a space for the kids to speak. I'll let them know I'm there as a police presence. I'll give them a sense of the seriousness of what we're dealing with and the potential consequences of both coming forward and staying silent." She shrugged. "It might work, it might not. But we need a lead." She looked at Jordan. "And I want to support you in this. There are some serious allegations around this Unharm group. I don't want any of them anywhere near it."

Jordan felt the offer of friendship through the tension. She wanted to take it, but she also wanted to run away from it. "Yeah, okay. I can end practice early. We'll see what happens."

"We'll see what happens," Rachel echoed and gave Jordan's shoulder a quick squeeze. Then she turned to Ali and stuck out her hand. "Counselor, it's been good working with you," she said with mock seriousness, her eyes dancing.

Ali shook Rachel's hand and said in a similar tone, "Same with you, Constable."

Chapter Fourteen

Jordan—Twenty-one

Fight night, and it's hot, so hot. Jordan is all sweat and muscle and fear. Perspiration is already collecting along the satin waist of her boxing shorts. The insides of her arms are coated, a layer of heated fear. Her scalp itches and burns. She's not yet used to the tight cornrows that make her look fierce and fight-ready. They make her feel stretched and taut, one pluck away from breaking.

Jordan stares at the carpet of the hotel room floor, counting shades of blue and grey. Bento is rubbing a roll of tape between his hands in a rapid, practiced movement. It warms the fibres, he says, in his growling Portuguese-Quebecois accent. Jordan finds a fifth shade of blue as sweat collects at the base of her spine under her tank top. She searches for the word that means these irregular patches of colour as Bento lifts her left hand without a word and begins to wrap gauze around her knuckles. The pattern is the same every time. It's all patterns, Jordan thinks. The word for colour still eludes her. She wishes Bento would turn on the air conditioner. He will, of course. On their way out to the fight. She'll sleep in a frigid icebox tonight. Maybe a winner, definitely bruised.

The tape is next, and Jordan watches as Bento smooths the tape against her skin with wide sweeps of his thick thumbs. Their skin is nearly the same colour. Bento is gruff and curses at her in Portuguese when she loses focus. He sets a punishing schedule to keep her body conditioned for each bout on her way to the division championship. But she feels the care in this small act. It is not love or family. Jordan does not have those. But this care is important to her, and she absorbs it through her wrapped hands.

"You're ready."

It's not a question. It never is with Bento. It's also not the truth, but Jordan stands anyway.

Jordan's anxiety intensifies as they make their way into the arena. Jordan pulls herself up onto the mat, the smell of dust and sweat and hurt filling her senses. Each step of the pre-fight routine is familiar: the sound of the disinterested crowd, the starkness of the lights, and the hazy and oppressive wall of heat and expectation.

Then the gloves. Shards of fear spike painfully against her ribs. The softness of the gloves is unbearable, and their weight makes her weak. Bento slips them over her wrapped hands and begins the lacing pattern. They do not speak. Jordan's heart pounds out a rhythm she has heard for so long.

Imposter, imposter, imposter.

Her opponent is in the ring, going through the same routine. She bounces and flexes and postures, the intricate French braid of her long hair and the lilac sparkle of her skirt shining in the overhead lights. Jordan drops her gaze to her own black sports bra and black shorts with MCADDIE in white letters across the front. The show does not matter. Jordan knows even the beauty queens turn into beasts in the ring.

One last tug on her gloves, and Bento drops her hands. The extra eight ounces quadruples with the weight of her fear and uncertainty. She cannot do this. Not again.

"You will fight well."

Jordan closes her eyes as her coach seals her fate. A command and a prediction. They are the last four words she will hear until the fight is over. Jordan makes space for the words in her chest beside her traitorous, disbelieving heart. The war inside becomes fuel, becomes tension in her arms, becomes the heat and flex of her muscles.

Jordan raises her gloves.

❖

Jordan was tense and jumpy. She felt like one of her kids, distracted by every sound and unable to sit in her living room for longer than a minute. Music thumped in the background through the shared wall with the gym as Jordan tried yet again to sit and focus on her assignment. Ali was curled on the couch with her laptop, alternately typing rapidly and watching Jordan pace.

"You're a disaster, McAddie," Ali said after Jordan had jumped up once again to look out the window at her empty parking lot.

"Forecast said rain. That always keeps kids away."

"Then you and Rachel will talk to the kids who show up," Ali said with a calm confidence.

Jordan wasn't interested in logic. "Maybe we should wait for a day when more kids are going to be here."

"I don't think Rachel wants to wait. Things are moving, Jordan. She wants the kids to get the message sooner rather than later."

Jordan pressed her forehead against the cold glass of her newly replaced window. She didn't want the kids to get the message. That was part of the problem.

"I don't even know if Madi is going to be there tonight."

"She said she was."

Jordan turned around. "You heard from Madi?"

"A little while ago. She asked if I was coming tonight or if I was…" Ali picked up her phone and scrolled through it. "Or if I was 'kicking international corporate ass' tonight instead." Ali smiled as she put her phone down again. Jordan wanted to return her smile, but it wouldn't surface.

"Okay, good."

Ali tilted her head. "That doesn't sound like it was good." When Jordan didn't respond, Ali put her laptop on the coffee table and approached. Jordan warred with herself to stand still. Accepting closeness right now was a battle. Ali stopped about a foot away from Jordan.

"Easy. Tell me what's going on in your head."

Jordan didn't move. It would be so easy to back away from this conversation. Jordan swallowed.

"I don't know where to start."

"Can you tell me your worries about tonight?"

Jordan blew out a breath. "God, so many."

Ali took a step closer and touched Jordan's arm. "Give me one. The biggest one."

"That I'm turning them in. Betraying them."

"Are you?"

The question hurt, but it was exactly the right question to ask. Jordan wanted to say yes. Talking to Rachel, to the police, had been a betrayal. Her suspicion was a betrayal. But it wasn't, not really.

"No."

"Then what are you doing tonight? Explain your intent." Ali's voice was direct and commanding, but her touch was gentle as she moved her hand from Jordan's arm to her waist. Jordan anchored to the warmth.

"I want to give them a safe space. Remind them they cannot mess up enough for me to stop loving them or being there for them. I want to show them what support looks like." Ali nodded, but Jordan needed to finish the thought. "But I also want to remind them there are consequences to their actions and show them a way out of whatever they're caught up in. If they'll take it."

"So, basically what you always do for your kids. What did you call it? A war of constancy."

Jordan hadn't thought of it that way. Tonight was not really that different. Maybe the stakes were higher, but her intention and her goal were the same. Love, support, problem solving, safe space. Jordan felt herself relax.

"Yeah. Thanks. That helped."

Ali leaned in and kissed Jordan lightly. "You're welcome."

Jordan thought about that kiss as they headed down to the gym to set up a little while later. It wasn't the most intense kiss they'd had, but it had been tenderness and understanding. It was the simplicity of saying she was here, and the certainty of saying she always would be. She would try to let Ali carry some of the load. She would try to believe the same way she was asking her kids to believe.

The rain held off, and the gym was packed. Searching now for collusion and secrecy, Jordan saw almost nothing different in the way the teens interacted in their after-school routine. They argued over the Taylor Swift selection for warm-up music, they lazed and lagged through the most hated stations and lingered over their favourites. They teased and fought, postured and laughed, engaged and entertained. Just another day at the gym.

Madi, however, was different. Jordan wasn't sure she would have caught it if she hadn't been looking. Madi was in her workout gear tonight, and though she laughed and directed and cajoled like she usually did, Jordan could see the effort. Madi looked spent, her veneer of energy thinning as the evening went on. Jordan watched and fretted and tried not to read too much into it. Madi had always had highs and lows, but she'd learned to ride them, to allow for the dips, to pay attention to her heart and brain and body and fight for equilibrium, not camouflage. Tonight Madi was working to conceal, and it made Jordan nervous.

Rachel came in about ten minutes into the warm-up. The mood had shifted slightly then, but the kids bounced back and accepted Rachel into their midst as they usually did.

About fifteen minutes before their usual ending time, Jordan caught Rachel's eye. With a definitive nod from Rachel, Jordan walked over and started the cool-down music, giving no response to the questions and exclamations of surprise. They'd know soon enough what this was about.

Five minutes later, Jordan cut the music. This alone was enough to get the attention of the teenagers. Jordan was usually a stickler for serious warm-ups and cool-downs.

"Grab some food and water, guys. Then come join me over here. There's something I want to talk to you about."

The mood shifted to suspicious in an instant. The majority of them searched Jordan's face, then checked in with each other.

"Come on, guys," Ali called out by the table she'd set up with vegetables, crackers, and a few small crates of orange clementines. "I went shopping this week, so lay all your complaints about the food on me."

Either Ali's voice or the sight of the food broke the spell. The kids grabbed handfuls of food and balanced them on industrial brown paper towels before making their way back to Jordan at the front of the gym. Rachel joined them, sucking on a water bottle and wiping sweat from her face. Jordan wasn't sure where to start. Nerves ate her voice. Ali approached with a clementine for both Jordan and Rachel before smiling and stepping back. Jordan accepted the distraction and the smile as well as the silent offer of support.

"Constable Shreve and I wanted to talk to you guys about something. Give you a space to talk or reach out if you need to. No one needs to stay, no one needs to speak up. But it's been a while since we had a community forum like this, and some things have come up that make me think we should have one."

Jordan pierced the orange rind with her thumb and stopped herself from asking if it was okay. They were doing it regardless.

"And I'm here," Rachel jumped in, "because I have some worries about things that are going on in the city." The gym went somehow even quieter as Rachel circled closer to the specifics. "I'm here because you know me and I know you. I'm a community officer, and to me, part of that means intervening in small problems before they become big problems."

"Do we need a lawyer present?" one of the teens called out, obviously hoping for a laugh. A few kids complied. Most didn't.

Before Jordan or Rachel could address the question, Madi spoke up.

"There *is* a lawyer present." Madi's voice was very clear and completely devoid of emotion. Jordan's heart sank.

"Not that kind of lawyer, Mad," Ali said. She smiled at the group. "But if you're asking, my advice would be there's no harm in listening."

The kids swiveled from Madi to Ali, and back to Jordan and Rachel.

"I know you've all heard of the protest group calling themselves Unharm that has popped up in Halifax in the last few weeks," Jordan said. The kids stared and ate their food. "Their movements have gone from public mischief to criminal activity. We have noticed that the focus of the group certainly overlaps some of the same circles you guys do." Jordan began to list them. "Vulnerable population, precarious housing, safe access to food and water, wait lists for addiction programs." Still none of the kids spoke, just stared at Jordan as if waiting for her to accuse them. Or at least get to her point. "I'm worried—we both are—that some of you are involved."

A heavy beat of silence.

"Involved how?" Madi's voice was ice and she stared unblinkingly at Jordan.

"I don't know exactly."

"Nice. So, you just think a bunch of deviant kids are the most likely source of the problem. Way to pick at the low-hanging fruit, Jordan."

The rest of the kids squirmed as Jordan and Madi stared at each other.

"You know that's not what I think of you," Jordan said.

"It's not what I think of you, either," Rachel added.

"I'm not sure your opinion counts, Constable Shreve," Madi said without taking her eyes from Jordan. "At this point we're all suspects, and we're all fully aware of how cops treat suspects." Madi pushed her hair out of her face and addressed the group. "I don't know about the rest of you, but I don't need this shit. You can keep your celery sticks and shitty crackers. I'm out."

No one else moved as Madi walked to the far wall, grabbed her backpack and phone, and headed toward the door.

"It's a nice speech," Jordan said, without turning around. Her heart was in her throat, trying to navigate this pivotal moment. "And a nice attempt at a diversion."

"My opinion is not a fucking diversion."

Jordan turned around to face Madi, whose hand already on the door. "You can insult my vegetable platters all you want. You can insult my gym, my occupation, my words. But I think you know full well, I think you *all* know full well, that I just want you guys to be safe and have a chance. If something's going on, I want to help."

Jordan held her breath as Madi stared at the floor for a moment before looking up. Her heart sank. Madi's eyes were blank.

"You want to help?"

Jordan nodded, waiting for Madi's final blow.

"Stay the fuck out of it."

It was meant to be a final word, a definitive cut, a silencing. Jordan refused.

"I won't. Ever."

Madi stared. "Is this the Disney movie moment, Jordan? Might need to get your girlfriend holding your hand for this one. It will scan better for the audience."

"I'm not going away, Madi."

"Great. You stand your ground. The reluctant goddamn hero, Jordan McAddie. I don't need your charity or your accusations. I'm done."

Madi slammed the metal door, the sound clanging across the gym.

It was the drama and finality Jordan was sure Madi had been looking for. As she looked back at the rest of the teens, she was pretty sure which way the theatrics had swayed them.

"It's not an accusation," Rachel said to the remaining group. It was an effort to salvage the evening though Jordan was convinced they'd either missed their chance or they'd never had one to begin with. "But if you guys know something, if you think there is some kind of danger to you or someone else, I hope you'll bring it to me or Jordan. Anonymous is fine." Rachel looked up at Jordan, as if seeking agreement to end this disaster of a community forum. Jordan nodded. "I'll leave my number here. You can call either of us, anytime."

The kids scrambled to their feet with an odd quietness. Their usual boisterous energy was gone, replaced by a shifting of glances, and apologetic or embarrassed looks as they all filed out of the gym.

As the last kid left, Jordan looked at the half-peeled orange in her hands. The smell of the citrus oil was sharp, and dried juice flaked on her palm. She could hear Ali and Rachel talking, but Jordan focused on the rind under her fingernail. She must have been digging her nail into the peel as she spoke, trying to connect with these kids. Her life's work. Tried to fulfill her duty to them, to keep them in her circle of influence and protection. To keep Madi there.

Jordan didn't want to look up. Panic sat in her chest, rising with a sure swiftness that crippled Jordan's ability to cope. She didn't want Ali or Rachel to see it. And she didn't want to see the acknowledgement of her failure, to have them try to salvage some good from what had been an obvious display of incompetence.

"They're involved," Ali said as she and Rachel walked closer. "Obviously. But they also aren't going to talk. So what's next?"

"We wait and see if anyone bites," Rachel said. She looked between Ali and Jordan. "One of you should try and connect with Madi. I think she's our best in."

"I can do that," Ali said. She was looking sideways at Jordan as if expecting an argument. Jordan didn't have it in her at the moment.

Rachel sighed and rubbed her eyes. "There's something else."

Jordan looked up, alerted by the exhaustion and caution in her friend's voice. "What?"

"We're looking at Helena Cavio as a person of interest. I can't tell you much more than that. But I think I should warn you that given what we can find—or more importantly, can't find—in her history, it's safe to say Helena Cavio is not who she says she is."

"Jesus," Jordan said.

"Seriously?" Ali said. "We just saw her the other night."

"Yes, we know," Rachel said evenly.

"You were there?" Jordan said. Accusation and suspicion still hung heavily in the air. Apparently it hadn't left with the teenagers.

"No, not me. But we were monitoring who was going in and out. I was surprised to see your names when I read the report the other morning. So was Staff Sergeant Buck."

"We were there to see Madi," Jordan said, straightening a little and meeting Rachel's eyes. "We were worried about her, so we tracked her down at the meeting. Helena invited us in, and we participated in a group discussion about home."

Rachel nodded. "That lines up with the scenario I floated by Buck."

"Okay, good," Jordan said cautiously. "Is there anything else you want to ask me?"

"How close are Helena and Madi? I'm just wondering. We have no connection between Madi and the Unharm group right now."

Jordan thought back, tracing their history together. "We hooked Madi up to Helena's services just under two years ago. I know Madi attends her groups." Jordan shrugged. "She doesn't talk about it much. At least not with me."

They both looked at Ali, who shook her head. "She doesn't talk about that with me either. She didn't seem altogether comfortable with Helena the other night. Their relationship seemed…imbalanced somehow."

"What do you mean?"

Ali looked like she was searching for the words. "In a business relationship, I'd say Madi was a commodity Helena needed, not the other way around. Does that make sense?"

"Yes, it does," Rachel said. "Perfect sense."

Jordan agreed. Ali had articulated her own discomfort with seeing them interact. Knowing what she did about Helena's possible involvement in the group made Jordan feel nauseous.

"I'll need you to let me know if you see or hear from Helena," Rachel said. "She agreed to come in for questioning this morning, but no one has seen or heard from her."

Jordan shook her head. "She's really involved in this."

"It looks like it," Rachel said. She looked down as her phone rang. "I should get going. Call me, about anything." She was already answering the phone and walking out the door before Jordan had time to answer.

The door of the gym slammed shut, and Jordan stared at the last clementine in her hand. She remembered her mom placing the small citrus in her purse on the way to the hospital the night Steven died. The scent was still a reminder, an ache in her chest.

"Jordan?"

Jordan tucked away the small orange in its wooden container and looked up at Ali. "Yeah, I'm good. I'm going to put the food away." She took a breath and hoped she wasn't about to fuck up. "Then I think I'm going to study for a bit, then crash."

Ali cocked her head to the side and took a moment before she answered. "I think you're asking for some space tonight."

"Yeah. I think it's a good idea."

"I can get another hotel for tonight, no problem."

"No," Jordan said quickly. "That's not what I meant. You can stay with me. I'd like you to stay with me. I just…" Words failed to materialize.

"You just need space. It's okay, I get it." Ali came around the table and stopped next to Jordan. She gave her a small kiss on the cheek before stepping back. "I'm going to head into the office and work for a few hours, and then I'll come by your place. If you're still up for company, I'll stay. If not, I'll find a hotel. Okay?"

"Yeah," Jordan said gratefully. "Okay. And thanks."

Ali smiled. "Thanks for trusting me enough to say it."

Trust and understanding. Jordan wondered if there was enough of it in the world to get herself and everyone she loved through all this.

Chapter Fifteen

Jordan dreamed of drowning. Water filled her mouth and eyes and lungs, pressing against her chest and making her limbs ponderous and slow. She was struggling, fighting for the surface, lifting and dragging a dead weight, a body. No, more than one. Jordan couldn't count, just knew she had to reach the surface and hold everyone there. She did, and it was a dream victory as her head broke the surface. But no. More people, dark water, flailing limbs, and crying. Jordan felt the bodies sinking even as she screamed at people to keep kicking.

Jordan woke in darkness, heart pounding against her ribs, anxiety soaking her shirt in a cold sweat.

"God," she breathed out. A dream. Just a dream. She rolled over and was about to turn on the light when she remembered Ali was beside her, curled asleep, hands tucked under her pillow. Jordan thought about waking her, sharing the awfulness of the dream. Finding a way to laugh at the predictability of her anxieties, the unimaginative transparency of her not-so-subconscious worry. She didn't. She allowed her breathing to slow, matching the peaceful rhythm of Ali's breath.

After a moment, Jordan grabbed her phone, blinking at the harsh brightness of the screen. It was just before three in the morning. Without stopping to think, Jordan sent out a message to Madi. An apology for their fight, a repeated request to check in. Jordan was just about to put her phone down when Madi responded.

Why are you awake?

Anxiety dream. You?

Hate those dreams, Madi texted back. *What was it?* It didn't escape Jordan's notice that Madi hadn't answered her question.

You'll like this one. I was trying to save people from drowning. Failing spectacularly. It was an offering of sorts, sharing this vulnerability. Exposing herself to Madi's further ridicule or anger.

You don't fail. The only reason some of us sleep at all at night is because of you. Whatever happens, don't forget that.

Thanks, Mad. Would really love to talk to you tomorrow.

Madi never texted back. Jordan eventually put her phone down and curled back under the covers. She rested one hand on Ali's waist, smiling at the small sound Ali made as she shifted closer to Jordan, then lay still. Jordan closed her eyes, searching for sleep as she reveled in the warmth of Ali in her bed.

Jordan didn't think to worry about the ominous feel of Madi's last words until she descended into sleep.

❖

By the time Jordan was walking to work the next morning, everyone was talking about the fire that had broken out at Lucky Seven convenience store. Jordan hiked her bag higher over her shoulder and gripped her travel mug of coffee as she walked past police cruisers angled across an intersection near her office. An acrid smell drifted with the occasional shift of the wind, and the lights of emergency vehicles reflected off windows and lit up the dull grey streets of downtown. Jordan pulled out her phone and quickly flicked to a news site, hoping some information would ease the disquiet in her chest. It didn't.

Four people were suspected dead, including the two owners, in a fire that broke out just after three a.m. The blaze had taken nearly four hours to extinguish, and buildings on both sides of the convenience store had been evacuated. Police and fire were offering no more details, and the downtown core would be blocked off for investigation for at least a day. They suspected foul play, no suspects in custody.

At the office, Jordan tried to focus on her work. It was hard, given the constant buzz of colleagues discussing the fire down the street, information and speculation mingling with an ease that annoyed Jordan. She tried to drown it out, putting in her earbuds and listening to music while she finished a report and began her month-end Ministry reporting data. A number throbbed in her temple, a reverberation like a headache that dully echoed her heartbeat. Three a.m. She'd been awake then. She'd been drifting back to sleep, calm and warm and safe once she'd freed herself from the clutches of her nightmare. As she'd dropped down through the layers of consciousness maybe a match was being struck, a fuse blown, a heat source sparked into life and a fire raged. It was all noise, fire and voices, rising into panic, splintering and banging as the fire trapped and fed.

"God," Jordan breathed out, wrenching her thoughts away. She yanked her earbuds out, the soaring violins replaced by ringing phones, a photocopier, and voices.

"You okay there, chicken? You're six kinds of pale."

Jordan looked up as Cay entered their shared cubicle. She was unwinding a colourful and seemingly endless scarf from around her neck.

"Yeah, I'm okay."

Cay raised an eyebrow. "No, no. Try again."

Jordan wiped a hand across her face. She was cold and sweating.

"Just the fire. Waiting to hear more information."

Cay turned her chair around to face Jordan before she sat down. Their knees almost touched in the small space.

"Tell me your worries, Jordan. What's got you caught by the throat?"

Jordan released a breath, only now recognizing how tightly wound she really was.

"The kids hang out there sometimes. Panhandle."

"You're worried one of them was there," Cay said.

Jordan nodded.

"Likely not at that hour. But I understand your fear. What else?"

Jordan cleared her throat. "I'm sure it's the Unharm group. I don't know the connection yet. Madi was awake at three, when the fire broke out. I'm worried we pushed them too hard last night. Or not enough."

Jordan knew she wasn't making sense, her words and worries twisted and conflated into a nonsensical mass of anxiety and deeply rooted fear.

"Madigan has had insomnia for years," Cay reminded Jordan gently. When Jordan began to speak, Cay held up a hand. "You need to wait, you need to breathe, you need to focus. Whatever is coming for Madi and the rest of our kids, we will be there. Stay present, Jordan McAddie."

Jordan exhaled. Then she took in a deep breath, full down to the bottom of her lungs before she spoke. "Yes. Okay. Thanks."

Cay smiled. "Now, then. Why don't we do a bit of a roll call? Just to ease our minds about the kids. Make a few phone calls, that kind of thing. It's an appropriate action, given the circumstances, don't you think?"

Before Jordan could respond, the phone on her desk rang. Kayla from the front desk said Constable Shreve was here and needed to see her immediately. Jordan's pulse spiked, and the cold sweat returned. She told Kayla to send Rachel back.

"Rachel's here," Jordan managed to say. Cay's eyes widened, and Jordan was sitting close enough to read the fear in her friend's eyes, in the tightness of her lips, the clench of her jaw.

"Breathe, Jordan." It was the only advice Cay had time to give before Rachel was striding up to their cubicle.

"Hey," Rachel said shortly. Her obvious stress ratcheted up Jordan's anxiety another three notches. "Sorry to drop in, but I needed to talk to you both."

"Is it about the fire?" Jordan said. "Is it one of the kids?"

"Not the kids," Rachel said quickly. "Shit, sorry. No, nothing like that."

Jordan let out a breath. "What do you need?"

Rachel pulled up a photo on her phone and turned it around. It wasn't a great photo, obviously shot on the street at night, but Jordan recognized a man she'd seen with Helena at the university and at the group the other night. Before she could speak up, Cay jumped in.

"Roderick Connors. I've known him a long time," Cay said. "That boy was up and down so many times. Is he in trouble?"

Rachel looked grim, and Jordan knew what she was going to say before Rachel even spoke.

"We believe Rod Connors was one of the deceased in the fire. I'm sorry, Cay."

Jordan heard Cay's quick intake of breath and saw her tremble.

"Sweet Jesus," Cay breathed out.

"I'm so sorry," Rachel repeated. "I need to ask if either of you knows where he lives."

Jordan shook her head and so did Cay.

"You should check with Helena Cavio," Cay said, grabbing a

tissue when Jordan held out the box. "I know he helps out with her groups. And you should tell her in person. She'll be devastated."

Jordan and Rachel exchanged a knowing look. Jordan's heart hurt. She really didn't want to add this to Cay's day.

"Cay," Rachel said gently. "We're investigating Helena Cavio in connection to the Unharm group." She paused, obviously waiting for Cay to react in some way, but Cay just stared blankly. "That's why I'm looking for Rod Connors's address, to see if she's there."

"More connections," Jordan murmured and Rachel nodded.

"Roderick Connors had a sun and knife tattoo on his left shoulder, and there is some preliminary evidence that a sun symbol was found inside the convenience store as well."

So it was connected. Of course it was. It was as if the city had been taken over, held hostage by this group of radicals who didn't seem to understand that in their efforts to draw attention to those who had been marginalized and hurt, they were inflicting a hurt far worse. Or maybe that was the point.

"What do you want us to do, Rach?" Jordan held her head, as if that would somehow stop the spinning.

"For now, just carry on. Ask around about Helena, whatever sources you have. Or Rod Connors. Text me anything you've got. I may not be able to respond, but I'll pick it up."

Cay and Jordan both murmured their assent, then Rachel stood, squeezed Cay's shoulder, and gave an apologetic look to Jordan before turning and quickly walking away. Jordan wondered how she did her job, facing the unexpected, the hurt, and the danger while under incredible pressure. For the hundredth time, she hoped Rachel would have some time to rest soon. She hoped they all would.

Cay had turned back to her own desk, and Jordan could hear her sniffling quietly. She assumed this meant her friend needed a little time and space to process what they'd just heard. Jordan grabbed her jacket and phone, pausing only briefly before touching Cay lightly on the arm. Cay reached up without turning around and briefly squeezed Jordan's hand. Then Jordan left the cubicle, feeling the need to get out of the space and the noise.

Outside, the sun had broken through the greyness of the November morning. Clouds raced past the sun, and blue sky dominated the dome above them. Jordan wound her way through the crowds on the sidewalk, businesses and offices still open even on the streets that were closed to vehicles. The excitement was still in the air as it had been hours earlier when Jordan had arrived at work.

Jordan blocked out the whispers and words, keeping her head down and taking side streets until she was close to the block where the Lucky Seven convenience store had stood until approximately three o'clock that morning. The smell of burning was stronger here, acrid and chemical. Jordan wanted to get away from it, but she stood and stared at the blackened three-story brick building, almost completely covered with a thick coating of ice that shone in the midday sun. There was no heat here any longer, no urgency or threat. No rage or passion or purpose. Just coldness, emptiness, loss. A well of unanswered questions.

Jordan wanted an end to the stranglehold the protest group held on the city. On her kids. She looked down at her phone. No text from Madi. The silence felt heavy and portentous, but Jordan chalked it up to the day, the environment, and the news. Breathe and focus, that's what Cay had said. And make a connection. Jordan opened her message app and found Ali's name. She had someone to connect with, she had someone to lean on. Right now she intended to do just that.

❖

"Has this ever happened before?"

Jordan looked up from her post at the gym door. Ali was inside, still optimistically arranging mats even though no one had arrived yet.

"No," Jordan said. "This has never happened before." She turned away from the empty gym, the sight of it making her sick with worry. Instead, she stared out at the night. The streetlights had just come on, though they revealed nothing other than the occasional car driving past the entrance. The evening was quiet and Jordan was afraid.

The silence felt ominous, and the rapidly descending dark only heightened the sensation. Something was very, very wrong, and Jordan didn't know what to do. She wanted to fight and yell, draw out her opponent, look it in the eye and channel her fear into anger before she lashed out with purpose. But there was only silence and darkness and Jordan's hurt. She'd spent her whole life boxing shadows.

She felt Ali's presence at her side but didn't turn around. "Think we scared them away last night? Punishment for the accusation maybe?"

Jordan quashed her anger at Ali's use of "we." These weren't Ali's kids. This wasn't her fight.

"Maybe a few of them," she said, trying to keep her tone neutral. "It doesn't make sense they would all stay away."

Ali touched Jordan's arm but dropped it a moment later when Jordan failed to respond to her touch. "What do you think it is, then?"

Jordan just shook her head and stared at the empty street.

"Talk to me, JP."

The flash of anger again. "What do you want me to say?" Jordan said, turning around. Staring at the street was unhelpful and pathetic. And she was letting all the heat out. Jordan moved away from the door and let it swing shut behind her with a final clang. "I don't know what's happening. I don't *know* anything."

"Okay," Ali said, following Jordan back inside but keeping her distance. Jordan was both grateful and annoyed Ali was here. "Then what do you want to *do*?"

There was always an action with Ali, always an achievable goal, a measurable outcome. But Jordan felt like she was back in survival mode, constantly on the defensive, pivoting off her back foot in an effort to duck and avoid whatever was coming at her. Planning a counterattack was so hard when you were under pressure.

"There's nothing I can do. Nothing."

"What about calling Rachel?"

"And tell her what, exactly? 'I'm nervous'?" Jordan shook her head. "No, Rachel is dealing with enough already." The four victims of the fire had been identified: the couple who owned Lucky Seven convenience store, a bouncer stopping for cigarettes on his way home from work, and Rod Connors. The media was already reporting the link to the protest group. Rachel and the rest of the investigation team would be working overtime trying to find Helena.

"Where are they, Jordan? The kids."

Jordan started to reiterate that she didn't know. But the concern etched in Ali's expression made Jordan's heart break a little, and she took a breath and voiced her fear. "I think…" Jordan cleared her throat and tried again. "Whoever texted them that night, whatever link they have to the protest group…I think something is happening tonight. I think the kids are there."

"The next target," Ali said. "That could be anywhere. The police have no leads?"

Before Jordan could respond, the sound of the gym door clanging made Jordan and Ali both turn. Hope and fear leapt into her chest as someone dragged the metal door open.

Sierra walked in. She was out of breath and looked like she'd been crying. Jordan and Ali both ran to meet her.

"Don't answer the message," Sierra said, gulping in air and trying to speak. "It's a fake. Madi says they took her phone, so it's not her and she's fine and don't answer it."

Jordan glanced at her phone, concern and confusion mixing in her belly. "Did you get a message?" she asked Ali.

"No."

"What message, Sierra?"

Sierra gulped air. Ali brought her one of the water bottles, and Sierra took a long drink.

"Maybe start at the beginning," Ali said.

"Yeah, okay. So, I got a call about an hour ago, but I ignored it because I didn't recognize the number, and who calls anyway, you know?" Jordan nodded though she didn't know really. "I finally remembered to check the message, and it was Madi. She sounded kinda weird, but she said they'd taken her phone and it was really important you and Ali knew so you could ignore the messages coming from her phone."

"Is that all she said?"

"Basically. She said it was important you guys knew it wasn't her, that she was fine. But I was out at the mall. It's Brooklynn's birthday next week, and I want to get her some books. That's why I forgot to check the message and then my battery died, but I was worried so I just thought it was faster to come here."

Sierra took another drink from the water bottle. Jordan and Ali looked at each other, both obviously evaluating the sketchy information.

"Did she say who took her phone?" Ali said.

Sierra shook her head.

"Do you know where everyone is tonight, Sierra?" Sierra blinked at Jordan's question but didn't respond. "You don't seem surprised that the gym is empty."

Sierra shrugged. "Madi told me to stay home tonight."

"Why?"

Another shrug from Sierra.

"Tell me what everyone has been hiding, Sierra. Tell me why you're scared."

Sierra dropped her eyes to the ground, her hair partially hiding her face.

"I don't know anything."

"You know more than we do," Jordan coaxed. "Whatever reason you were given for keeping this a secret, people in danger trumps that. No matter what Madi says."

Sierra looked up. "No, Jordan, you don't get it. I don't know anything because Madi won't tell me anything." She sounded angry now, frustrated. "She said I should stay out of it, that it was better if I knew nothing. That way, Social Services couldn't hold it against me when I petition for more time with Brooklynn. So, I stayed out of it. Until tonight." Sierra sniffed and wiped her nose on her sleeve.

The chime of a notification on Ali's phone sounded loud in the empty gym. Jordan's heart pounded as Ali looked down at her screen and opened the messages app. Everything seemed to take so long, she wanted to scream with frustration and impatience.

"It's Madi," Ali said. Then she paled and Jordan saw her hand shake. "Shit," she said quietly. "The message says, 'I need help. I'm on the bridge and I'm not okay. Can you come get me?' "

Jordan was frozen, ice in her veins, her head throbbing. Madi on the bridge, Madi hurting. The force of logic made her listen to what Sierra had just told them. Then a message popped up on her phone. Jordan opened it.

"I got one, too. Madi's phone, same message. I'm going."

"But it's not Madi?" Sierra said tentatively.

Jordan was grabbing her jacket, checking for her keys. "Either it is Madi and she's on the bridge, or it's someone pretending to be Madi to draw us in. Either way, Madi's in trouble."

Ali was putting on her jacket as well and looking at her phone. "Should we respond?"

"No," Jordan said. "*We* should not. You stay here with Sierra and get her a cab home. I'll text when I know something."

"Fuck that. I'm coming with you."

"No, you're not." Jordan turned and headed toward the door, thinking that if she just left, Ali would go away. It had worked before.

Jordan heard scrambling behind her as Ali and Sierra grabbed their stuff and followed her out. The steel door slammed shut. Jordan's heart pounded, fear chasing confusion. The sun had gone down, and dusk had turned to a damp, cold night as she walked around the gym to her car. The crunching of gravel behind her made her angry as Ali and Sierra followed.

"Go away, Ali."

"No, Jordan." Ali wasn't just stubborn, she was completely immovable. Wind whipped her blonde hair around her shoulders and Ali pushed it away. Sierra stood completely still, looking back and forth between them.

"Goddamn it," Jordan muttered. "We don't have time for this. Both of you get in."

They did, scrambling for seat belts as Jordan started the car and pulled out of the parking lot.

"Give me your phone, I'll call Rachel," Ali said.

Jordan handed it over and kept her eyes on the road as Ali scrolled through her contacts and connected the call. Jordan focused on the wet streets, the traffic, the lights. Anything to stop herself from thinking about Madi up on the bridge.

The sound of ringing interrupted her thoughts as Ali put the phone on speaker.

"Not a good time, Jordan." Rachel's voice was loud and slightly garbled through the speaker phone.

"We got a message from Madi," Jordan said, trying to project her voice through the phone speaker and keep her eyes on the road. "She says she's on the bridge and she needs help. But we also just got information saying someone took her phone and—"

"The bridge?" Rachel said. "You got a text from Madi saying she was on the bridge? Is that all she said?"

"Rachel, it's Ali. I got the same message." Ali pulled out her phone and read the text message word for word. "But like Jordan said, Madi sent Sierra to tell us that someone took her phone and the messages are a fake and to ignore them."

The sound of Rachel's muffled cursing filled the car. Jordan could hear voices in the background, wind through the speakers, the sound of car doors slamming.

"Where are you right now?"

"We're on our way to the bridge. About five minutes out, maybe a little more with traffic."

"Shit, okay. Yeah. Look, we started getting calls about twenty minutes ago from commuters saying there was a group of demonstrators on the bridge. They've shut it down now, and it's a shit show. Traffic backed up, and we're trying to get close but the protestors have a line of their own vehicles blocking both ways."

"Can you say that again?" Jordan said. The background noise through the speaker was loud.

"Stay off the main routes, try Novalea Street." Rachel's next words were drowned out by a loud, thumping, continuous noise. It filled the car as Jordan pressed down on the gas and shifted into a higher gear. She had no idea what was happening. She needed to know.

Without warning, the sound died, and the phone gently chirped to say the call had disconnected.

"I think that was a helicopter," Ali said quietly.

Silence permeated the car, just the sound of Jordan downshifting as she came up against traffic. She mapped out a route in her head, trying to move around the block of rush-hour traffic backed up from the bridge closure. Jordan needed to find her way there. Needed to find Rachel.

"What's happening, Jordan?" Sierra sounded scared, and Jordan saw her pale face in her rearview mirror.

"I'm not really sure. Sounds like the protest group is demonstrating on the bridge. They've shut it down. I'm going to try and get close."

"Why? Because of Madi?"

Because of all of them, Jordan wanted to say.

"We'll find Constable Shreve," Ali said calmly, answering Sierra's question. Jordan could hear the undercurrent of strain. "We'll find out what's happening."

Jordan wound her way through and around traffic, breaking more laws than she cared to admit until she was on the nearly dead residential street that paralleled the highway entrance to the A. Murray MacKay Bridge.

A sudden sound from the back seat made Jordan turn around quickly. Sierra was staring down at her phone, the small speaker blaring voices and nonsensical noise.

"Someone's posted something to YouTube," Sierra said. Jordan could just make out the sound of garbled cheering and shouts.

"Do you see anyone you know?" Jordan said, pulling her car half over the curb and jamming on her hazard lights. She could see some emergency vehicles with their whirling lights just down the hill.

Sierra stared at the screen for a few seconds longer. Jordan wanted to scream at her.

"No, it's stupid dark. There are comments, though. 'Bring it all down,' 'block the bridge,' 'you're all dickwads.'" Sierra looked up. "Maybe that last one isn't super relevant."

Jordan got out of the car and Ali and Sierra followed. She climbed the small rise and looked down through the chain link fence that separated the residential block from the highway entrance to the bridge below. A cluster of police cruisers and emergency vehicles blocked the entrance to the bridge. Farther up, a confusion of cars and trucks were trying to turn around, with a transport truck wedged sideways across the bridge as it attempted to retreat. Cops in neon high-vis jackets were trying to direct traffic off the bridge. A helicopter suddenly buzzed overhead.

Rachel was right. This was a shit show.

"You two stay here," Jordan said, climbing the fence. She hadn't worn gloves and the metal was a crisscross of cold pain against her palms and fingers. She gripped the top bar to steady herself as she swung a leg over. She could feel the fence shake and looked over to see Ali and Sierra climbing on either side of her. Jordan said nothing.

The grassy hill at the base of the bridge was steep and slippery, not intended for pedestrians. Jordan, Ali, and Sierra all slipped their way down, each of them taking at least one fall. As they skittered to a stop at the edge of the highway, they were met by a young officer, his face enraged.

"What do you think you're doing? This is an active scene and you can't be here."

"My name is Jordan McAddie. Constable Shreve asked me to come down. I have information relating to individuals on the bridge." It was an approximation of the truth.

The young officer eyed Jordan with suspicion.

"Constable Shreve asked you to come down?"

"She's the one who told me to use the side streets," Jordan said, throwing a thumb over her shoulder at the hill they'd just descended. "I really need to see her."

"Stay here," the officer said. "I mean it, or you're going to find yourselves in the back of a police cruiser."

Jordan stepped to the side as a group of officers in dark tactical gear moved en masse to the front of the vehicle line.

"Jesus," Ali breathed.

Jordan glanced at Ali. Her expression was focused. And just the edge of scared.

"Jordan!"

Rachel was waving her over, the young cop by her side.

"I shouldn't be surprised you muscled your way onto the scene. Jesus, McAddie," Rachel said when the three of them approached. "Have you heard anything else from Madi?"

"No, nothing. Have you seen her? Have you seen any of them?" Jordan had to shout to be heard above the racket around them.

Rachel shook her head. "No confirmation. We've got helicopters overhead trying to get footage, and we've got two police boats circling underneath. So far we've got around a hundred head count. Placards and chanting. No demands at this point, which, I have to say, is making me nervous."

"You don't think blocking the bridge during rush hour is the final goal of this demonstration?" Ali said.

Rachel shook her head again and was about to answer when the two-way radio attached to her lapel crackled a message Jordan couldn't hear. Rachel spoke into the two-way and listened to a garbled message. Jordan saw shock and fear take over Rachel's expression before it was replaced by grim focus.

"Officers on the Coast Guard boat are reporting activity on the struts of the bridge."

"What kind of activity?" the young officer said.

"They're not sure. But I can't think of a reason for any protesters to be down in the structure of the bridge if all they're trying to do is bring awareness to their cause. Can you?"

The young officer silently shook his head. Rachel closed her eyes briefly.

"Jordan, I'm going to ask you to come with me. Constable Jeffs, can you escort Sierra and Ms. Clarke back to their vehicle, please?"

Jordan nodded her agreement but Ali was already building her case.

"Sierra should go, yes. But I got a message from Madi as well. Let me stay until we know why Jordan and I were asked to be here. There's a plan, let's see if we can co-opt it."

Jordan watched as the two women squared off, Ali standing her ground even though Rachel had all the power.

"Okay, you can stay," Rachel said. "For now. Let's go find Staff Sergeant Buck."

Jordan and Ali followed Rachel around vehicles and clusters of cops and firefighters until they reached a large van with "Emergency Response Team" emblazoned on the side. Staff Sergeant Buck was conferring with the tactical team, looking down at a tablet playing video footage.

"Staff Sergeant Buck," Rachel said, and the officer looked up before handing the tablet to the tactical officer. "You know Jordan McAddie, and this is Alison Clarke. They both received texts from Madigan Battiste trying to get them on the bridge tonight."

Buck stepped in closer as the helicopter made another pass overhead. He shouted as Jordan and Ali leaned in to hear. "I need to know if Ms. Battiste is part of the protest group. A leader or a follower, it doesn't matter. Her allegiance in this is central to any plan we have moving forward."

Allegiance, a tricky word. It implied ties and loyalty, love and family. Jordan hated that she hesitated, a complete betrayal of Madi. But maybe that was her answer. Ali touched her arm and shook it a little until she had her attention.

"Tell him, Jordan. You know the answer to this."

Jordan looked briefly at Ali, and then she turned to Buck. "I think Madi has known what's been going on with this group for a long time. I think she's involved to protect the other kids. I think she's involved to keep me as far away as possible. I think someone took her phone and sent that message so we would be here. But I don't know why."

Staff Sergeant Buck nodded once curtly. "That's Constable Shreve's opinion also. I needed to hear it from the source." He gestured to the truck and they all followed him.

The space was cramped, walls lined with monitors and equipment and gear Jordan only recognized from movies. But it was quieter here, even with the various screens streaming footage obviously taken from the helicopters and the boat. Jordan stared at the screens, seeing the protestors at the apex of the bridge, some waving placards, some cheering, most moving in a ponderous, massive circle. She tried to find familiar faces, but she couldn't.

Rachel seemed to follow Jordan's gaze. "Norton, can you show us what you've got zoomed in?"

The officer sitting at the controls clicked on his keypad and pointed at a monitor above his head. The aerial footage was magnified.

"There," Jordan said suddenly, breaking the tense silence as she pointed to the screen. "That's Philip and Rupert. Jasmine. Dylan. Seamus. Raya." Jordan named some kids she'd seen just yesterday in gym as well as a few that had aged out of her programs.

The picture zoomed up and away as the helicopter raced past and turned around mid-air. The sensation was nauseating, but Jordan kept staring at the screen as the helicopter returned. She was looking for Madi, tiny and fierce Madi.

"We can switch to the boat footage," Rachel said quietly. "It can give us another—"

"I see Helena," Jordan said. "Right there."

Rachel and Buck both leaned closer.

"Capture that image, Norton," Buck said.

They all stared at the screen in silence. Helena was surrounded by people, but two looked like they were acting as bodyguards, positioning themselves between Helena and the crowd. They had their hoods up and their faces were obscured. But Helena, in her pea coat and scarf, had her head bare. She seemed to be smiling.

Ali moved a little closer to the screen. "Is that…?" She pointed at a figure sandwiched between one of the bodyguards and Helena.

Jordan saw Madi's face. She couldn't make out all the details, but she recognized her pale face and defiant body language.

"Pause it, please, Norton," Rachel said quietly. The frame froze, and Rachel pointed. "Madigan Battiste next to Helena Cavio." She looked at her superior officer. "I think you need to let Jordan in on a few details."

Buck ran a hand over his mouth as if considering Rachel's request. Then he turned to Jordan. "The protestors have blocked the bridge with vehicles in both directions." Norton, the video guy, pulled up images without being asked. "The ones that concern us most are the four rental vans, two on each side of the bridge. Their contents are unknown, and we're treating them as suspicious until we can get more intel. Those vans coupled with activity on the understructure of the bridge means we are moving real careful on this one. With a hundred people on the bridge, a couple dozen of them minors, we've got the potential for a real situation here."

Jordan squeezed her hands in her pockets, clenching and unclenching her fists as a wave of dread threatened to engulf her. "What do you need from me?" Jordan said. "I'll help in whatever way I can."

Buck regarded her before he nodded decisively. "All right. We want you to make contact with the protestors, specifically with Helena Cavio. We assume that's why she used Ms. Battiste's phone to get both of you down here. I am very hesitant about asking you to go on that bridge. I have very little idea what I'm sending you into, but my gut is telling me a police presence or show of force will only add fuel to the fire, and we need eyes and ears up there."

"I'm in," Jordan said. "Let's do it."

"Me, too." Ali held up a hand as Jordan spun to face her. "Save it, McAddie. I'm not interested in your argument."

Jordan felt all eyes on her as she glared at Ali. In response, Ali just lifted her chin in silent challenge.

"Hand me a mic and earpiece, will you, Norton?" Rachel said.

Jordan didn't move as Rachel hooked a battery pack to the back of Jordan's jeans and threaded a wire up her back and over her shoulder. "You know," Rachel said conversationally as she worked, "as much as I don't want to see both of you walking toward that protest group on the bridge, I'll feel a hell of a lot better knowing you've got backup." She handed Jordan an earpiece. "Especially backup that has already proven she can kick ass if necessary."

"There are a hundred people on that bridge," Jordan said,

adjusting the rubbery piece of plastic in her ear. "No one can kick that much ass."

"I don't think they're all a threat," Buck said from his position by the door.

Rachel grabbed another set and started wiring Ali. Jordan felt sick. She focused on Buck's words.

"What do you mean?"

"I think more than one agenda is playing out right now. Hell, I think there's been more than one agenda this whole damn time. I think most of the people on the bridge, most of the folks who have been involved in the graffiti and demonstrations, truly believe they're fighting a cause for justice and change. I don't think their motives are violent. My guess is a core few, like Helena Cavio and her henchmen there, have no issues with injury or loss of life to further their cause. The convenience store fire proved that." He pointed at Jordan and Ali. "I need you two to find out who is a threat and what do they have planned."

As Jordan and Ali, both fitted with mics and earpieces descended out of the ERT truck back onto the windy and loud bridge, those words kept repeating in the back of Jordan's head. *Who is a threat, what do they have planned.* Rachel and two officers in tactical gear escorted them to the front of the line of the emergency vehicles. Then, with a few last words of encouragement, Jordan and Ali began making their way up the slope of the bridge.

It was an odd feeling, silently climbing the deserted four-lane highway as wind swept over the massive structure spanning the Halifax harbour.

"I love you, Jordan McAddie," Ali said as the wind whipped in a downward draft, bringing the sound of the protestors in an anger and energy-fueled wave. "And I'm not going anywhere."

For a moment it all hung in the balance, past and present and future, as Jordan's heart struggled to place Ali's words where they needed to go.

"Your timing is impeccable, Alison Clarke," Jordan said.

Ali grinned, her eyes shining.

"I love you, too," Jordan said. "But I won't pretend I'm happy you're here right now."

Before Ali could respond, Rachel's voice came through Jordan's earpiece. "As much as I'm looking forward to the wedding invitation, I thought I should remind you two that you're being broadcast to the ERT base here."

Jordan felt herself blush, and Ali's eyes went wide and she mouthed "oops" to Jordan.

"Sorry, Rach," Jordan said. "How should we play this, exactly?"

"Don't play it," Rachel said immediately. "You can be completely honest about your motives for being there. We're not trying to fool Helena or whoever is running this. You want a peaceful resolution, end of story."

"Okay."

"Just be yourself," Ali said, briefly squeezing Jordan's hand. "Treat Helena like you always have. She respects you because you've always shown her respect."

Jordan's steps felt heavier as they passed the first set of struts that held the suspension wires over the Halifax Harbour. Jordan couldn't hear the water far below but she could picture it, inky and cold and deep. She shivered.

"Fifty metres from contact." Jordan heard an unfamiliar voice in her ear.

"If you're with the police, that's close enough."

Jordan tried to find the source of the shouted command, finally isolating it to a figure in a bulky jacket standing by the hood of one of the rental vans. He popped his head over the hood, and Jordan recognized him immediately.

"Creaser, it's me. Jordan."

Creaser immediately walked around the hood of the van, smiling broadly.

"Jordan? Hey! I didn't know you were joining us. The boss said no one else was allowed on the bridge. What the hell are you doing here?"

Jordan passed the line of cars and shook Creaser's outstretched hand. "I should be asking you the same thing."

"Ah, you know. Just doing my duty," he said good-naturedly. Everything about Creaser had always been good-natured. "*Vive la révolution*, and all that," he added in a terrible imitation of a French accent. He switched his gaze to Ali. "Who's with you, Jordan?"

"Creaser, this is Ali. Ali, this is Creaser. We grew up in the same housing project together."

Ali shook Creaser's hand and smiled. "Nice to meet you."

"Same to you, ma'am." Creaser looked over his shoulder and yelled out. "Jamie, come cover the van for me. I'm going to take these two to the boss lady."

The man Creaser had called over glowered first at Creaser and then at Jordan and Ali. Jordan looked at him impassively, trying to remain neutral and unaffected by the urgency and undercurrent of tension.

"Fine," Jamie said curtly.

Creaser waved them over. Jordan tried to look at everything and everyone, counting cars, detailing locations, trying to decipher intent from the expressions of everyone around them. The vans were most heavily guarded, and the stationary guards seemed to have the coldest and most serious expressions. The main group of protestors was surrounded by these hardened, immovable men and women. Jordan caught sight of a few of her kids, though they were too caught up in what they were doing to pay attention. They were imprisoned, not protected. Jordan doubted they knew.

Ali had her chin tucked into her jacket, as if she was cold. But Jordan was fairly certain she was relaying everything she could see into her mic.

"Boss lady is just back here with her lieutenants. Well, two of them. You heard about Roddie Connors, didn't you, Jordan?"

"I did. Was he a friend of yours?"

"Yeah. I mean kinda? Guess I'm just surprised. He just seemed so set on doing whatever the boss lady said, you know? She was so clear with everyone that our group wasn't about revenge. But when Rod heard about how those people at Lucky Seven treated Helena when she was on the street…" Creaser gave a low whistle and shook his head as he ducked around more people and more cars. "He wanted to get back at them even though Helena said not to."

"Was she upset? Helena?" Jordan said just as a cheer went up with the protesters.

"They're really having a blast," Creaser said, smiling at the antics of the group. Then his face fell. "She was mad. Real mad." Creaser gestured at the side of the bridge. "Here we are."

A few men shuffled back as Jordan and Ali approached, giving them a clear view of Helena.

"Hello, Jordan."

Helena's voice cut through Jordan. She looked at Helena Cavio standing calmly in the midst of the chaos. Madi was nowhere to be seen.

"Hello, Helena. I think you wanted to see me."

Helena smiled. "I'm always happy to see you." When Helena looked at Ali, her expression grew noticeable colder. "Ms. Clarke, I see you got my message also."

"I did."

Helena nodded briefly in acknowledgement and turned her attention back to Jordan. "I knew you would ignore a message from me, but not from Madigan. I hope you'll forgive the trickery. It really was very important to get you here. You straddle worlds in a way I have never been able to. I need you to do that now since you have a voice people will listen to."

"I don't know about that," Jordan said. "But I want to help in whatever way I can."

Helena nodded, her face becoming more animated. "I always admired your willingness to help. Not just a willingness, a selflessness."

"These kids are important to me, Helena."

"Yes. Exactly. They are important. Which is why we need to make changes now. Demand change. Force change." Helena spread her arms wide, as if glorying in the cold confusion of this dance she had orchestrated.

"I'm worried about my kids. They've had a chance to be part of this protest and use their voices. But I'd like to take them home now."

Helena's eyes had become distant with that far-off stare Jordan had come to recognize. It no longer looked like a simple quirk. It seemed like the marker of someone no longer able to connect with reality. That gaze filled Jordan's chest with fear far more than the shouts and stomps of the protestors behind them or the glares of Helena's bodyguards.

"Where's Madigan?" Helena said suddenly. One of the men gestured to someone behind Jordan. "Her voice is important in this." She laughed, but the sound was off to Jordan, just this side of shrill. "You know that already, of course. You helped give Madigan her voice."

Madi walked into the small circle of people, her expression oddly blank. Her hood was pulled up against the wind. She looked at Jordan and stood in the vacant spot next to Helena. Jordan's heart pounded.

"Hey, Madi," Jordan said.

Madi nodded an acknowledgement.

"You okay, Mad?" Ali said.

"You didn't need to come down here."

"You said you needed help."

"I don't." Madi looked at Helena. "Let them take their guys out of here. We had a better turnout than we expected, we don't need—"

Helena held up a hand, and Madi stopped talking. She looked pleadingly at Jordan and then she dropped her gaze to the ground.

"A brief story for context," Helena said, her voice sharper than it had been a moment ago. "Eight years ago, I decided I would become the person I had always needed on the streets." Helena stopped and seemed to scrutinize Jordan's face. "You don't look surprised."

"I always knew you were connected to the people you supported in a way most folks weren't."

"Yes," Helena said softly. "I know their powerlessness, and I promised myself I would do what I could to shift the balance. So I paid for a new identity and took a bus and a ferry to Halifax to start over. I lived in a shelter in Dartmouth, worked on my résumé, found a job. I dressed up in donated clothes, I even carried the same Starbucks coffee cup for two weeks and refilled it at the shelter every morning. I pretended to fit in, but I was a sheep in wolf's clothing. I mimicked the tones and postures of the people who worked in Social Services, bemoaning the lack of resources when all I saw were misspent riches. I feigned exhaustion at the end of the day when people went home congratulating themselves on their hard work. Instead, I walked the streets and used my paycheck to hand out food, and all I wanted to do was sit with them, be one of them. But I needed to keep my cover. I played the game just enough to hide. I wanted the world to see a wolf among wolves."

"But you *are* a wolf, Helena," Madi said. "You've always been a wolf."

Helena smiled sadly. "I was born a sheep, Madigan." She pointed at Ali. "That one is a wolf. Born a wolf, lives her life amongst wolves, congratulates herself on being a wolf. She is all pride, that one."

Jordan didn't like the way Helena had focused on Ali. Her eyes had gone cold, and though Ali was silent and impassive, Jordan needed to bring Helena's focus back.

"What am I?"

Helena switched her gaze back to Jordan. "What *are* you, Jordan? You tell me."

"A sheep," Madi said, before Jordan could find the words. Her dark eyes bored into Jordan, alive now with anger. "Content to be a sheep though the world keeps offering her a chance to be a wolf."

Helena looked at Madi approvingly. "Yes, very good. Exactly."

Jordan steeled herself against the hurt of Madi's words. She blinked as Rachel spoke quietly in her ear.

"We've got a problem. Intel on the convenience store fire shows an incendiary device was used, which means this group has had access to the materials needed for explosives as well as the knowledge and capacity to put it together." Jordan risked a quick look at Ali, who had obviously heard the same thing. Ali shivered. "We're assuming the bridge has been set with explosive charges. We need whatever intel you can give us. Fast."

Jordan tuned back in to the chanting and the wind and the bright overhead lights and the dark sea around them. She felt shuddering beneath her feet, the instability of fear, of facing an opponent so much bigger.

"They're asking something of you," Helena said, sounding more curious than concerned. "What is it?"

"The police know about the explosives," Ali said, her voice calm confidence. "They want to know your demands."

"Really," Helena said. "And are you volunteering to relay my demands to the police?"

"Yes, I am. I'm an excellent negotiator," Ali said. "And I speak wolf."

Helena's eyes glittered dangerously. "Don't fuck with me, Ms. Clarke."

"I'm not. You've set the stage for a takeover, all the stakeholders are here. We've all agreed the power lies in your hands. We're all just waiting here for you to tell us your demands. Show us your teeth, Helena."

Each of Ali's words seemed to hit like a blow to Helena. She shrank visibly as Ali handed her the power and outlined the magnitude of the moment. Helena took a step back.

"Let Jordan and Ali take the kids off the bridge," Madi said, obviously seizing Helena's moment of indecision. "Give Jordan the manifesto we wrote. She'll read it to the media. There will be change. Just let my friends off the bridge."

Helena blinked and grabbed Madi's arm. "Madigan?"

"The manifesto, give it to Jordan," Madi said quietly. "Give the all-clear to let them off the bridge. They've played their part. They have come to meetings, they have taken risks and built up their voices. They need to take their own messages out into the world."

"And you?"

"I'm right here."

Jordan began to protest, but Madi shot her a scathing look and Jordan swallowed her protest. She had to trust Madi knew what she was doing.

Helena reached into her oversized pocket with a shaking hand and pulled out some folded papers. She gazed at them with incredulity, then confusion eclipsed the happiness and she reached into her other pocket and pulled out a small flip phone. She stared at them both.

"It's not enough," Helena whispered, her words nearly carried away by the wind. "Words on the page, spoken to the uncaring media and viewed by an uncaring community."

Helena was getting her strength back, and Madi looked distraught.

"We have to tear their hearts open, Madigan. Tear them open, and they'll understand layers of pain. Then we'll see change. Then we'll see caring. Then we'll see collaboration." Helena gestured at the two men standing beside her. "Escort these two over to the black box, please." She looked at Jordan. "You can say goodbye to your kids on the way. Don't forget to tell them they've been strong and good."

"Helena, no—" Someone yanked Jordan's arms painfully behind her back. Jordan struggled and then dropped her weight. Her knees hit the ground painfully, but Jordan pivoted and kicked out with her leg even as she blocked a swing from above. Her kick landed with a satisfying thud, but Jordan was soon lost under a flurry of legs and arms, at least three men now trying to subdue her. An elbow to the eye had her seeing stars and a kick to the gut made her double over in pain.

Her face pressed to the cold, wet pavement, Jordan gasped for air as her arms were once again wrenched and bound behind her back. They hauled her to her feet and held her there with a bruising grip.

Ali was on the ground with a man kneeling on the small of her back. "Jesus, Ali. No! Get the fuck off her." She saw the blow coming at her from the corner of her eye, and she turned her head just in time to avoid a broken nose.

Ali was still struggling but then she too was hauled to her feet. Her face had a long red scratch down one side and she was shaking, her eyes murderous. Jordan shook her head to clear the pain and fear.

Helena was staring at Madi, who was being held from behind by a huge man, one hand over her face, one wrapped around her small frame. Madi struggled and tried to scream.

"Black box," Helena said. "All of them."

They spun Jordan and Ali around and pushed them forward across the bridge. The line between them and the demonstrators, hard men and women with anger and resolve etched into their expressions, melted away as Helena approached. The demonstrators were lifting their voice in protest, completely unaware of what was happening around them. Which was obviously the point, Jordan thought. She imagined Helena had convinced them they were safe in this circle. Her kids and the others, maybe forty in all, did not know they were trapped. This line of defense was meant to keep them here, a circle of sacrifice.

"Jordan? What the hell?"

Jordan didn't recognize the voice, but she saw some of the protesters turn and watch as she and Ali and Madi were pushed along. She saw Rupert's face briefly, his goofy grin quickly replaced by shock. Jordan said nothing, just concentrated on what was ahead of her. If she was going to keep her kids safe, she needed to figure out Helena's plan.

Jordan needed to talk to Rachel. She shook her head but couldn't feel the earpiece in her ear anymore. Shit. She tucked her chin into the neck of her coat and felt the microphone rub against her chin. Jordan whispered, hoping like hell the guy behind her couldn't hear over the din.

"No earpiece, I can't hear. Ali and I restrained, taking us to east side of bridge. Called it a black box." They pushed Jordan the last few steps, and the crowd cleared so Jordan had an unobstructed view of a heavy plastic box taking up most of the space on the bed of a truck. Jordan whispered all the details of what she could see into her coat.

"Why'd you piss off the boss lady, Jordan? I thought you were on our side."

Creaser pushed off from where he was leaning against the pickup truck, looking confused and hurt.

"Creaser, I *am* on your side," Jordan said quietly. "What's in the van you were guarding?"

Creaser's face lit up. "Snacks. Helena said we'd need fuel for the protest, and because so many teenagers were here, I'd have to make sure they didn't eat them all."

Jordan closed her eyes briefly. "It's not snacks, Creaser. Go look in the van."

The man holding Jordan shook her, and Jordan bit back a cry of pain as he wrenched the muscles in her shoulders. "Shut up and listen. Creaser, fuck off."

The chants of the protesters had died down, and Jordan could feel the crowd like a silent presence at her back. Ali was being held on the other side of the semicircle. The cut on her cheek dripped blood and her top lip was puffy.

"I'm sorry," Jordan mouthed to Ali.

Ali mouthed something back. Jordan shook her head; she didn't understand. Ali did it again, slower.

"Five minutes."

It must be a message from Rachel. They needed five minutes. How to delay what Helena had planned?

Helena now stood beside the black box with Madi still held captive beside her. She waved away the huge man until it was just the two petite, powerful women.

"This is a proud moment," Helena said, her voice lifted and carried in the wind. "I hope you all feel it as I feel it. You have used your voices, your minds, and your hearts to get us to this moment. I am proud to call you all family."

Some cheers and clapping met Helena's announcement, and her expression became infused with benign resolve. The look terrified Jordan, and her fear leapt into her throat as Helena reached for the sniffling, broken Madi, who stood complacently beside her.

"Madigan represents our future, the moving forward in our fight to be seen and heard. And as our future, Madigan will be making the decision for what happens next."

Helena took the phone out of her pocket again. Madi reached for it, but Helena smiled and pulled it out of reach. "Your friends can leave the bridge before our final announcement," Helena said, and Jordan had to strain to hear the words. "But you have to choose either Jordan or Alison to lead them. One will stay and be witness, immortalized in the message we have to send."

Jordan saw the moment Madi broke.

"I can't," Madi said, staring at the ground.

"You must," Helena said, quietly triumphant. "Who stays, Madigan? The sheep or the wolf?" Helena leaned in closer to Madi, and Jordan could just read the words on Helena's lips as she whispered, "Who lives?"

Jordan couldn't breathe. It couldn't end like this. All of them needed to walk off the bridge. *We just need minutes*, she thought. *Rachel has our backs. Minutes.*

"I'll stay," Jordan called out. Madi lifted her head and Jordan saw her defiance. Good. "Madi, I'll stay. Tell Ali to get the kids and go."

"Not your decision, Jordan," Ali said. "I'll stay."

Jordan noticed a movement out of the corner of her vision. She thought she saw Creaser moving toward the front of the truck, but she didn't want to give him away by looking. She just hoped like hell she'd convinced him.

"Madigan? You see my vision, don't you?" Helena said. "You always have. This burden will be carried by the many. When the bridge goes, we fall and we rip their hearts open. They *see* what they have done to us. We will use the sun to light the dark and help them see. They will carry your name and your memory along with the burden. You will be beloved as you have always wanted to be beloved. We all must sacrifice in our own way."

Madi looked at Helen, and Jordan read eerie calmness. And resolve.

"I see your vision, Helena. But I don't agree with it. I—"

The sound of helicopter rotors drowned out Madi's words. A chopper with lights blazing rose up out of the darkness, just out of reach of the suspension wires, a confusion of lights and noise. The pressure of the downdraft made people duck and cower. The chopper gained altitude and dropped again, blasting everyone with a downdraft so hard most fell to their knees.

Jordan used the moment to turn on her captor, kicking him hard between the legs as he fell. Ali was fighting as well, using the back of her head to smash into the nose of the man holding her. Where was Madi? Jordan fought through the chaos of noise and movement. She heard the sound of a revving engine and looked up to see Creaser pulling away in the truck, smashing through other vehicles and careening against the railings of the bridge.

Jordan caught a glimpse of Madi, squaring off against Helena, who still held the cell phone in her hand. Then someone hit Jordan from behind, knocking the breath out of her as she hit the ground again.

"Lie still! Lie still! Police!"

Jordan's shoulders screamed in protest as she tried to lift the weight off her back. She managed to get her head up just enough to see Helena try to take Madi out, the cell phone clenched in her hand. Madi blocked Helena's strike with her forearm, ducked under the intended blow and landed a perfect, solid right hook into Helena's solar plexus. Helena folded under the punch, and Jordan stopped struggling as officers in tactical gear swarmed Helena and grabbed the cell phone.

Madi sank to the ground and covered her face with her hands. Jordan wanted to go to her, but she was so tired and everything hurt and her heart was shredded. She closed her eyes, feeling every piece of rocky asphalt press into her cheek, the smell of gasoline and seawater. Her muscles were jelly as an officer hauled her to her feet, asking her questions as she released Jordan's hands from the plastic ties cutting into her wrists.

Jordan ignored the officer and looked around, dazed and unsteady. Scuffles and fights were still happening around her as officers subdued the last of Helena's lieutenants. Jordan could see her kids huddled together, Rachel in their midst shouting orders and sheltering as many of the kids as she could. Then Jordan's eyes landed on Ali, also unbound now, crouching down next to Madi and holding Madi's head between her hands.

Jordan forced her legs to hold her for the few feet it took to sink down next to Madi and Ali and hold them in her arms with all the love and strength she had left to offer.

EPILOGUE

"I don't know about this."

Jordan watched Madi fidget with the sleeve of her black sweater. Madi was looking nervously around the ballroom of the posh downtown Chicago hotel hosting Centera Corp's annual general meeting. Men and women in suits and ties, expensive shoes and pressed shirts filled the space along with the near-deafening din of chatter and the smell of coffee.

"Hey, I have to present, too," Ali said, looking utterly relaxed in her summer-weight grey suit and light blue shirt. "Every one of the executives is nervous about their homework assignment."

Madi didn't look convinced.

Jordan exchanged a look with Ali, seated on Madi's other side. They'd talked endlessly about whether or not this was a good idea. It had been six months since the incident on the bridge. They'd all healed from the cuts and bruises, but Madi's confidence had taken a huge hit and was still in recovery. Her and the rest of the kids being cleared by the police of any wrongdoing had helped. Spending time with Jordan and Rachel outlining her involvement with the Unharm group had helped as well, releasing some pent-up secrets.

It had helped Jordan, learning that Madi had only joined when she'd heard some of the kids were involved. She'd used Helena's twisted attachment to her to try and keep the others safe. And keep Jordan out of it. Knowing Madi was expected to testify at Helena's trial in eight months was still a worry. Madi see-sawed up and down, steady and not. She was working so hard, and Jordan wished she could start feeling the payoff for all her effort.

"You two all ready? We'll be getting started in a moment."

Tom Lawrence leaned on the back of a vacant chair, looking eager about the day's event.

Madi nodded. "I'm ready," she said quietly.

Tom looked at her sympathetically. "It's okay to be nervous, Ms. Battiste. I recognize I've put a lot of pressure on you as our first speaker. But I think your message will set the tone for the day. I can't thank you enough for being here. For being a mentor to Alison."

Madi cocked her head to the side, and a small smirk emerged. "You're thanking me even though you're losing one of your top executives? Your project turned into corporate headhunting. Bet you never expected that."

Tom laughed, and Madi's eyes sparkled with some of her old spirit. "No, you are very right. But I've known for a long time Alison was ready to move on. I wish her nothing but the best." Tom and Ali exchanged an understanding smile.

Ali would be starting at a small start-up firm in Halifax in August. She'd sold her condo in Chicago and was making her move home permanent in just a few weeks. Jordan's heart thudded a happy-scared rhythm. They were looking for a place together. It was finally time.

Tom straightened and clapped his hands together once. "We need to get this show on the road. I'll say a few words and then you're up, Ms. Battiste. Break a leg."

Madi nodded, this time with a set to her shoulders that reminded Jordan of her old confidence.

Jordan shifted in her seat and took a sip of her nearly cold coffee in the small china cup. She straightened the lapel of her new blazer. Madi caught her fidgeting and rolled her eyes.

"Cut it out. You don't have to present and you look hot in that outfit." She turned to Ali. "Doesn't she?"

Ali smiled and raised her eyebrows. "Yes, she does."

"Shut up, both of you," Jordan muttered, making them both laugh. She wished Ali was sitting beside her right now. She tried to remember these were still Ali's colleagues and this was still her place of work.

Up at the podium, Tom called for everyone's attention and cracked a joke about the similarities between executives and preschoolers. The room quieted, and the lights dimmed as Tom launched into a short speech about why they were all here. He pulled no punches and Jordan respected him for that. He spoke of their previous failures without judgement or excuse. He outlined the purpose of the mentorship project and the itinerary for the day.

"First on the agenda is a young woman from Halifax who I have had the honour of getting to know over most of the last year. She is a poet and a leader, and when she speaks, we should all listen. Madigan Battiste, the stage is yours."

Madi stood and approached the stage as Ali and Jordan clapped and whistled. Jordan thought her heart would burst with pride as Madi climbed the steps of the stage and shook Tom's hand. Jordan felt Ali slip into the seat beside her and was grateful for her closeness. Madi looked at the height of the podium, then pulled the mic free of its stand and walked a few steps away. The spotlight followed her and the clapping died down. It was just Madi on the stage, and Jordan could see as she closed her eyes, took a breath, and started to speak.

"I wake each morning. I evaluate my body, consciously connecting my cerebrum to my limbs and lungs and lips. I try to calculate which synapses are firing today, which receptors are taking in not enough or just enough or too much. I ask myself, will I balance today? Or will I tilt, rushing headlong into a high that feels so right and so terrifying at the same time? Will I fall, will I lay myself out under the weight of a thousand feet, trampled and invisible. Hurting. Will I balance today?

"You ask if I will accept your help. I will not. Not again. You have weighed me down for too long. Each letter of each diagnosis another weight you hand me when I have just cracked open my ribcage along its fault line and revealed to you that I am already drowning. You weigh me down and then you shake your head when I refuse your help, refuse to express my gratitude. But I cannot speak. I am already filled with water.

"Never forget I only smile because you demand proof of life. I stretch my lips and reveal all my teeth, leaving you self-satisfied and me empty. That is not love, or help, or understanding. I will no longer bare my teeth to make you feel better.

"I wake each morning. I remind myself I have learned to tread water. I remember there are days I reach high ground. I ache for the day the water will hold me close and hold me up. Until then I find gratitude in my chest for the people in my life who understand that there are moments I hate them for loving me. I am nearly convinced their love is a perpetual motion machine. Soon I will let those words pass my lips. But not yet. I wake each morning."

The crowd was stunned, a silence so pervasive it was as if Madi's words had beat them down like a concussive force. Then the room seemed to take a collective breath, and they clapped. Jordan, recognizing only now that she was clenching Ali's hand so tightly she could feel the delicate bones, released her and clapped along with the crowd who rose to applaud Madi's words and her bravery.

Madi bowed her head briefly in acknowledgement, then searched the crowd, finally finding Jordan and Ali standing and clapping along with everyone else. She grinned at them and raised her fist in a silent salute. Jordan swallowed the tears and the pain and let herself feel the joy of Madi's moment. And as she took her seat and took Ali's hand, Jordan's heart thumped in contentment with the security of knowing home.

About the Author

Jessica Webb spends her professional days working with educators to find the why behind the challenging behaviors of the students they support. Limitless curiosity about the motivations and intentions of human behavior is also a huge part of what drives her to write stories and understand the complexities of her characters and their actions.

When she's not working or writing, Jessica is spending time with her wife and daughter, usually planning where they will travel next. Jessica can be found most often on her favorite spot on the couch with a book and a cup of tea.

Jessica can be contacted at jessicalwebb.author@gmail.com.

Books Available From Bold Strokes Books

A Fighting Chance by T. L. Hayes. Will Lou be able to come to terms with her past to give love a fighting chance? (978-1-163555-257-7)

Chosen by Brey Willows. When the choice is adapt or die, can love save us all? (978-1-163555-110-5)

Gnarled Hollow by Charlotte Greene. After they are invited to study a secluded nineteenth-century estate, a former English professor and a group of historians discover that they will have to fight against the unknown if they have any hope of staying alive. (978-1-163555-235-5)

Jacob's Grace by C.P. Rowlands. Captain Tag Becket wants to keep her head down and her past behind her, but her feelings for AJ's second-in-command, Grace Fields, makes keeping secrets next to impossible. (978-1-163555-187-7)

On the Fly by PJ Trebelhorn. Hockey player Courtney Abbott is content with her solitary life until visiting concert violinist Lana Caruso makes her second-guess everything she always thought she wanted. (978-1-163555-255-3)

Passionate Rivals by Radclyffe. Professional rivalry and long-simmering passions create a combustible combination when Emmet McCabe and Sydney Stevens are forced to work together, especially when past attractions won't stay buried. (978-1-63555-231-7)

Proxima Five by Missouri Vaun. When geologist Leah Warren crash-lands on a preindustrial planet and is claimed by its tyrant, Tiago, will clan warrior Keegan's love for Leah give her the strength to defeat him? (978-1-163555-122-8)

Racing Hearts by Dena Blake. When you cross a hot-tempered race car mechanic with a reckless cop, the result can only be spontaneous combustion. (978-1-163555-251-5)

Shadowboxer by Jessica L. Webb. Jordan McAddie is prepared to keep her street kids safe from a dangerous underground protest group, but she isn't prepared for her first love to walk back into her life. (978-1-163555-267-6)

The Tattered Lands by Barbara Ann Wright. As Vandra and Lilani strive to make peace, they slowly fall in love. With mistrust and murder surrounding them, only their faith in each other can keep their plan to save the world from falling apart. (978-1-163555-108-2)

Captive by Donna K. Ford. To escape a human trafficking ring, Greyson Cooper and Olivia Danner become players in a game of deceit and violence. Will their love stand a chance? (978-1-63555-215-7)

Crossing the Line by CF Frizzell. The Mob discovers a nemesis within its ranks, and in the ultimate retaliation, draws Stick McLaughlin from anonymity by threatening everything she holds dear. (978-1-63555-161-7)

Love's Verdict by Carsen Taite. Attorneys Landon Holt and Carly Pachett want the exact same thing: the only open partnership spot at their prestigious criminal defense firm. But will they compromise their careers for love? (978-1-63555-042-9)

Precipice of Doubt by Mardi Alexander & Laurie Eichler. Can Cole Jameson resist her attraction to her boss, veterinarian Jodi Bowman, or will she risk a workplace romance and her heart? (978-1-63555-128-0)

Savage Horizons by CJ Birch. Captain Jordan Kellow's feelings for Lt. Ali Ash have her past and future colliding, setting in motion a series of events that strands her crew in an unknown galaxy thousands of light years from home. (978-1-63555-250-8)

Secrets of the Last Castle by A. Rose Mathieu. When Elizabeth Campbell represents a young man accused of murdering an elderly woman, her investigation leads to an abandoned plantation that reveals many dark Southern secrets. (978-1-63555-240-9)

Take Your Time by VK Powell. A neurotic parrot brings police officer Grace Booker and temporary veterinarian Dr. Dani Wingate together in the tiny town of Pine Cone, but their unexpected attraction keeps the sparks flying. (978-1-63555-130-3)

The Last Seduction by Ronica Black. When you allow true love to elude you once and you desperately regret it, are you brave enough to grab it when it comes around again? (978-1-63555-211-9)

The Shape of You by Georgia Beers. Rebecca McCall doesn't play it safe, but when sexy Spencer Thompson joins her workout class, their nonstop sparring forces her to face her ultimate challenge—a chance at love. (978-1-63555-217-1)

Exposed by MJ Williamz. The closet is no place to live if you want to find true love. (978-1-62639-989-1)

Force of Fire: Toujours a Vous by Ali Vali. Immortals Kendal and Piper welcome their new child and celebrate the defeat of an old enemy, but another ancient evil is about to awaken deep in the jungles of Costa Rica. (978-1-63555-047-4)

Landing Zone by Erin Dutton. Can a career veteran finally discover a love stronger than even her pride? (978-1-63555-199-0)

Love at Last Call by M. Ullrich. Is balancing business, friendship, and love more than any willing woman can handle? (978-1-63555-197-6)

Pleasure Cruise by Yolanda Wallace. Spencer Collins and Amy Donovan have few things in common, but a Caribbean cruise offers both women an unexpected chance to face one of their greatest fears: falling in love. (978-1-63555-219-5)

Running Off Radar by MB Austin. Maji's plans to win Rose back are interrupted when work intrudes, and duty calls her to help a SEAL team stop a Russian mobster from harvesting gold from the bottom of Sitka Sound. (978-1-63555-152-5)

Shadow of the Phoenix by Rebecca Harwell. In the final battle for the fate of Storm's Quarry, even Nadya's and Shay's powers may not be enough. (978-1-63555-181-5)

Take a Chance by D. Jackson Leigh. There's hardly a woman within fifty miles of Pine Cone that veterinarian Trip Beaumont can't charm, except for the irritating new cop, Jamie Grant, who keeps leaving parking tickets on her truck. (978-1-63555-118-1)

Death in Time by Robyn Nyx. Working in the past is hell on your future. (978-1-63555-053-5)